THE SOLUTION GAME

A Short History of Man

J. S. TROTH JR.

ISBN: 0985284609
ISBN 13: 9780985284602

Table of Contents

The Solution Game

A Short History of Man

Did the uncovering of the earliest human ancestor begin with Lucy or was Australopitheus Sediba the earliest human? Whether it was either means the human lineage is approximately three million years old; a mere drop in the ocean when measuring the first forms of life on Earth which date back three billion eight hundred million years. While some scientists still believe man is a descendant of the apes there are huge unexplained gaps between the two groups. Are we really linked; the probability is that we are not.

The Solution Game's "A Short History of Man", the first of three or more books, puts the fascination of discovery in the hands of two teens who want to know more about the Earth and man and the history behind their existence. It is critical that we all understand the path we have followed, to bring us as far as we have come, that will allow us to continue on.

Man's ability to survive as long as he has was predicated on small groups whether it was a small family structure, a tribal community or a small town. Every individual in a community relied on each other; you either worked together or you didn't survive. Today, Earth is comprised of many different highly segmented groups with totally dissimilar backgrounds all working independently; instead of working together we are fighting one another.

Can man forget his differences and work together for his own survival?

I want to thank over 200 scientists and historians whose work has allowed me to present this fascinating story in a form that ties our world today together with out past.

Chapter One

THE CRASH

*T*he snow melted along the roadside creating a dirty brown slush. The date was February 11th, a completely unimportant date for most; for Fred, however, it was an anniversary that would change his life. For the moment, the date eluded Fred and had it not been for his secretary's discrete, "Oh by the way, I guess you will be taking your wife out for dinner tonight," he would have completely forgotten.

"Oh my God, Mary, would you please make reservations at the Candlelight Inn for us tonight. Also, ask them to have a bouquet of fresh flowers on the table."

"Yes Fred and you have a call on line 9."

"Fred Willing."

"Fred, James, what is going on this morning?"

"Mr. James, the retail sales figures are not good and consumer confidence is taking a nose dive. Our country is running on credit and if the consumer pulls back and reduces his spending, the economy will have a difficult time."

"You know Fred, our government never learns. We experience the same problems over and over. They seem to have less understanding of business and our economy than does the average person. They couldn't see the housing bubble? Did they think prices could climb to the sky? It's the fifteenth century tulip craze all over again. Perhaps, everyone forgot that as prices of houses go up so do taxes. Our local governments need revenues as much as our federal government, which means local governments jump all over the opportunity to raise school taxes and property taxes. Where did our government think everyone would get all this money not only to buy the more expensive house but in addition to pay the higher taxes? There is just no common sense in Washington and absolutely no understanding how business works. In my opinion, I think our elected officials look at being elected as a priestly ordainment rather than a tough watchdog job. They must believe all they have to do is kiss babies, shake hands, smile and collect a pay check. Why do they think they should get paid for that? They should have been all over the housing and credit bubble before it got out of hand. Fred, what is your call for the opening this morning?"

"It looks lower; Nasdq, Dow and S&P futures are all down."

"Fred, buy 25 March 370 puts on the OEX at the open."

"Mr. James, do you want to put a stop in?"

"I'll watch it closely, Fred."

"Mary, put this ticket in."

"Hello, Fred Willing."

"Fred, Tom, does the market look up or down on the opening?" Fred looked at his two monitor screens in front of him. The data on the screens was changing constantly as the information was being updated. One monitor displayed the quotes of many stocks and indices Fred watched while the other had the latest information on many different companies and the latest national and international news on the world and world economies.

"Tom, all three futures indexes are lower."

"Fred, I want to buy 60 march puts on GM. Talk about management wearing rose-colored glasses. Their sales forecast is for sales to jump; I just don't see it. Who is going to buy expensive $30,000 gas guzzling cars when our economy appears to be falling off a cliff? On top of that, the world is depleting its oil supplies. It annoys the hell out of me when people who should know and get paid big bucks to know, don't know what they're doing."

"Tom, I agree but GM stock has lost a lot of its value already and I don't like the risk to reward ratio. I don't want to talk you out of the trade, because I don't know how low this stock will go. However, I do want to give you both sides."

"Fred, I think GM will wind up in bankruptcy; you have the same management running the show now that is responsible for driving the company into the ground. T. Boone Pickens, you know the converted oil billionaire, says we can't afford foreign oil any longer. That will mean alternative energy vehicles that are light weight, smaller and more energy efficient. India even has an alternative energy vehicle that costs $2,500. How will GM make any money with competition like that?"

"I'm putting the ticket in Tom".

"Mary, did you make those reservations for tonight?"

"Yes, Fred, you are all set for 7:00. Bob is on line 3.

"Fred Willing."

"Fred, Bob. What does the opening look like?"

"Lower, the Dow futures are down 50 points, Bob."

"Damn, I'm long 10,000 shares of Caterpillar. You know, I am so fed up with our government, I could ring their necks. The problem is we have a form of government that was devised in the horse and buggy days. Our present form of government is just not up to the complex problems we face today. The reason the market keeps going down is that people have lost faith in their leaders and the system. If you apply for a job at a company, the first thing they want to know is what experience do you have that qualifies you for this position in our type of company? The people we elect to represent us, in our highly complex world, come from backgrounds that wouldn't qualify them for such a complex job in any company. Why are we electing them to manage our future? We elect someone right off the street to run a very complex system. It's like pulling someone off the street and asking him or her to run a nuclear power plant and our government is many times more complex. What does a lawyer know about business unless he has run a company and yet we want people with no top level business experience to tell business people how to run their business? We just have to demand a change if we are going to survive and honestly, I don't know if we will. We are supposed to be a Republic not a democracy. Our founding fathers knew that a democracy would never work, that is why in our pledge of allegiance we say 'I pledge allegiance to my flag and to the Republic for which it stands'. We are following the same road the Roman Empire followed and we know what happened to that empire. They started out as a republic and ended up in a democracy which does not work and, of course, it collapsed. Are we dumb enough to do exactly the same thing?"

"Bob, we have turned out to be a bunch of hot air balloons, in my opinion. I have never heard so much hot air when I turn on the radio or T.V. People are getting paid big bucks for all this hot air but I don't see any action, just hot air. To effect a change, we all have to come together with the same objectives and we have to take action or our efforts are useless. The common denominator is survival."

"Sad, really sad, Fred. Do you see the bottom to this market?"

"Bob, I don't know. Some say there is no bottom in sight and others say the market will make a V bottom and rocket higher with the stimulus package. If I had to make a guess, I would have to say the market will go lower. I don't know where the heads of our leaders in Washington are. I still have not heard anyone say this is the problem and this is how we can solve it. In my mind, the problem is a dysfunctional government that is asleep at the switch. The housing bubble was caused by easy credit and buyers who over extended themselves with massive amount of debt. Now our government wants to solve the problem with more debt. I guess it's like giving a drunk more to drink until he sobers up."

"That doesn't make any sense, Fred."

"I guess you need more to drink Bob," chuckled Fred. "Bob, do you want to put a limit on your position?"

"No, I'll call you later."

"Fred, Charlie Whisler wants you to call him. He didn't sound very happy."

"No one is happy. I feel more like a shrink than a stockbroker. However, in a market like this, where you can lose a fortune, I have to know my clients, it's vital. My clients' financial status is changing constantly and I have to make sure they can take the risk. This is not fun stuff. People can get into real financial trouble and guess who gets blamed if one of my clients says I misled him or I didn't pay attention to his financial state."

"Charlie, Fred Willing returning your call."

"Fred, this is not a good day for me."

"What's wrong Charlie?"

"Remember two years ago our government was begging investors to invest in ethanol. We had to become more environmentally conscious and more energy independent, they said. So, I invested in one of the largest ethanol plants and bought a farm to help supply the corn. Well, you know what happened; we took corn from being a food to being energy. It shot the price of corn and other food crops sky high and people all over the world started yelling they couldn't afford to eat. Now our government has fallen asleep again and allowed this sub-prime mess, which is causing the economy to fall off a cliff and with it the price of gasoline. The demand for ethanol is so far down that my ethanol plant is going bankrupt and closing down. My farm had contracted with the ethanol plant to buy my corn. Now, they have canceled our contracts. I'm left with a huge loss on my ethanol plant and the price of corn has plunged from over seven dollars a bushel to around three dollars and seventy cents a bushel. I might have to sell the farm to boot."

"I'm sorry to hear that Charlie. Don't you think the price of corn will come back?"

"I'm sure it will in the future but I have to pay a mortgage on the farm now."

"Charlie, we are electing the wrong people to represent us in Washington. These politicians are way over their heads and they are just grasping at straws. Our whole system, in my view, has to be updated. Charlie, are you going to sell your holdings in Microsoft?"

"I was thinking about holding Microsoft right now but I do want to sell my shares in GE."

"Do you want to sell all your shares in GE? According to my records you have twenty-five thousand shares."

"No, sell ten thousand."

"Charlie, do you want me to put the ticket in at the market? You know GE stock has been weak and a good size order could get you a lower price."

"Fred, I've got to sell so just put it in at market."

"It's done Charlie." Fred turned towards Mary to hand her the ticket.

"Have you told your wife you are taking her out to dinner tonight?" asked Mary.

Fred thought for a moment. "I don't think so," he said with a puzzled look on his face.

"Maybe you should call her just in case so she can make plans."

Fred sheepishly replied, "You're right."

Fred called Susan while the two monitors in front of him flashed as they were being updated and a phone line lit up with an incoming call. Fred motioned to Mary to get the incoming call.

"Hi honey, do you know what today is?"

"Don't tell me your mind is actually thinking about something other than business. Why don't you tell me what today is?"

"It's our seventeenth anniversary. It's hard to believe."

"Well, Fred, it's nice you remembered. Your sales assistant must have reminded you. Last year you both forgot, remember?"

And I paid for it for months thereafter, Fred thought to himself. "I made reservations at the Candlelight Inn for 7:00. Will that work for you?"

"That's fine Fred, what time will you be home tonight?"

"I'll leave early and catch the 4:25 train. Can you pick me up at the station?"

"I can, if you catch that train but I also have to pick the kids up from their sports and start cooking dinner for them before we go out."

"Lacy is fifteen, can't she cook?"

"Fred, she is about to turn sixteen and I am in the process of teaching her but I didn't tell you, however, she almost burned the house down last week."

Fred gasped. "What?" Fred ran his fingers through his hair while his lower jaw dropped.

"Don't get all excited, she was cooking hamburgers in oil and somehow the oil caught on fire. When she went to put the frying pan under the kitchen faucet to put the fire out, and turned the water on, the fire flared up and caught the curtains on fire. Fortunately, I was home and when I heard her scream, I dashed to the kitchen. As soon as I saw the curtains on fire, I grabbed the fire extinguisher and put the fire out. Thank God, you put a fire extinguisher in the kitchen."

"Doesn't she know not to put water on a grease or oil fire?"

"She does now."

"I didn't notice any damage or smell anything," said Fred.

"I got a little pry bar from your work shop, took the window trim off and went to Home Depot and got some more. With a little paint, it looks as good as new. I opened all the windows to get the smell out and used a spray to kill the odor but you didn't notice the curtains are different."

"How about that. How did you cut the trim?"

"I just used your miter saw. I put it to cut a 45 degree angle and it did. It is so simple. You can even go on the Internet and they have a video on how to use one. You know men aren't the only ones who can use them."

"Honey, did you wear eye protection?"

"No Fred, it didn't take very long."

"Susan, you have to wear eye protection every time you use a piece of machinery. Did you protect your ears with hearing protection and what about a respirator so you don't get all that saw dust in your lungs?"

"Oh Fred, it didn't take that long to cut the molding."

"Susan, I love you and the last thing I want is a blind and deaf wife who has a problem breathing."

"Fred, don't be silly. I am fine."

I live on the edge of chaos, thought Fred. "Susan, I have to run but I will see you later."

Fred had a lump in his stomach. He reached in the bottom drawer of his desk and pulled out some Pepto-Bismol. The bottle was half empty. He kept a napkin and a spoon for immediate access to relief next to the bottle. Economic times like this were hard enough, but your daughter almost destroying the house too, well, that calls for a full table spoon of cherry flavored Pepto, Fred thought to himself.

"Fred, you have a call on line 1."

"Fred Willing."

"Fred, my name is Gretchen Swivel and a friend told me to call you. I am trying to get more interest than I can get in a CD at my bank."

"Gretchen, have you ever invested in anything other than a CD?"

"I have a little stock in a company that doesn't pay a dividend."

"Gretchen, can you tell me a little about yourself? How old are you and are you married?"

"Well, I'm 27 and engaged and we are hoping to get married this summer."

"Are you working?"

"Yes, I am in sales for a software company."

"Are you trying to save for a down payment on a house?"

"Yes, but Fred, it is so hard these days, house prices are out of sight for someone just starting out. I don't know how anyone can afford these high prices and on top of that the taxes are out of sight."

"I agree Gretchen, what does your fiancé do for a living?"

"He is in sales too, but he has a band on the side also. The band is really good, Fred, you should hear them."

"Are you both college graduates?"

"Yes."

"Gretchen, interest rates are very low right now for everyone; no matter if you are in certificates of deposit, treasuries, even triple A rated bonds. I hope you know the old adage, the higher the return the higher the risk."

"That's why I only use CD's. I can't afford to lose any money."

"Have you been keeping up with what is going on in our economy?"

"I know things are not good. Unemployment is going up and Wall Street is in a mess because of too much greed and probably corruption. I don't trust Wall Street, they are focused only on one thing and that's making as much money as they can. They really could care less about anyone else."

"Do you need this interest income to live on?"

"No."

"How much money were you thinking of investing?"

"I have ten thousand dollars that is coming due in my CD in a couple of weeks."

"Gretchen, I would be very careful right now. You can look at those ETF's that pay a higher dividend than you can get on a CD. However, you are taking a risk that your ETF can go down in value and or the companies that make up the ETF could cut their dividends."

"What is an ETF Fred?"

"ETF stands for exchange traded funds. These are funds that represent a basket of stocks or bonds. In fact, you can find an ETF that represents almost anything. If we look at a stock ETF we are looking at a basket of stocks. Instead of buying one stock you can buy an ETF so you are spreading your risk among many stocks. Instead of betting on one stock you are betting on a basket of stocks. You can do the same thing with bonds. You can get some ETF's that pay a dividend much higher than you can get in a CD, however, if the ETF goes down in price and you have to sell, you will take a capital loss. Gretchen, it is like a roller coaster. Sometimes the price goes up and sometimes the price goes down. As long as you can wait for the price to be equal to or greater than the price at which you bought your ETF you will make a better return than you will in a CD. If you can take the risk emotionally and financially, you will probably make the most money nibbling at good stocks or ETF's when they are way down. Historically, stocks have always rebounded, so in the long term, at least 5 years; you should make a lot more money by investing in good companies than you will from a CD. Do you have any debt, like credit card debt?"

"Well, we are trying to get it down but we still owe on our student loans and we ran up over a thousand dollars on credit cards but we have that down to about five hundred dollars now and we each have a car payment."

"Gretchen, debt is your worst enemy as you can see in our sub-prime mortgage meltdown right now. The interest rates on debt are always much higher than what you can get on any interest bearing investments. I would concentrate on paying off your credit cards first, that will be your best investment. Cut your credit cards up and get a debit card which draws money directly from your checking account. You can't spend more than you have in your account. You will be surprised how much more attention you will pay on your purchases when you know it's coming directly out of your account and if you over spend you will get a great big over draft penalty which will really hurt. Second, make a budget for both of you and stay within it. Third, I would pay yourself first every payday. Save as much as you can afford to but at least $100. Put the $100 in a savings account even if you are not getting a lot of interest. Fourth, if you use your car for business make sure you keep track of the mileage you use for business and all your other business related costs which are deductible from your income taxes. I am not a tax adviser so get a good book at the library on this topic and call the IRS and see what help they can give you. They publish a lot of information that most people never get or read. Fifth, call your local HUD office, that's the Housing and Urban Development office, and see what help is available for first time home buyers that you may qualify for. Then finally, once you get your credit card debt paid, I will look for a bond ETF and a stock ETF that pay a higher yield than you are now getting, which you can start to nibble on. Does that plan seem reasonable?"

"Yes. Thanks."

"Call me once a month so we keep you on tract."

"Thanks, Fred."

"Fred, Dick Solijing called and he has a problem with his account."

"I'll call him. I have to leave earlier than normal today Mary, will you take messages and handle any trades that have to be made?"

"Of course, Fred."

Later, as Fred maneuvered through the crowds on his way to Grand Central Station, the same nagging thoughts kept running through his mind. Would the stimulus package work? What will happen to our economy? Will I have a job? These were questions only time could answer as Fred ran past the electronic track boards showing the track numbers of all incoming and departing trains. "Seats in the rear" yelled a conductor. Fred made his way to the rear of the train. The only available seats were on the isle. Fred tossed his coat into the overhead compartment and sat down as many other travelers pushed by him. He pushed the recline button and pushed back on his seat. He withdrew his lap top from his briefcase and started to review the day's events. Why are we trying to bail out failing companies? If they are in trouble

there must be a reason. Management must not be doing its job.
Maybe the company should fail? Maybe, management needs to
be replaced; maybe, they need to get consultants in to define the
problems or, maybe, their product mix is wrong or their products
are outdated or poorly manufactured. It could be a case their
own management is stealing them blind with huge salaries and
bonuses. There is a reason a company fails. AIG, CITI Bank,
GM and GE all got too big. There should be a limit on the size
a company can get. Man is only so smart, he has his limits and
to allow companies to get too big is just asking for trouble. Look
at our government it is way too big and inefficient. If a company
fails it's not the end of the world. Companies that get into trouble
can go into Chapter 11 bankruptcy and restructure themselves;
parts sold off, new management brought in, salaries and bonus
restructured so executive compensation is based on profitable
performance. If you are going to give an executive a golden
parachute, what is his incentive to run a profitable company? It's
tantamount to saying here take control, ruin our company, throw
our hardworking employees out on the street and we will just
smile and pay you a king's ransom to boot. Man must be losing it.
Our society depends on profitable well run businesses for the jobs
they create the dividends they pay and the taxes they generate not
to mention the money that goes to charities and churches. Since,
our government is run by people who don't understand business
and have never been in business or run a business, why are they
getting involved? Why haven't we updated our own government?
Why haven't we put together a new form of government for this
day and age? Our government was devised in a different era. Our
present form of government is broken, dysfunctional, much too
inefficient, way to slow, and structured incorrectly. Why don't
we have four year terms for those retiring business executives
in each state who are at the top of their particular field instead
of electing officials in a beauty contest who come from other
backgrounds and have little to no idea what the problems are or
what the solutions are? Talk about insane.

Fred's mind continued to whirl with the many facets of our economic world as the train jerked forward as it started to move.

One of the things our economy needs is a larger vulture sector, a larger distressed asset sector. The reason there are vultures in nature is to clean up the inevitable; age, failure and death, a sector that is funded by private funds that everyone can invest in. If a company goes into bankruptcy and can't restructure itself for survival there is nothing else you can do but bring in the vulture detail. You could have the General Motors Distressed Asset Fund or the AIG Distressed Asset Fund and so on. People like Wilbur Ross, who can see the value in distressed assets and knows their value, could be brought in to salvage what value there is still left. But we have to keep government out of the private sector because they don't know what they are doing. If there is a profit to be made, why not let investors reap the rewards? It could be very profitable. Isn't this a capitalistic system? Wasn't our government designed to give the private sector a legal outline of what is acceptable but leave the rest up to the people? If we fail we fail, we can't save every sinking ship. It's like a father and daughter relationship. I want to sit on the front porch with a shotgun to keep the wolves at bay from my daughter. My wife says "you can't do that". She says, "Our daughter has to make her own mistakes and pay the price if she is wrong. We set the guidelines, instill in her good morals and the rest is on her shoulders." If our own daughters can make mistakes and pay the price then why the devil can't crummy companies and crummy management pay the price? "Damn," said Fred out loud.

"Excuse me," quipped the person in the adjoining seat.

Fred looked over, not having noticed who was sitting next to him. "Sorry," he replied.

For the first time, Fred noticed the person sitting next to the window, half hidden behind a Playboy magazine. She put her magazine down and started to wiggle out of her long red tailored coat. She revealed a beautiful silk embroidered blouse and a young woman who could be in Playboy magazine. "Wow," Fred thought subconsciously but it came out loud anyway.

"What?" said the woman startled.

Fred sheepishly replied, "I said ow as in ouch. I think something bit me."

"Now what could have bitten you?" replied the woman.

"No, no, I must be under a lot of stress these days with the economy the way it is."

"I know," said his seat mate. "I am very uncomfortable with the situation also. My generation will have to pay for this mess, not to mention our energy and environmental fiascoes. I am very outspoken, do you mind?"

"Not at all," said Fred as he started to relax back into his reclined seat. "I am too. Do you work in Manhattan?"

"Yes, I'm a broker with Pierce Withers."

Fred's eyes rolled. "Are you afraid of losing your job?" asked Fred thinking about his own worries.

"If our government will keep their fingers out of our pie, we will be fine," she stated. "Our own government is turning out to be our worst enemy. Can you believe a government official would say 'they may have to nationalize some banks for a short time?' Think how many American lives have been lost at war defending the capitalistic system and now they say they may nationalize the very core of the system. The market fell off a cliff when that was reported and the bank and brokerage stocks fell apart. Don't our government officials think before they open their mouths? Do you know how many people depend on the dividends from these companies to live? How irresponsible can anyone be?"

"Don't get me started ah," Fred said tilting his hand towards her.

"Linda and yours?"

"Fred".

"What do you do Fred?" asked an inquisitive female.

"I'm a broker with Bean Walters."

Linda took a better look at Fred. "Are your clients worried?" she asked.

"Of course. Look what has happened in the first two weeks of a new administration. We got a Commerce Secretary nominee who withdrew due to corruption charges, a tax cheat nominee for Chief Performance Officer who withdrew under charges of cheating on her taxes, a Labor Secretary nominee who withdrew under charges of unethical conduct and a Secretary of health and Human Services nominee who withdrew under charges of cheating on his taxes and a Treasury Secretary who had to apologize for an oversight on his taxes. And that's just in the first two weeks. How can you have any trust in this system? Wouldn't you think they would all have had a background check and been cleared before they were nominated? It makes the nominees and our government, look like fools. And we think they can fix our problems?"

"Fred, it is a disgrace, however, more importantly, we have to update our government. It has gotten way too big to manage, too complex for mere mortals to control and way to corrupt. I majored in anthropology at college and the human is just a simple hunter/gatherer. We are meant to live as we have done for several hundred thousand or more years and now we find ourselves way over our heads. The scary part is that our problems are snow balling and we either can't or are unwilling to face reality. We have fooled ourselves with our technology. We have jumped ahead of our own abilities. We have created technology for the sake of technology without any plan for the future. We are basically the same animal we were in the beginning. We have not lost our basic and original instincts and no matter how smart we think we are we have the same minds we had when we were living in caves and trying to discover fire. Fred, we have trapped ourselves."

"You are a very perceptive young woman," said Fred. But I am not quite that pessimistic. Perhaps, I am a dreamer, but all the countries on planet Earth are having terrible problems too. We are ruining our environments, our populations are out of control, man has fooled himself thinking technology can fix everything and everyone everywhere is making a mad dash for the most worthless stuff on planet Earth called cash. The pendulum just has to start swinging the other way or it's over."

"Fred, the problem goes to the very core of mankind which is, man does not have any common sense. Look at Wall Street. These people were supposed to be so smart. Obviously, there is a huge piece of the pie they are missing. Maybe they have sharp pencils but certainly myopic minds. They didn't or couldn't see the implications of the products they developed. They didn't even understand them completely and neither did anyone else. We have allowed our greed to rule our judgment. Man has not come to the simple revelation that his mind is not as smart as he thinks it is and is only able to handle so much. We are not an intelligent animal but a reactive animal like all animals. Look at all these takeover artists who thought they were so smart. No matter whether you call it a hedge fund or private capital or leveraged buyouts the result is almost always the same. Instead of creating jobs they throw hard working tax paying people out on to the street so their greed can be satisfied. Everyone is the loser except the firm collecting the huge fees. Few of these take overs ever make money but they throw people out on the street, they disrupt lives, they rob tax dollars from local, state and federal governments and for what? I know some companies have over staffed themselves and some people may have to go. Management, in some cases, may be less than stellar and may need to be replaced but there is a fine line between what is good for the company and what is good for our country. Just think about this; when you tighten on the cost side of a company by laying people off, you are ruining the middle class which is the backbone of our capitalistic system. In other words, you are cutting your own throat, if it continues, on a longer term basis, unless the economy can grow fast enough to keep up with the demand for jobs. Everyone needs to answer this question. Are we working for the good of all or for the good of a few? If we are working for only a few the system won't work. Private capital can serve a useful purpose; however, three questions should be answered before a company is allowed to take another company over. First, is it in the best interest of the consumer, second, is it in the best interest of society and third, will it make a stronger more efficient company? However, efficiency means producing more with less people, in many cases, so if the economy isn't growing, the end result will be higher taxes, more unemployment, a declining GNP and the cycle will continue until we bankrupt ourselves. Isn't that exactly what we are doing now? We can see what is happening all over the world. People are waking up, they want more equality. The reason the capitalistic system has worked, was everyone felt they had a piece of the pie. Now the system has been so distorted that many people feel they are being left out. We have to ask ourselves, does man have a social conscience? Our capitalistic system was originally designed so everyone could share in our country's growth. Man can create but then he ruins what he has created. But what I really fear is, man doesn't realize that for the last ten thousand years, he has, through blood, sweat and tears built his country's histories and dynasties, his coat of arms so to speak and to think, all of a sudden, with no more than a snap of his fingers, time has taken him out of his past and dumped him into a world in which he is a total alien. Does he realize that all of his past endeavors have been severed by his own over population, disregard for the environment and technology? The problem with man is each generation lives for such a short period in time that everything he experiences is just a split second in time. He can't experience what went on before him or see what will come after he dies. He doesn't realize how myopic he is. There are two major questions in my mind that we have to answer. Has man surpassed his limit of ability and can man survive without common sense?"

"Linda, it is really scary. I have a young family and I break out in a cold sweat every time I think of the problems man has caused himself. Can't man see that all his past knowledge and thinking is outdated? Man is way behind the learning curve.

Einstein even made the observation eighty years ago 'you can't solve today's problems with the same thinking that created them.' Man is still opening up the same old books with no new thinking. We are no more than a robot and that type of thinking will not allow man to survive in the world we have created. Man seems to lack any ability to think outside the box or use any common sense. You can see this lack of common sense in our whole economy," continued Fred. "We have gutted this country of its manufacturing and we have become just paper shufflers and service industries. What has happened, in my view, is we have stepped into a huge bear trap of debt and greed. We have priced ourselves out of the world markets; we have over taxed our industries forcing our industries to move abroad so they can compete with the rest of the world. While I believe in the principals underlying the capitalistic system, I also believe the root of our problem is our government. We absolutely have to update our government for our times. We need to restructure our whole system. Part of our problem is our corporate tax rate which is the second highest in the world. But our over taxation doesn't stop there, we have to lower our corporate state tax rates also to be more competitive giving companies a reason not to leave. However, we are so far in debt that we need every penny we can get. Man is a horrible strategist unless he believes that all nations will ultimately have no choice but to wipe all debt off the books by defaulting on their debt obligations. If that is the case then every lender should be asking who is going to be the last man in. Who is going to be left holding the bag? Our national debt here in the U.S. is greater than our entire GNP or gross national product. In addition we have mountains of household debt that can't be paid unless people have jobs and student loans that can't be paid if the graduates can't find work. God forbid that interest rates should rise. But the other problem is our wages and salaries are not competitive with the rest of the world. We are not playing on a level playing field. Either our wages and salaries have to come down or our productivity has to go up. However, the rest of the world is using our technologies and catching up to us and perhaps even surpassing us in productivity. On top of that, the world is becoming so focused on their economies the planet's environment is suffering because of it. We are at the point where we either unify the planet so we work as one or the inevitable will happen, in my opinion. We can no longer take what we have for granted. We can't get raises based on inflation but only on productivity. We can't allow takeover artists to ruin our companies so they can make a buck. We need to encourage and nurture our companies not tear them down. We need to use the Warren Buffett approach and allow the management of well-run companies to continue without the threat of a hostile takeover. Private capital has a place, I think, in buying poorly managed companies and bringing in new management that sees the problems and can nurture the company back to health. Compensation to management has to be based on their ability to increase the bottom line." Fred paused from his excitement. "I get a little wound up on this subject, would you like a drink?"

"You stole my thoughts," replied Linda.

"What would you like?" asked Fred.

"A glass of house wine would be fine. No, make it a White Zinfandel."

Fred headed for the bar car. I wonder why someone majoring in anthropology became a stockbroker, puzzled Fred. He nimbly maneuvered back to his seat with a drink in each hand. Handing the glass of Zinfandel to Linda, Fred said "cheers" and touched the two glasses together. Hesitating for a few moments Fred said "Why did someone majoring in anthropology become a stockbroker?"

"Thanks for the wine. I need to unravel a little. I can only stand so much talk about our totally dysfunctional system," she smiled. "It is so upsetting to me but our problems are mounting and if we don't face them there is no hope for the future. You know, I could ask you a similar question. What brings you to this lopsided jungle?"

"Linda, there aren't many anthropologists on Wall Street, that's why I asked."

"There should be with this collection of clowns," smiled Linda. "Can you think of a better place to study man? This experience is a real eye opener. Wall Street is an inside look at barebones man. We see greed; myopic thinking and reactions, the struggle for financial survival and a fantasy world dislocated from reality and pegged to a quarterly earnings report."

"But you must be a very aggressive woman. Wall Street is not for wilting flowers."

"You must be very aggressive for a man?" smiled Linda.

"Touché. I see you reading Playboy, do you read that magazine often?" asked Fred.

"Why, does it bother you?"

"No, I just"

"Does it make you feel uncomfortable?" smiled Linda.

"Can I get you another drink?"

"No, but it looks like you want one."

"It's my 17th anniversary today and my wife is meeting me at the station, so, I don't think I will. Do you take this train every day?"

"It depends on how much work I have at the office. If you have a bad day and want to discuss it call me at work. I'm the only Linda Z at Pierce Withers in Manhattan and perhaps we can catch the same train. Linda went back to reading Playboy while Fred relaxed deeper into his seat with an empty plastic glass dangling from his fingers as the scotch and water helped to make his eyelids somewhat drowsy.

The time passed quickly until the conductor broke the relative silence with "next stop Greenwich". Fred reacted more from the loud voice of the conductor than from cognizance. Climbing out of his seat he reached overhead for his coat, bid his seat mate adieu and headed for the door.

"Fred," yelled Susan, his wife, as Fred descended the stairs of the train. A cute woman of Asian descent wearing a long winter coat and scarf was flailing her arms over her head in the cold evening air. Fred looked up as he stepped down. Walking quickly over to his wife with a smile he said, "Hi honey" wrapping his arms around her smaller frame and giving her a kiss that even shocked Susan; "Happy anniversary."

"Thanks," she said looking up at him with a warm affectionate smile; "Happy anniversary to you too."

Partly oblivious to the army of commuters rushing around, they walked arm in arm to their car.

"Fred, I got a baby sitter for tonight because Lacy is going over to a girl friend's house for the night."

"Who did you get?"

"Christina Smith, the cute little girl we had about a month ago. The kids said they liked her."

Twenty minutes later Fred turned into his driveway that led to his Tudor style house that overlooked Long Island Sound.

"Where are the kids?"

"They are at the Halls. Kathy picked them up at sports for me so I could come down to get you. Her girls are playing sports at the same time. Both our boys just love her two girls."

"That's because they can climb trees faster than our two boys. Do you think there is any hanky-panky going on between them?"

"If there is it's only on a very inquisitive basis," said Susan with a slight giggle as she glanced back at Fred."

Opening the door to their house, Fred said, "I think I better have a talk with them on how to treat girls."

"Fred, Freddy is only eight years old. You haven't even had a "birds and bees" talk with Lacy and she will be driving this year."

"Oh, yes I have."

"You have, when?"

"Oh, from time to time I mention some things."

"You mean like not wearing tight fitting clothes?"

"How do you know that?"

"Lacy, mentioned that you thought her sweater was too revealing."

"Well, it was. She happens to be very well endowed if you haven't noticed," muttered Fred as he closed the door.

"Honey, she is starting to take more interest in her appearance and she is feeling more womanly."

"Oh God," replied Fred, "Would you please talk to her about not being too obvious in this day and age. You know it has become a much more dangerous world today."

Susan put her arms around Fred's neck and said, "All girls want to feel wanted, me included. After all, our job is to attract the male. And sweetheart she knows everything has a time and place. I have to go over and get the kids so you better shower and get ready because it is a good twenty minute drive over to the Inn."

"You mean we can't have our own hanky-panky?" said Fred glancing at Susan.

"Fred, not now, but if you play your cards right," Susan said striking a sexy pose, "maybe later. I have to get the children now."

Freddy and Tommy got out of the car looking as if they had been through a war. Their coats were caked in mud as were their pants. "It looks like you guys have been through a war," exclaimed Fred when he saw them.

"Those damn girls," exclaimed Tommy with a grimace.

"Wait Tommy, let me tell Dad what happened," moaned Freddy.

"I can tell Dad what happened," snapped Tommy.

"No Tommy, I'd better tell Dad what happened, I'm older," replied Freddy.

"Would someone please tell me what happened," ushered Fred.

"O.K. Freddy, you can tell Dad what happened," said Tommy taking off his muddy coat and dropping it on the floor.

"Fred, are you getting ready?" called Susan from upstairs.

"The kids are going to tell me what happened to their clothes, they look like they went through a war," yelled Fred back.

"Well, they will have to tell you later. Christina will be here any time and we are going to have to leave as soon as she comes. Will you please come upstairs and get ready."

"Mother," called Lacy, "you have a phone call from Mrs. Beasley."

"Tell her I will call her back tomorrow; tell her Fred and I are just running out the door to celebrate our 17th anniversary."

"She sounds all up set almost hysterical. I think you better talk to her."

"Sally, Lacy says you sound very upset, what's wrong," said a concerned Susan.

"Susan, Matilda called me and she is beside herself. She could hardly talk. Her husband, Jack, and their son Jimmy were in a head on car accident and have been taken to the Greenwich Hospital."

"Oh my God," said Susan with tears starting to form in her eyes."

"Will you meet us there?"

"Of course, we are leaving now."

"Fred," Susan yelled with emotion, "Jack Fredericks and their son, Jimmy, were in a head on car accident."

Fred ran upstairs. "What?"

"Sally just called me. We will have to postpone our anniversary and go right over to the hospital," said a very emotional mother of three. "Lacy, you will have to stay here until Christina comes."

"Jimmy was in a head on car accident?" blurted a shocked and saddened young girl. "Oh my God."

"Fred, for God sakes; go start the car." blurted an emotional mother.

It was a nerve-wracking twenty minutes before they reached the hospital. They ran to the emergency waiting room where Sally and Matilda were holding each other in shock. Matilda's eyes were flooded with tears and Sally was an emotional mess.

"What's the latest news," asked Susan, distraught.

"They had to use the Jaws of Life to get them out," sobbed Matilda.

"We haven't been told much. They are working on them now," said Sally.

Susan's eyes welled up in tears. "Do they know what happened?" she asked.

"They think it was a drunk driver. They said the cars were almost fused together," said Sally, choked with emotion."

Fred paced the floor along with Sally's husband Hank. "I feel so useless," whispered Hank.

"We can only pray," said Fred softly. "Only God is in charge of miracles."

The door to the emergency room opened and a nurse motioned to Matilda. "I want you to know we are doing everything humanly possible but it is a grave situation. Do you want a sedative?"

Matilda could only shake her head as tears flowed down her face. She sobbed quietly within herself. She couldn't help but see the remains of their car splattered in the blood of her husband and child. "Why?" she kept asking herself. "Why, is anyone allowed to leave a bar drunk and drive a car? Why is anyone allowed to be distracted by a cell phone or anything else when driving?"

A very long hour passed and the nurse entered the waiting room again and went over to Sally. "Do you know the church Matilda and her husband belong to?"

Sally nodded. "I think it would be nice if you called to see if the priest or minister could come down to be with Mrs. Frederichs."

Hours passed with the severe strain showing on the face of each. The minister had arrived to be with Matilda. He held her hand and tried to hold out hope. Finally, the door to the emergency room opened and a doctor walked over to Matilda.

Putting his hand on her shoulder, he said, "Your husband is in grave condition. He has been murmuring Mattie, Mattie. He needs you. He has been calling for you. We have done everything we know to do, but he is not responding. It really is in the hands of the almighty. Perhaps you would like to be with him in his final moments. Sometimes a touch can do more than a room full of doctors."

Matilda could feel her legs buckle and almost give way. Her mind was in a chaotic state; confused, stunned and in disbelief. She managed to nod back to the doctor with her tears almost blinding her. Her minister held her hand and the two walked together down the hall to her husband's bedside. She reached out to her beloved husband and took his hand in hers. He stirred for a moment and opened his eyes and then they closed and his hand fell limp. The minister read from his bible as the doctor tried to listen for Jack's pulse. The sheet was pulled over the bed and Matilda trembled and collapsed over her husband's body as tears streamed from her face. "No, no, oh please God no" she cried. Minutes seemed like hours until Matilda had the strength to turn to the Doctor and ask emotionally "what about my son?" sobbed Matilda shaking uncontrollably."

The doctor summoned a nurse for a sedative.

"You've been under a tremendous amount of strain Mrs. Frederichs," said the doctor, "I think this will help."

"He suffered a spinal cord injury and can't seem to move his lower legs. But he is alive and we think we can save him. We will know more in a few hours."

Matilda pulled herself up and with the help of her minister dragged herself back to the waiting room. Matilda's eyes were glazed over with tears as her wobbly legs carried her to the closest chair. Her minister sat down next to her and held her hand. In a flash, life had changed. Life can never be taken for granted. It is only by the grace of God that man exists at all. We hang by an environmental thread and a will to live. Matilda's life now revolved around her son, Jimmy.

"My son," she murmured to Susan, "my son, my only child. He's paralyzed."

Susan was beside herself. She couldn't control the tears that ran down her face and fell to her dress. "But he's alive Matilda," she said in a choked and muffled tone. Do you want us to take you home so you can get some rest? We can bring you back as soon as the Doctor calls."

"I can't leave my son?" cried Matilda.

Fred went over to Matilda and Susan, and said "I know we are all emotionally drained. Hank and I are going to find a Chinese restaurant and get some food to bring back. I am sure we all could use some energy to see us through the night."

Susan smiled through her tears, put her arm around her husband and kissed him. "Thanks," she murmured.

The night was long and dark. Minutes seemed like hours and hours an eternity. The only news they had received was "He has a huge will to live. He is a real fighter." The nurses stood watch throughout the night. No one slept. It was a matter of dozing off here and there. Their seats became uncomfortable, their backs groaned and broken hearts sobbed quietly to themselves. It was not until the sun was starting to fill the room with light that a nurse opened the door and said to Matilda, "All his vital signs are strong do you want to see him?"

Matilda's eyes filled with tears again and she nodded to the nurse.

"Do you need more tissue?" asked the nurse.

Matilda nodded.

"I wouldn't take too long, he is still groggy and his body needs all the energy he can give it."

Matilda nodded again.

"Unless he asks about his father, I wouldn't bring it up," said the nurse softly.

Matilda's legs started to buckle until she caught herself.

"Do you think you will be alright?" asked the nurse.

"In a minute," replied Matilda

Matilda entered Jimmy's room. Her son was black and blue and he tried to look over as she walked in. Matilda used every bit of whatever energy she had left not to break down.

"Sweetheart, I love you," she said touching his face. She bent over and kissed him.

He looked up at her and asked, "How's Dad?"

Matilda's heart almost stopped. Her legs trembled and she had to prop herself up on the bed. She pinched her side as hard as she could. "He's fighting too," she murmured.

"I saw him; he was on his phone texting, Mom."

"The driver was on his phone texting?"

Jimmy nodded.

Matilda leaned over again and kissed her son. "I love you sweetheart; I want you to get as much rest as you can. I'm right outside if you need me."

Matilda dragged her exhausted frame out to the waiting room. Tears started to stream down her cheeks and she collapsed into a chair. Susan and Sally came over and sat down next to her. They each took a hand and squeezed tightly. Silence, other than sniffling, filled the room for what seemed like hours until Susan asked "was he awake?"

Matilda nodded.

"Was he able to say anything?" asked Sally.

"He asked me how Dad was". Matilda broke down and started to sob.

Sally looked at Susan and their eyes filled with tears that rolled silently down their faces. Hank looked at Fred and whispered "your worst nightmare." Fred just shook his head with sadness in his face and tears in his eyes as he grit his teeth.

Time passed and the door opened and the nurse came out and went over to Matilda. "Mrs. Frederichs, we think Jimmy is out of the danger zone, why don't you go home and get some sleep. If anything should change we will call you right away."

An emotionally uncomfortable week followed. A week no one wants to live. Matilda knew she had to tell Jimmy about his father. Every time she thought about it she broke down in tears. She was an emotional wreck herself. Her nights were spent weeping and her pillow became wet with tears. Her life was in a shambles all in a flash. Things you never think can happen; happen, things you can never prepare yourself for happen and things that happen only in one's own worst nightmares happen. She kept asking herself why, why would man allow anyone to drive a vehicle, at high speed going in opposite directions only feet apart, to be distracted by cell phones or texting or drinking hot coffee, anything that could cause a mind to lose its focus? Susan and Sally also spent sleepless nights and worked their own lives around their children and being with Matilda. It was a long week that seemed to drag on forever. It was hard to talk to Matilda because everyone was so emotional. Tears appeared easily, nerves were being overloaded and the mind shuttled thoughts regarding anything else to another out of the way location.

Jimmy improved day by day and Matilda lived in limbo between her house and the hospital. She had been putting off the day of truth.

The day arrived when the doctor said "Mrs. Frederichs, Jimmy is making good progress and we are going to release him on Friday. He has been in therapy and he will have to continue to receive therapy as many times per week as possible but I would recommend at least five."

"Can he walk?" asked Matilda

"Mrs. Frederichs, a spinal cord injury is one of the most difficult injuries for doctors to cope with. The spinal cord and the peripheral nervous system carry all the electrical wiring throughout the body. Any damage or even bruising to that system can cause it to malfunction. In fact, the system seems to want to shut down completely after it has been damaged in many cases."

"Was his spinal cord damaged?"

"He has what looks like damage to L3 which is his third disk in his lumbar region. Below that region there is no communication between his upper leg muscles, the hamstrings and the quadriceps, and the lower leg muscles."

"Why?" asked Matilda, "if it hasn't been cut?"

"We don't know. What we do know is the neurons that are supposed to communicate don't."

"Will he ever be able to walk again," asked Matilda teary eyed.

"If the cord was cut, I could tell you no. Since it wasn't cut, I can only say there have been cases where people have regained mobility and sometimes even years later. However, it is somewhat of a rarity. Because, I don't know, we have to do everything we can to keep him positive. We have to make sure all his muscles get their needed exercise so they don't atrophy."

"Can I see him?" asked Matilda.

"Of course."

As she walked down the hall to her son's room, she bit her lip and told herself, you have to be strong.

"Hi Sweetheart," she said as she entered his room.

"Mom, I want to go home. Is Dad ready to go home too?"

Matilda's heart collapsed. She had told herself she had to be strong, but tears appeared and her nerves became as taught as violin strings. She did her best to control herself and she said in a whisper, "Sweetheart, it's just going to be you and me."

Jimmy's face changed, tears appeared in his eyes and he said "Dad didn't make it, did he?"

Matilda shook her head; it was all she could do. She put her arms around her son and squeezed as tears ran down their faces. "I love you," she murmured and kissed him.

Chapter Two

THE ANNIVERSARY

Over a month passed and the merry-go-round of life picked up its rhythms where they had left off. Susan's pain of the tragic accident faded and the knots in her nerves were slowly becoming untied.

"Fred, let's celebrate our anniversary this weekend," suggested Susan.

"Do you want to try the same Inn?" questioned, Fred.

"It wasn't the Inn, Fred that caused the accident."

"Some people are superstitious, that's why I asked.

"I like that Inn," replied Susan.

"Why don't you call Christina and see if she can come Saturday?"

Saturday came and the same record played.

"Fred, are you ready?"

"The kids were just going to tell me something."

"Fred, they can tell you later. Christina will be here any time and we are going to have to leave as soon as she comes. Will you please come up stairs and get ready."

Fred stooped over as he trudged back upstairs in his underpants and white button down shirt as Susan came down looking beautiful in her black low square cut front dress.

"Fred, did you shower yet?"

"Honey, I'm already. Just give me a minute to put on my pants and a tie and jacket."

"Tommy, why did you take your coat off and dump it on the floor?" asked Susan.

"I always take my coat off when I come inside."

"But I always tell you to hang it up."

Tommy frowned, picked his coat up and put it in the closet on a coat hook made just for him.

"Was that so tough," said Susan smiling.

There is a knock at the front door.

"It's Christina," yelled Freddy looking through the window.

"Hi, Christina," yelled the boys as they opened the front door.

Christina, a cute fifteen year old was wrapped up in a winter coat and wearing a wool hat that covered her ears. "Hi boys," she replies.

"Christina, Fred and I have to run or we will be late. I left some snacks in the kitchen for you and the kids. We should be back early but if we are late, please put the kids to bed. If you put them in their pj's please put all their dirty clothes in the wash hamper."

Susan yelled upstairs, "Fred, what are you doing?"

"I'm right here," said Fred appearing at the top of the stairs. "Hey guys, I got a new game for your Xbox360."

"What is it," exclaimed Tommy.

"I got NHL 09. I know you like hockey so you should really like this. Christina, do you know how to use Xbox360?"

"Yes, of course, everyone my age knows how to use an Xbox360," said a fifteen year old with a confident smile.

"This new game should keep them busy for you," said Fred.

"Come on Fred," said Susan opening the door.

"Fred, I have to take my car into the shop," said Susan as they drove out the driveway.

"What's wrong with it?"

"All I know is the kids were fooling around in the car when I was inside the house. Tommy said Freddy was trying to stuff something up the heater. However, whatever it was, broke the heater, at least now the heater doesn't work"

"Well, I doubt the kids could do anything to the heater in a 51 Ford Woodie Country Squire Wagon. It's built to last. It's a battleship on wheels, but I'll take a look at it. If the kids did break a part, it will take some digging to find a replacement. You will have to tell them they are not allowed in my Ford unless one of us is with them."

"Fred, we are just going to have to replace that car. It is too hard to get parts for now."

"What, replace my Woodie Squire, that car has been in my family for years. It's a classic. You mean retire it, and I am not going to get another car that burns fossil fuel other than natural gas. Our country is going broke, in part, because we import seventy percent of our oil. Our country has way out stripped its own supply. Talk about stupid or blind, I don't know which. But the bottom line is we are transferring our wealth to other countries at the fastest pace in human history and many of those countries don't even like us. It's like holding ourselves up at the end of a pump gun so we can supply our enemies with bullets. Not to mention, we are ruining our atmosphere. When I can get natural gas at the gas station is the day I will get a new one."

"Fred this is our anniversary, do you think we can forego a long tirade about oil. I know all the major oil fields are in decline. Mexico's seventeen largest wells are all in decline. Every year the world's oil wells are losing at least six percent of their total reserves and we can't even be sure the reserves in other nations are what they claim. Man has built his whole civilization on a finite resource. At some point, demand will drive the price higher which will dictate how fast our economies can grow. But the real problem is our system. These people in Washington have done nothing except lead us down the garden path. They are either totally blind or just plain dumb. If we didn't have a billionaire like Pickens willing to spend immense amount of his time and more than sixty-two million dollars to make everyone aware of the problem, what would have happened? I know it's a mess and I don't understand what our congress and the car companies have been thinking about but obviously they are not part of the solution. Everyone is upset about it but let's talk about happier things."

"How is Mustard doing?" asked Fred.

"Oh, the kids just love her. She follows them around all over the house. She is the cutest little thing."

"I thought she might cheer everyone up after the accident. Do you think the kids made the right choice?" smiled Fred.

"Fred, they were right on. She is the most beguiling little ball of fluff with the cutest disposition."

"Golden Retrievers are known for that. How is the potty training going?"

"She's made a couple of mistakes but when I scold her, she looks up with the sadist eyes, like she knows she made a mistake and I just fall apart. I just want to pick her up and kiss her instead of saying "no" in a meaningful way and putting her outside."

"I don't know if I like the name Mustard. It really doesn't fit her," said Fred.

"The kids agree and they have shortened it to Mussy. It sounds more female, don't you think?"

"That's much cuter," replied Fred. Tell the kids to make sure she doesn't run down to the water. It's cold this time of year and I don't want her catching pneumonia."

"Fred, you make it sound like we just had a new child."

"We did. A little puppy is a new member of the family with all the same responsibilities."

"Fred, she is so cute. She will do anything the kids want her to do. She is the most trusting dog I've ever seen."

"Everything except sleep on Freddy's bed," quipped Fred. "She loves Tommy's quilt for some reason and I think she'd have a nervous breakdown if we tried to get rid of it."

"Fred, it's not funny. We're going to have a fight over that quilt. Freddy wants Mussy to sleep on his bed and she won't. One of these days Freddy is going to discover that Mussy goes where ever the quilt goes and then he is going to take Tommy's quilt and there is going to be a big fight with lots of tears."

"What are you going to do?" smiled Fred.

"What am I going to do? You mean what are we going to do, and I don't know," sighed Susan.

"Do you think we can find another quilt just like Tommy's?" asked Fred.

"I don't think it would make any difference because Tommy's quilt must have a particular odor that Mussy is attached to."

"Well, let's look for a quilt that looks similar and when the kids aren't around we will rub the two quilts together and see if that doesn't work" said Fred. "What do you think?"

"We can try. Fred, there's the Inn. It looks like they painted it since we were here last and it looks like they have valet parking now. Oh! How nice."

Susan snuggled up to Fred grabbing his hand as they walked into the Inn.

"My name is Willing and I have reservations for two at seven."

"Yes, Mr. Willing, this way please." The Inn was glowing in candle light that highlighted the colonial raised paneling and cornice. The old random width hardwood floor had several oriental rugs covering them. It was lovely and warm with several other couples in different parts of the dining room.

"Will this table be satisfactory?"

"Perfect, thank you," replied Fred.

"Oh Fred, we are right in front of the fire place, it's so romantic."

"Good evening, my name is Charles; do you care for a drink?"

"Yes, we will both have a Bloody Mary," answered Fred.

"Oh Fred, don't you just love candlelight and look at these beautiful flowers," said a mother of three who had just become a little girl full of romance and excitement. "Honey, is it possible to start investing with only a hundred dollars?"

Fred's eyes shifted from looking at the glowing embers in the fire place to his wife.

"What," replied Fred tugging at his ear with a surprised expression on his face?

"Would it be possible to start investing with a hundred dollars?" replied Susan meekly.

Fred couldn't believe his ears. My wife never had much interest in investing and now, in front of a beautiful fire and candlelight, she brings it up?

"Sweetheart, did I hear you say something about investing? As I recall, the last time you ever mentioned anything about investing was when Tommy was born."

"Oh Fred, I know this is our anniversary but I just wanted to know if it could be done?"

"Sure, why not? What brought that up?"

"I was talking to Matilda and she mentioned that Jimmy loved the stock market."

"And," said Fred with a nervous fidget.

"Well, now that he is confined to a wheelchair, he is either in therapy or on his computer all day and he wants to start investing."

Oh no, thought Fred. Not on our anniversary. "Susan, I love you and we have a beautiful fire flickering right here making a very romantic setting. Can't we talk about this another time?"

"Oh Fred, I know, but Matilda asked me and I feel so bad about what happened that I told her I would find out. He wants to go to college in a couple of years and they don't know how they can afford it."

"Susan this is a very tough market to invest in. I have seasoned well capitalized investors who are losing their shirts. I certainly think Jimmy should put his money in a bank CD. There are lots of scholarships available also. This is not a good time for someone who only has a hundred dollars and no income to speak of to start investing; in fact, he is a minor and cannot legally invest anyway. Susan, my heart goes out to Jimmy but this is just not the time. Tell Matilda this is not a good time to invest but it is a good time to learn about the markets. Tell her to get Jimmy to do as much research as possible and to paper trade and see how he does. Now can we get back to enjoying the fire and the candlelight and maybe a little romance?"

"Oh Fred; why is life so complicated?"

"Well, you know as well as I do, life is a crap shoot. It is totally unpredictable. Life is like everything in nature. There is no way to know where the next bolt of lightning will strike or where the next hurricane will pop up. People are just as unpredictable. You think you know what someone is going to do and then they do just the opposite. How many times have you told the kids to do something and they either didn't do it or they misinterpreted what you meant. That unpredictability is what makes the stock market as volatile as it is. If you combine that unpredictability with a failing economy you are just playing with dynamite. Now, can I tell you how much I love you and how important you are to me?" said Fred, as he leaned over to his wife and kissed her.

"That's so sweet Fred. I love you too."

"It's so nice to get away and just be with each other, isn't it?" said Fred.

"It is heaven," said Susan. I can feel the warmth of the fire and it feels so good. Fred, I thought you said that as long as the market is moving, whether it is up or down, you can always make money? How can you have a bad or tough market if it is moving?"

Fred was caught in the wrong gear. His face showed the confusion. It took him a few seconds to change gears.

"Honey, I'm trying to be romantic and make a happy and romantic anniversary for you."

"I know sweetheart but I can't stop thinking about Jimmy. He is paralyzed and may well spend the rest of his life in a wheelchair; whether he will ever regain the use of his legs nobody knows. That means he may not be able to find work and competition for scholarship money is so competitive these days. Not only that but what happens if he takes out a student loan and then can't get a job after he graduates because the economy is falling apart? I heard on the radio that many students can't pay their loans back and our government will be facing upwards of a trillion dollars in unpaid loans. How can we afford that Fred?"

"We can't Honey. Is he smart?"

"Matilda says he is average."

The waiter came over to the table with a half hidden hand signal from Fred.

"Two more Bloody Marys, please," said Fred before Susan could say anything.

Fred looked a little perplexed.

"I hope you are not suggesting that I try to invest his college money especially in a market like this?"

"Fred, you told me that the worst market is a flat market when nothing is moving. The market is moving all over the place now. Someone is making money, right?"

"And a lot of people are losing it too. Susan, there are two kinds of people who use the markets to try and make a better return than they can in bonds or U.S. Treasuries or C.D's. You have the investor who is looking to invest in a good company with good growth potential over the long term, five years or longer. Then you have the speculator who doesn't care about long term investing and just wants to make money on the fluctuations. He can be in and out in the same day, in fact, most trades on the floor of the stock exchange are only for about four minutes and are made by computers. The individual speculator has a very difficult time making money and the vast majority of speculators do not. Speculating is exceedingly difficult. I am not a speculator and every time I try, I lose."

"Someone must make money Fred or they wouldn't do it."

"Susan, there is always someone who is wired to be able to take advantage of every type of situation not to mention luck.

That's true in everything. There is always someone who is wired differently than the rest and excels where the rest fail. I would say fewer than ten percent of all speculators ever make money; especially consistently."

"Why not buy good companies when they sell off?" asked Susan.

"That is, in my opinion, the only way to make money consistently."

"Then why wouldn't now be a perfect time to buy a company whose stock has sold off?"

"Normally, I would have to say yes. But our economy right now is in no man's land. Greed was allowed to run rampant. Greenspan used the phrase "irrational exuberance" which was really a nice way of saying greed is about to kick us in the rear end. Of course, no one really heard him, the phrase was repeated over and over but it was a superficial cognizance. In fact, no one was really listening; the phrase went in one ear and out the other. It seemed everyone thought prices of houses and everything else could, at least, reach to the moon. The regulators fell asleep at the switch, our Congress was totally out to lunch, the bankers were making so much money they got caught with their pants down out in left field, basically our whole system fell apart. What really worries me is these are the people we count on. These are our best and the brightest supposedly. I don't think anyone will believe them anymore."

"What do you think is going to happen?"

"Paulson was brought in to head the Treasury from Goldman Sachs to fix things under very difficult circumstances but many say he really hasn't shown any creativity, nothing new. His opponents say he looks more like a fish out of water than a financial savior. So the long term investor is continuing to take a bath right now and we don't know how low the market will go or what will happen to the market. I would be loath to recommend buying even at these levels."

"Didn't the Governor of New Jersey come from Goldman too?"

"Yes," replied Fred.

"How can anyone forget, right Fred. The Governor races down the highway at about 100 miles per hour; crashes and is almost killed and endangered the lives of others. What a role model. How can someone be smart enough to run a major bank and yet lack any common sense? Even he had to apologize to the public for his stupidity. There seems to be a total disconnect between running a company or country and so called intelligence or maybe it's common sense but that disconnect happens over and over and almost always in our government decisions. No wonder our economy is in trouble."

"Susan, I am sure they are asking themselves many of the same questions in hind sight."

"Fred, the problem with hind sight is it can kill you."

"Susan, how do we define intelligence? Is man's problem intelligence, a lack of common sense or not being able to think outside the box or all of them? What do we mean when we say thinking outside the box? Man must lack a critical part of what we call intelligence but we don't even know how to define intelligence or even test for all its parts. Part of the problem is the very structure of both business and government. You don't go into business to be a philanthropist, and you don't become a politician not to get elected. In both cases the structure is set up for the person or entities' own self-interest. In business all they want is continuation of the business to make money. In government both the politician and the party he or she represents, wants continuation. Continuation doesn't necessarily mean change. The only reason either changes is for survival."

"Anyway Fred, Matilda asked if you would help him invest a hundred dollars?"

"Susan, Matilda asked you if I would help him invest a hundred dollars." Fred's face could be read a hundred miles away with an "I don't believe this expression."

"Yes, Jimmy and Matilda just wanted to know if my husband would consider helping him. Perhaps you could find time to talk to them and explain that he may be smarter to keep his money in the bank and that while it would be safer it would not enable him to pay for college."

Oh no, thought Fred, she is on his side. She doesn't understand what a slippery slope the market and our economy is on. Minds are so different; some can see what others can't even if you tell them.

"I take it you are on his side and not mine," remarked Fred who knew he was being snared. "Won't he get something from the insurance company?"

"Matilda says the other driver didn't have any insurance and their insurance doesn't cover uninsured motorists. Fred, I just want you to talk to him and explain what would be best for him. I love my husband and I'm always on your side," said an adoring wife, "I also have a lot of faith in my husband."

Fred was shell shocked. How could he say no?

"But I am no magician sweetheart. I am just trying to do a very difficult job the best that I can. Can we go back to having our anniversary now?" asked Fred touching his wife's soft face in an adoring manner.

Fred signaled to the waiter.

"Another round of Bloody Marys."

"Will you talk to Jimmy and Matilda at church?"

"Yes. Do you know, I think you are the most beautiful woman in the whole world? All I want to do is undress you piece by piece," Fred whispered as he leaned over to kiss her.

Susan gave her husband a blushing flirtatious smile.

"You're bad," she replied. "Someone might be listening."

"Good, I'll make them so jealous their ears will fall off," replied Fred as he leaned over and put his arm around her.

Susan giggled as she looked at her husband with a sexy throw me down on the floor look.

"Honey, I'm not that sexy am I?" inquired a coquettish wife.

"I just want to tear your clothes right off you," said Fred in a low sexy voice, "and throw you right down on the floor."

"Oh, stop that," smiled Susan. Fred, would it really be possible to build a hundred dollars into enough to pay for college in two or three years?"

"What," exclaimed Fred, "how can you change gears like that? I'm telling you how much I want you and all of a sudden you're thinking about something else? How did we jump from romance back to this problem you've gotten sucked into?"

"Well, it intrigues me. After all, if it could be done then why wouldn't everyone do it?"

"Of course. Unless he wins the lottery he will have to get student loans and or scholarships."

"But could it be done?" asked a tipsy but adoring wife.

"I don't know if it would be even theoretically possible. He would have to have an incredible feel for the mood of the market; a sensitivity and feel for mass psychology that goes off the charts... But who knows what is possible unless one tries. After all, what are the chances of an Andrea Bocelli? A man who is blind; a man who has a photographic memory; a man who can hear a piece of music and forever remember it without missing one note and a man who also possess a fabulous voice to boot. But it happened."

"I love Andrea. When he sings Somos Novios I feel so romantic. I think he is the best overall singer of this century, even Pavarotti. He can sing anything with such feeling, I just fall apart inside."

Oh, I guess I should have had the Inn play Somos Novios, thought Fred, nothing else is working.

"Don't you love Andrea, Fred?" asked Susan getting more tipsy by the minute.

"I love him too, Susan. I never tire of listening to Andrea. But what are the chances of all those pieces coming together for that genius to happen? Life is a kaleidoscope with random pieces or, in our case, hormones, acids, sugars and thousands if not tens of thousands of other variables all falling randomly into place guided by a sketchy DNA molecule. We have three children and all three are like night and day. None of them seem to be like their parents at all. You wonder where they came from."

"The milk man, the plumber, the electrician," giggled a romantic wife looking into her husband's eyes giggling.

Fred motioned for the waiter again. He pointed to the two almost empty Bloody Mary glasses and signaled two more.

"Where could you invest only a hundred dollars?" asked Susan as she became tipsier.

"You choices are few. You can gamble on a penny stock, however, the reason they are a penny stock, more than likely, is because they are low on capital and are in dire need of more. In this market with the banks unwilling to lend and with the price of stocks so low, it would be very difficult to raise more needed capital."

"What about General Motors, they can get bailout money from our government," reasoned Susan.

"Honey, as gambling goes; it probably is not a bad gamble. However, they have to pay all that bailout money back if they survive, so, in my opinion, it will be years before their common stock moves higher. Moreover, the economy is still falling and taking car sales with it. But, if the stimulus plan starts to work and car sales take a turn for the better, GM could bounce higher."

"So, what can he do?"

"If I had to place a bet with only a hundred dollars to my name, my thinking would go like this. We have had a bubble which means peoples' emotions got over extended on the upside, so, more likely than not, they will get extended on the downside as well, which means GM is going to have a very difficult time.

What I would do is, gamble on my outlook and buy an out of the money put on the Spider."

"On the spider." Susan burst out giggling. "Fred, you have had too much to drink. I hope you have arranged for a cab to get us home?"

"Yes, I will, but I'm not drunk. Spiders are bench marked on the S&P500. It is a derivative, a basket of stocks that mirrors, in this case, the S&P 500. Its value goes up and down along with the S&P500 index. You can buy a put option or a call option on the spider."

"Is it risky?"

"Of course; if he bets wrong, he is out of luck. This is not investing. This is pure speculation. It's like going to the casinos unless he has some hidden intuition that we don't know about. His first move has to be right on the money or he is out of the game."

Fortunately for Fred, the waiter asks, "Are you ready to order?"

"What are you going to have Susan?"

The evening passed quickly with a warming fire and a couple who were rekindling their love for each other. Each looked into the eyes of the other, joked and acted as if they were Romeo and Juliet all over again.

Chapter Three

A NEW SCHOOL ROOM

"Fred, don't forget to talk to Jimmy and his mother today at church," reminded Susan.

"How could I forget?"

"And don't forget, we have to take your car."

"Oh," thought Fred, "I have to check the Ford and see what is wrong with it. I wonder what the kids could have put up the heater."

Fred finished his juice and opened the door in the kitchen that led to the garage. Fred's 1951 Ford Woodie Squire Wagon that had been completely restored over the years, sat polished and gleaming in its dark blue coat of nine layers of paint. He went over to his classic and opened the door. "Oooh, what an awful smell," he exclaimed.

Fred lowered the windows to get some circulation through the car and then went back inside to get the keys which he had forgotten and a coat hanger. Freddy and Tommy were seated at the breakfast table.

"What did you guys put up the heater in the car?" questioned Fred.

"Freddy put his frog up the heater in the car," exclaimed Tommy.

"Freddy, why did you do that?" asked Fred.

"Tommy, you have a big mouth," retorted Freddy.

"Well, it was your fault," snapped Tommy.

"Freddy how would you like to be stuffed up a heater?" asked Fred. "If you do anything to your hamster there is going to be hell to pay. Do you understand?"

"Yes," said Freddy with a long face knowing he had done something he shouldn't have.

"Have you fed Mussy this morning, Tommy?" asked Fred searching for the car keys in a drawer full of stuff.

"Yes, and I gave her a treat too."

"What kind of treat?"

"I gave her one of our chicken nuggets, she loves them."

"Susan, can Mussy have chicken nuggets?"

"I guess, why not, Fred? She seems to love them and they haven't come up yet. If the kids can eat them, I guess a puppy can." Mussy came out from under the table with her little tail wagging and looked up at Tommy, as if to say, what else do you have that's tasty? Susan couldn't resist. She leaned over, picked her up, and kissed her. Then she put her down and gave her another chicken nugget. Fred shook his head and having found the keys to the Ford, went back to the garage. Minutes later, Susan heard a loud, "Oooh God." What happened, Fred?" exclaimed Susan, as she poked her head into the garage.

"I put a wire coat hanger up the heater and fished around to see if there was something clogging the vent and I pulled out a dead decaying and smelly frog," exclaimed Fred.

"Freddy," yelled Fred, "you have to bury this frog as soon as you get your clothes on."

"I thought we were going to church?"

"We are, but you have to bury the frog first and at church you have to tell God you are sorry for what you did to the frog."

Freddy trudged off upstairs with a long guilty face.

After the frog was buried and with an appropriate head stone put in place, the family was off to church. Fred and Susan left the kids at Sunday school and walked toward the main church, when Susan spotted Matilda and Jimmy.

"Good morning Matilda and Jimmy," said Susan.

Fred, looking a little nervous said, "Susan tells me you are interested in investing."

"Well Jimmy is," replied Matilda with a big smile on her face. "He just loves the markets and follows them every day. He even talks about becoming a stockbroker. I know very little about investing. Jimmy, why don't you talk to Fred about getting him to help you?"

"Jimmy, are you aware the economy is not doing well, the banks are having a hard time just staying solvent, the car companies are losing money hand over fist, the mortgage market is in disarray and the housing market is taking a nose dive? Have you thought about putting your money in a bank CD?"

"Oh yes, I listen to Bloomberg News every day," exclaimed an eager young man. "Interest rates are very low and I think I can do better than the banks. After all, banks are notoriously horrible at investing. All they want to do is collect fees."

Fred's eyes opened a little wider. "Do you know the difference between investing and speculating or gambling?"

"You mean like buying stock in our country's largest and most respected name in the auto industry for the long term and watching its stock go down to almost zero vs. buying low and selling higher even if it happens to be in a day or a week?"

"Yes, smiled Fred, "that is what I mean. Do you know a minor cannot open a brokerage account?"

"Yes, but I can get my mother to open an account."

"And will she do that?" inquired Fred looking over at Matilda.

"Yes, she said she would."

"Do you know if you are thinking about using options, all brokers require a minimum deposit of two thousand dollars? Jimmy, how much are you going to open your account with?"

"A hundred dollars. I know it's not very much but it is all I have. But my mother will open the account with two thousand and of that I can only use one hundred dollars."

"Jimmy, I am going to be very up front and honest with you. I would tell my own sons exactly the same thing. The risk in what you want to do is extremely high. The probability of you turning a hundred dollars into enough for college in two or three years is so tiny; I mean the odds of you doing what you want to do are almost impossible. If we had a more stable stock market that had a strong economy pushing it up and your parents wanted to invest for you over the longer term, at least five to ten years, I would be much more encouraging. Take a look at all the investment funds run by professional traders and of those only a small percentage can make money on a consistent basis let alone beat the market. The number of pros who can consistently outperform the Standard and Poors Index is small, and even they will have good periods and bad periods where they may well lose money."

"I know, Fred, but I am trapped in this wheelchair and I love to follow the markets."

Fred swallowed hard.

"Jimmy, I am not a magician," said Fred somewhat emotionally. "The only thing I can do is to give you my ideas and experience. Look at it this way, if I was a market genius and could call all the turns in the market, I would be retired and living on an island in the Bahamas. Have you given any thought on how you are going to invest your hundred dollars?"

"Of course," said a smiling young man. "I am going to buy a Spider put."

Fred almost jumped backwards, Jimmy sounded like he really knew what he was doing. He had a game plan. Fred smiled, "Jimmy, you are going to have to keep your commissions down or they will eat up your little capital."

"I know I am going to trade online, over my computer. If I use an online broker to put my orders in, I can save a lot on commissions and it's faster, usually only a second or two," said a very confident young man.

Fred grinned, "Do you have a low cost online broker picked out?"

"Yes. In fact, I have filled out the required paper work with Mom. I don't know why anyone would use a full service broker now. The cost for the broker to put a ticket in is almost negligible, so almost all the commissions or fees, is profit. Fred, I don't mean to degrade the brokerage field because I'd like to be a broker someday but I have always thought fees should be based on the amount of money a broker makes for his client, not for putting a time stamp on a ticket."

"Jimmy, it sounds like a great idea; however, the brokerage industry has never been able to figure out how to do that. Since, even the professional traders, who manage vast pools of money, have a difficult time making money, how could the brokerage industry survive on fees from client profits especially in down markets like this one? Brokers not only put time stamps on tickets but they have to know all their products and how and when to use them. They have to prospect to get their clients, which is no easy trick, and they have to keep abreast of each client to make sure he or she is staying within his or her stated goal. They also have to stay on top of all the research that pours out from their company's analysts. It is a very demanding job. Every firm has to make enough money, after they pay their brokers, to pay their analysts and overhead and management salaries."

Matilda puts her arms around her son and squeezes him. "Fred, we have to let him try."

Fred put his arm around Susan and they walked into church.

"That was nice of you," whispered Susan. "He sounds like he knows what he wants to do."

After church, Fred and Susan walked over to pick the kids up at Sunday school.

"Did you tell God you were sorry for what you did to that poor little frog, Freddy?" asked Fred.

"Yes, and he said it was alright."

"Oh, he did not," exclaimed Susan. "You are going to go into church right now and tell God you are sorry for what you did to that poor little frog." Susan took Freddy by the hand and led him into church and to a pew. "I want you to kneel down and tell God you are sorry," whispered Susan sternly.

Freddy knelled down with a long face and Susan could hear him say, "God, I put my frog up the heater in my Mom's car but I didn't tell him to get stuck but he did and he couldn't get back to me and I didn't know what to do so I left him there and I know I shouldn't have done it and I'm sorry."

"I want you to make sure you take care of animals from now on," Susan said softly as she led her son out of church.

Fred could see Freddy pouting in the mirror as he drove the family home.

"Fred is the heater in my car working now?" asked Susan.

"Yes, once I got the poor frog out, the heater is now working again."

"When we get home, I want both Freddy and Tommy to take Mussy out so she can get some exercise," directed Susan.

"I will," blurted Tommy.

"Aren't you going Freddy?" asked Susan.

"I guess so," said a sad little boy.

"Freddy, we all make mistakes but you have to learn not to do it again," said Fred.

"Well, we dump all kinds of stuff into our oceans that kill our fish and our wildlife and nobody seems to be sorry for what they are doing," said Freddy.

There was silence for a few moments while Susan and Fred thought of a reply.

"Freddy, you are right and it is inexcusable. Adults should be punished for not taking care of our planet Earth. There is an old adage "out of sight, out of mind". The human animal is visual and if he doesn't see it, the problem doesn't exist in his mind. Man forgets there is a huge problem just below the surface but out of his sight. One of these days, there won't be any fish left and man will start to starve and then he will start to ask why. All we can pray for is, he sees his mistake before it is too late," replied Fred.

"That doesn't sound very smart to me," said Freddy. "I thought we were supposed to be smarter than the other animals?"

Again there was silence.

"Honey, we know what is right but we often don't do it. We forget in our rush to buy the T.V.'s and the washers and dryers and all the other things that make our lives so much easier than they have ever been before, that there is an environmental price to pay. We forget all these things we buy use up the Earth's resources and we forget that when they wear out we throw them out. I think we prefer not to see our problems and we would rather fool ourselves into believing that the factories that make all these things don't pollute the Earth's oceans and rivers and streams and the air we breathe," said Susan.

"How can that be smart?" asked Tommy. "There better be enough clean air for Mussy to breathe and enough clean water for her to drink because if anything happens to her I'll just die. At school they tell us that everything has to be recycled. Why are we throwing things away when they get old?"

There again was silence.

"Tommy," said Susan, "man is extremely near sighted. We have to learn that everything we buy has to be accounted for and recycled. Your school is right and we all should follow their teachings."

A few minutes later, Tommy slammed the car door shut and ran to open the door of the house to let Mussy out. A little ball of fluff let out a little puppy bark and ran to Tommy.

"Freddy, do you want to take Mussy up to our tree house?" asked Tommy.

"Honey," said Susan, you can't take Mussy up a tree, dogs can't climb trees."

"Well, I'll carry her," explained Tommy.

"Tommy," said Fred, "If she should fall and hurt herself, you would feel awful, wouldn't you?"

Tommy thought for a moment and said, "I'd cry," said Tommy.

"Honey," said Susan, "when you get an idea, think of everything that could go wrong because, you will learn if something can go wrong, it will in life."

"Why".

"Things happen you never plan for. Accidents happen out of the blue. So it's important to take your time and think about what accidents could possibly happen because of your idea. You don't want to take any unnecessary chances. That is what makes man smarter than other animals and that is why we have to look out for them."

"Can Freddy and me run down to the water with her?"

"I don't want her in the water," said Fred, "It's too cold and she could get sick. Think about what your mother just told you. If something can go wrong it will. So how do you think you can make sure she doesn't go in the water?"

Tommy thought for a moment, "You could build a fence."

"Fred, that's a good idea," said Susan. "Why don't you build a nice little white fence so we don't have to worry about Mussy?"

"Susan, I was thinking about something far easier, like a leash. I know we have one."

"Oh," said Susan. "I like the fence idea. Can we build a nice white fence with a door? We could even plant bushes in front of it... Fred it would look so nice."

"Susan, we have a big yard, it would take a lot of work and the fence would have to go all the way around the yard. If we just put a fence along the water Mussy could just run around it. And we certainly can't have any sharp points the kids or Mussy could get hurt on. Don't forget when we play baseball or football our attention is focused on the ball which means we could run into something. And when Mussy gets bigger she will jump right over it unless it is a high fence. If we have a high fence, then we can't see the water and we certainly don't want a chain link fence."

"Oh Fred, it seemed like a good idea. I guess the leash is a better idea, certainly simpler. Maybe we can get an invisible fence. I think that would be even better."

"That is a much better idea, Sweetheart".

"Will you do it Fred?"

"I will think about it and put it on my "to do list," replied Fred. "Freddy, I want you to get Mussy's leash and then let's walk down to the water with her."

"Fred, if we don't do it soon, Mussy will grow up and I want to teach her not to run outside our yard when she is still a puppy."

"Susan, Mussy is a little ball of fluff right now but she is a golden retriever and she is an outdoors dog. She is not a house dog. She needs a lot of exercise and she will be attracted to the water. The reason I got Mussy was, we are fortunate to have a large yard and the water so she can play in it when it's hot. I think invisible fences are great if you have a smaller yard and you have to keep your dog confined."

"Like if you lived in a development or in town, right Dad," said Freddy.

"That's right Freddy."

"So, you're not going to put the invisible fence in," retorted Susan with a disappointed face.

"Well, she is an outdoors dog, do you want to confine her when we don't have to?" answered Fred.

"Mom, I want to be able to swim with Mussy this summer," said Tommy.

"It looks like I'm out numbered but I just thought it would be nice while she is little to be able to put her outside without one of the boys watching her."

"I don't mind Mom," replied Tommy

"I don't either," piped in Freddy.

"I'm going to remember that the next time I ask you to take her out to piddle," replied Susan.

It was a chilly mid-April day with nimbostratus clouds over head but with the signs of boating season approaching. There was enough wind to ripple the waters of the bay and several gulls sat on dock pilings surveying the landscape. It wouldn't be long before the boatyards became busy with boaters getting their boats ready for another summer season. As the family walked down to the water with Mussy on her leash Fred pointed to a sailboat in the harbor and said "If you want the boats in the water by the last week in May, we are going to have to start working on them."

"What has to be done?" asked Freddy.

"Blue Moon's bottom has to be scraped and painted which I hate doing. All the bright work, that's the mahogany that has to be varnished, has to be done and that is no easy job either. You and Tommy can wash off the sunfish and have them ready to go as soon as the water warms up. So, if nothing is broken and has to be repaired, we should be able to get the boats in on time this year."

"Oh boy, I can take Mussy sailing this summer," exclaimed Freddy.

"Mom, can I take Mussy sailing," asked Tommy.

"Well, we will have to go out sailing a few times first to make sure you are good enough. The sunfish aren't very big and you are going to have to keep Mussy in the little cockpit with you. Of course, we have to make sure Mussy is a good swimmer before she can go out with either of you."

"I'll be seven this year Mom, so I know I'll be good enough," replied Tommy. "I was pretty good last year. Mom, I thought dogs knew how to swim."

"Tommy, dogs know how to swim instinctively, but I want to make sure our little ball of fluff has plenty of practice so if she falls overboard she can swim back to the boat or shore. That also means you both have to stay close to shore," stated Susan.

"Since you are getting so old now, I expect both you and Freddy to take responsibility for the sunfish this year. You have to make sure they are brought out of the water every evening and that their sails are lowered and secured so a storm can't shred them," said Fred. "Freddy will be nine this summer so there is no excuse from either of you for not taking care of your sunfish."

The following evening Fred was in his upstairs home office working.

"Fred," yelled Susan, "the kids want to shave Mussy with their hair clippers."

Oh no, thought Fred.

Fred rushed down stairs to the kitchen. "What is going on?"

"The kids want to shave Mussy for the summer so she doesn't get hot," explained Susan.

"Hey guys," explained Fred, "golden retrievers are not supposed to be clipped for the summer, especially a puppy. Puppies need their hair to keep them warm."

"Well, you cut my hair," exclaimed Tommy.

"You are not a puppy and Mom makes you wear a hat when it's cold outside."

"But sometimes I forget and I don't get a cold. If you are afraid of Mussy catching cold, why can't she wear a coat? I see other dogs wearing hats and coats?"

"I've never seen a golden retriever in a coat or hat," Susan said smiling.

"I've seen other dogs wear coats and hats Mom,"

"Each dog breed is different," explained Fred. "The way you care for a golden retriever is a little different than you would care for a poodle. You don't clip a golden retriever but you have to brush her daily to get all the dead hair and knots out. In the summer she will automatically shed hair so her own body will compensate for the warmer weather."

"Tommy," said Susan, "look at it this way. Mussy is just like you. You and Mussy both have to take care of yourselves. She has to eat right just like you and both of you have to make sure not to get over weight, both of you have to see a doctor regularly for your check ups, and both of you have to get your daily exercise. If you shave her coat off, her body is not use to that and she could easily catch a cold. When you catch a cold you're miserable, your nose runs, sometimes you get a sore throat and sometimes a headache and sometimes even a fever and you have to stay in bed. Mussy goes through a lot of the same things. Do you want her to feel awful?"

Tommy thought for a short moment and said, "You mean she can get a sore throat and a headache."

"Yes, sweetheart, just like you."

Mussy, by this time, had responded to her name and was looking up and bouncing around with her tail wagging as if to say "won't anyone play with me." She grabbed Tommy's pants in her little teeth and started to yank on them. Susan could not resist this beguiling little golden ball of fluff. Mussy let out a puppy bark as she pulled on Tommy's pants and Susan leaned over and picked her up. Mussy's tail stopped wagging as she was smothered with kisses."

"You are going to spoil that dog rotten," quipped Fred.

"I know but she is just so cute." She handed Mussy to Freddy, "have you brushed her today?"

"No," replied Freddy.

"I want you to do it daily. It doesn't take that long. Look how little she is. I want you and Tommy to do that right now."

"Where is the brush, Mom?"

"I hope where it is supposed to be or certainly should be. Tommy did you put the brush back where you got it last time?"

"I always do," said Tommy with a slightly guilty look on his face.

"Then Freddy it should be in that drawer," pointing to the drawer that held a lot of miscellaneous stuff.

"Mom, there are two brushes, a wire one and a rubber one. Which one should I use?" asked Freddy.

"Honey, use the wire brush to get the tangles out. I think it's called a slicker brush and use the rubber one on her little pink tummy. If you see any fleas let me know right away and we will have to bathe her and put some flee powder on. If you find another brush in the drawer next week, it will be a porcupine brush which they tell me is good for her coat and makes it shine.

Use the slicker brush to get the tangles out, then give her a once over with the porcupine brush after I get it. You can use the porcupine brush on her ears and tail also."

"Should we use the wire brush on her ears?" asked Tommy.

"Just be careful and don't be rough with her. That reminds me, I've got to get an undercoat rake when she starts to shed or we will have hair all over this house. Fred, what are we going to do with her when she gets big?"

"When the weather gets better, I am going to build a kennel for her with lots of room for her to run."

"Oh, no," exclaimed Tommy. "If you build a kennel, then I won't be able to have her sleep on my bed. You can't put her outside," said a young boy with a long worried face.

"Tommy, she will get so big she won't fit on your bed," remarked Freddy.

"We will see honey," consoled Susan, but all baby animals grow up and get to be bigger. Mother Nature gives them everything they need to survive outside. Mussy is no different. She will become a big dog and she will need her exercise. Her instincts will start to take over and she will want to dig and run and listen for all the sounds of nature. She will want to hear the bark of other dogs too."

"What do dogs bark about, Mom?" asked Tommy.

"They talk about lots of things. Dogs communicate better than people. When you hear a neighboring dog bark, he or she is saying "I'm here, is there anyone listening and by the way this is my territory over here."

"I don't hear them say that," replies Freddy. "I just hear them bark."

"Oh Freddy, all animals communicate, it's just that you don't understand them," said Susan. "It's like talking to someone from another country speaking a foreign language. All you hear is a sound, but you don't know what they are saying."

"How do people communicate if they don't talk the same language?" asked Tommy. At least all dogs bark the same. When

I go to a pet store all I hear are barks, I don't hear any foreign languages. All dogs seem to understand each other. It seems to me they keep their conversations short and simple."

"Good Tommy," replied Susan, "that is exactly what they do. Between their body language and their barks other dogs know exactly what is being said and it doesn't take a lot of barks either. It is the animal called man who makes something that should be simple so complex. I want both of you to remember the word K.I.S.S., because it stands for keep it simple stupid."

"Mom is right, guys. Man likes to make things complicated. In fact, we make it so complicated sometimes we get lost in our own maze; the more complex we make our communication with each other the easier it is to get confused about what is really being said or to misinterpret what the other person means."

"On the news," continued Susan, "Washington reporters are always commenting that the devil is in the details when discussing a particular bill our congress is trying to cope with. Lawyers make things so complicated and contorted that the non- lawyer doesn't understand what the lawyers are talking about. In fact, man seems to want to impress everyone with a vocabulary that sends the listener to the closest dictionary. Why is it, we want to confuse the issue? Language in itself is confusing enough. Certain words can have several meanings, how a word is used in a certain context will give it an entirely different meaning. A facial expression along with a word can change the meaning of that word and in some countries there may be many different dialects within the same country. A word in one part of that country may mean something entirely different in another part of that country. People will go to a lengthy explanation to tell someone what they are going to do and guess what, they do just the opposite. Man makes communication questionable as it is."

"It's a wonder we communicate at all," said Fred. If we all don't start reading from the same page we are going to have a very difficult time pulling this world together."

"With the internet, satellites and cell phones the world will have to develop one common language," said Freddy.

"That's a very good observation, Freddy," said Fred.

"You mean dogs are ahead of us?" asked Tommy.

"Oh Tommy, don't be silly." replied Susan smiling. "You know man is the smartest animal on Earth."

"How can we be so smart if we can't communicate with each other, Mom?"

Susan had to think for a moment. "Dogs have been on mother Earth longer than we have and they have learned to work together. Man's ego gets in his way. He wants to feel special, better than his neighbors, so he can beat his chest and tell the world how great he is. All dogs and many other animal species think as a pack or group unlike man who thinks individually. You always know what dogs are thinking because they want to make it obvious so there is no guess work. Man, on the other hand, wants to confuse the issue and keep you guessing."

"Well, how can that be communication," asked Tommy. That sounds more like a T.V. show. Maybe man thinks he is making a movie."

"Yea," said Freddy, "like Dr. Jekyll and Mr. Hyde."

"Tommy," said Fred, "it's like all your computer stuff that often doesn't talk the same language and can't communicate with other programs. The software engineers wanted to make something that was different from their competitors without thinking about how useless it would be if it didn't communicate with everything else."

"You mean like that stupid program I'm trying to use to send pictures to my friends. I have a hard time making it work. Dad, I have to get another program," complained Freddy.

"You mean it's not user friendly?"

"No, it's user stupid."

"Fred, I don't understand why engineers can't make things easy to use and easy to fix," said Susan. "It seems they want to make it so difficult to fix that you either give up and throw it out, which our environment can no longer afford, or pay an outrageous price to have it fixed. If we look at what happened on Wall Street and we compare it to things engineers design there seems to be a common thread being a lack of common sense. I wonder why those who run our companies and those who design our products have a technical ability but don't seem to have common sense to go along with it?"

"I'm sure there are many people asking the same question," replied Fred. You would think the president of a company would get his own family to use his company's products to see how they work. Why wouldn't a design engineer ask "how can I make this product useful to the largest audience, is it user friendly, does it talk to other programs and also is it easy to switch components if they should fail or if they need to be upgraded?" And why doesn't the board of directors ask themselves these questions and get their families using the company's products before they sell them. Nobody is earning their big salaries these days as far as I am concerned. It's no wonder we are pricing ourselves out of the world markets."

"How do we change things?" asked Susan.

"Susan, that's a conversation for another time. I have to go up and finish what I was doing."

"Someone just drove up the drive, Mom," observed Freddy.

"It's probably Lacy. She has been at her girlfriends and her friend's mother said she would bring her home."

"Oh," replied Freddy.

Susan opened the door and walked outside and over to the car. "Jane, it's so nice of you to bring Lacy home."

"Oh Susan, we were having a great time together. I was teaching the girls how to make a pie from scratch. With the economy the way it is who knows what's going to happen. These girls better know how to sew and cook."

"I agree," replied Susan. "All the things girls thought were unimportant are going to become very important again, especially if the economy takes years to recover. The girls have only seen good times, they have no idea how tough things can get. All the things that made their grandmothers so important to the family may well become important again."

"Susan, my husband is tearing his hair out, he doesn't want to lay anyone off but he doesn't have a choice. He can't sleep at night which means I can't sleep either. My sister and her husband piled up so much debt with new cars and a new house and now she tells me his company is going out of business. This is a depression as far as they are concerned."

"Jane, Fred and I were just talking about the over extension of debt. It's a catch 22, we need the debt to power our economy and so the government can collect taxes and pay their bills. If we cut back on credit the economy tanks and the government can't get the taxes they need. What a mess. With all the brains we have in Washington, why didn't they see this problem in their strategy planning long ago? The more I hear people telling me how smart they are or how many degrees they have the more skeptical I become. Clearly, we seem to be incapable of thinking through a problem and that is a real worry for all of mankind. Why don't you come in while I make dinner and we can talk?" smiled Susan.

"I have to get back and start cooking dinner too but let's get together this week sometime. I am so depressed over this. I hope I am wrong, but I don't see the economy we had coming back. All in a flash; times have changed."

"I'll call you tomorrow, Jane," said a sympathizing Susan.

Susan's face turned from smiles to one of worry as she went back inside. She went upstairs and opened the door to Fred's nicely paneled office and said "Fred, I want to talk to you."

"What's wrong honey?" questioned a puzzled husband.

"Jane was just telling me that her husband may have to lay people off and it is keeping him up at night and Jane can't sleep either. She also told me her sister's husband's company is going out of business and they are awash in debt with new cars and a new house. What happens if you get laid off?"

"First, let's not jump to conclusions. Everyone is starting to stampede mentally. Consumer sentiment is very negative. What's happening is we are all beginning to realize that everyone in the industrialized world has been living above their means. We have given ourselves a false sense of wealth and security all built on credit. It really isn't any different than a Bernie Madoff Ponzi scheme. People run up their credit cards to the limit, pay the minimum and then apply for an increase in their limit. When things really get tight, they get another card to pay the interest on the first card and they keep doing the same thing over and over until they can't get another card. I know a woman who makes an average salary who has $230,000 of debt on many different cards. How she can support that much debt is amazing. She was just telling me she can't afford to pay the interest this month so she just got another card. There are a lot of people who just can't say no to themselves when they want something, and our system is more than happy to accommodate them. Somehow she continues to pay the minimum so she has good credit. It's a totally insane system."

"But isn't she going to have to pay the cards off at some point," asked Susan.

"Nobody thinks about that. They are only interested in being able to pay the monthly payment. The whole pyramid falls apart when she can't get another card and then the card companies are left holding the bag. Real estate experienced the same type of problem. People would buy real estate, jack the price up and resell the same property at a higher price. It's like who is going to be the last sucker in. Someone will be left with insanely overpriced real estate and if they have a mortgage which, you can be sure they do, a down turn in the economy, like this one, not only dries up the buyers but also the lenders. The consequence is what you are seeing now in our economy, a collapse in the housing sector."

"Why don't the card companies do something?"

"Greed; man never learns. Man started recording bubbles back in the 1500"s when we had the tulip craze and we have had bubbles up to the present. What really is upsetting to me is our elected officials, who are being paid by us, were totally asleep at the switch. They were out to lunch without punching their time cards; they were double dipping the tax payer as far as I am concerned; they got caught with their pants down while ringing the cash register; they were busy chasing little Ms. Jane around the office daydreaming while Rome burned. Now we have to build a new phoenix to arise from the ashes. Our political system just doesn't work, it is dysfunctional. It's not like it's a big surprise. We've known for a long time that our present political system is way too slow and way too costly and way to corrupt and inefficient. But man doesn't face his problems and fix them. Man is nowhere near as smart as he thinks he is. But instead of updating our present system to a new one made for the 21st century we will patch this one and try to make it work. The really big question is how long can we continue to kick the can down the road? The longer we wait to make the needed changes the more we will compound our problems and the more severe and disrupting the solutions will be. We, like every other financial company, track the housing affordability index which is usually around 2.5 times average income. Presently, it is way over that. Greenspan knew and used the famous phrase "irrational exuberance" but did anyone listen? Why do we even bother to have experts, if no one listens? When he testified before congress half our representatives attending looked like they were trying to catch up on their sleep or were playing games on their laptop. The questions they asked Greenspan could have been phrased better by a toddler or a sleepwalker. If our congress people worked for a company they would have been fired on the spot. Our elected officials have to be held accountable and not just at election time. We need to be able to fire our elected officials at any time we catch them asleep at the switch. After all, as far as I'm concerned, politicians are not supposed to make their time in Washington a job but a time of service to the community and to our country. That's why originally our representatives came from the land holders who had farms bringing in income. They didn't get paid so there wasn't a conflict of interest. But man ruins what he creates. He distorts or circumvents his original plan. There most certainly should be a limit of six years anyone can spend as an elected official."

"But Fred, what happens if you lose your job?" asked Susan.

"Honey, we have no debt and our mortgage is down to a point we can pay it off from savings. If I get laid off, we will have to be more frugal and we will have to consider our options. But let's not jump to conclusions; just keep spending down so we can save more for a rainy day."

"But what happens if things really get bad, I mean depression bad?"

"The first thing we have to do is install solar and wind energy to run this house. My biggest worry is no electricity. Everything in this house including our water pump is run by electricity, no electricity and we are back in the dark ages. We couldn't even flush our toilets. But the likeliness of that happening is minimal, I hope," said Fred.

"But it could happen," emphasized Susan.

"Yes, it could and with a dysfunctional government kicking the can down the road all the time, at some point, we will find ourselves in a major depression which we may never get out of. We have to take all the necessary precautions now just in case. God willing we won't have one now."

"Jane says, she doesn't think we will ever see our economy back to where it was."

"She may be right. Credit card companies are starting to cut lines of available credit; they are less willing to lend and if card holders default it will be very hard for them to regain their old credit standing. However, the latest household savings figures are increasing, people are worried and they are saving more. I think you will see the average amount of debt per household decline.

We have to realize that we stepped from one room called "oil and credit" to another room called "alternative energy and savings." Two completely different worlds and the question now is how fast can we make a transition from one to the other without toppling our entire system. You have the same problem in Europe. There is far too much debt not only at the household level but in governments too. It really is a perfect storm with no easy solution. We have leveraged ourselves and our countries with way too much debt and it will take time to de-leverage everyone. If you really want to have nightmares think about this. Our economies, in the industrialized world, have way too much debt and border on bankruptcy, at the same time people are starting to realize that our political systems are dysfunctional and not up to the job of fixing the problems. The balancing act of growth to debt is starting to shift, the seesaw is starting to tilt towards debt and at the same time there is a major portion of the population that will be retiring and spending less. With slower growth how can we raise the tax revenue needed to just keep up our aging infrastructure. If our infrastructure goes then the ball game is over. On top of that, the world is depleting its known oil reserves at about six percent per year. At some point, in the not too distant future, even if the world is still in a recession, we will still run low enough on oil that the price will go out of sight causing our economies to crash unless we have converted over to alternative energy. Add to that mix a health care cost estimated to be a trillion dollars or more in the next few years and student loans that can't be paid back which will run another trillion dollars and on top of all of that our Social Security Trust Fund will run out of money by 2033. We have pulled the rubber band back as far as it can go. We are teetering on the brink of total world bankruptcy."

"It's scary, Fed; but aren't they finding more oil all the time though?"

"You are probably referring to the deep basins of oil they found in Mexico and to the oil shale in the U.S and Canada.

Unfortunately, the cost will be so great to reach and extract those very deep basins of oil that it will require much higher oil prices to make it worthwhile for the drillers. Also, the technology needed has not been completely worked out as yet. Moreover, it will be years down the road and our atmosphere can't take much more pollution as it is. Honey, we have lived to the max and we are going to pay the price. If our economy stands a prayer we are going to have to change over to alternative energy in no more than a snap of our fingers. If there is a common thread to many of our economic problems it is oil. If we can quickly and dramatically lower our cost of energy, that would reduce a very big cost to our government, allowing more tax dollars to go into paying off our debt, stabilizing consumer confidence which would lead to increased consumer spending. Will we do it is the question?"

"Well, will we do it, Fred?"

"Honey, our government is dysfunctional and doesn't seem to be able to agree on anything. In order for us to make the switch over to alternative energy it will probably take government subsidies because the cost for new technology is more expensive than the old technology. But our government has boxed itself in with so much debt it will be difficult to do. That means we will be forced to do it without subsidies. It will have to be the largest and fastest transition in the history of the planet and most people are going to feel very uncomfortable about such a rapid change not to mention the cost. We are going to have to realize that our government is not the solution and we can no long count on them to fix our problems. In fact, they are part of our problem. We have given them way too much responsibility for our own welfare."

"Fred, I'm scared," whispered Susan.

"So you should be. We all should be so scared that we look at each other and say, no more of this, I've had it. Every dime has to be put into this transformation whether we like it or not. We have to convert our houses and factories, our power plants and our transportation systems. And also, the structure of our government has to be updated so this never happens again. We can't just sit around and argue. Our entire political system has to be streamlined so problems can be quickly acted upon."

"But aren't our technologies changing all the time?"

"Yes, but we can't wait for the perfect technology which doesn't exist. We have already waited so long that we are now balancing on a razor's edge. We have to do the best we can and update as we go along. We are told we have about one hundred years of natural gas, at our current usage rate, and we own that. We don't have to buy it from a foreign source. If we combine that with solar and wind and geothermal, I think that will give us enough time to discover better sources of energy. We also have to get our government to realize we have stepped into another room and get them to ask for our help. We need to car pool, we need to use mass transit and our buses and trucks need to be converted to natural gas immediately. Susan, think of this, just in the state of Pennsylvania the children are transported more than 346 million miles to school each and every year. That is almost two round trips to our sun and back and that is just one state. In my opinion, we have to start teaching our kids at home over the Internet, we have the technology, now we need the help and willingness of all mom's and dad's."

"But Fred, many moms work."

"Susan, remember we have just walked into a new and totally different room. What people did yesterday is not what they will be doing tomorrow. Remember, this transition will have to be done faster than any transition in our history. The real question is will man change gears and do it before it is too late?"

"Man can do anything if he puts his mind to," replied Susan. "The question is do we still have the same will our forefathers had when they had to conquer the ordeals of a new country. Just think of where we have come from. We lived in huts and log cabins with no sanitation, no refrigeration and we hunted every day for survival. If we can overcome that, then we can overcome this."

"Sweetheart that is the spirit we all need to take."

"But, if mom's have to stay at home while the kids go to school over the Internet, that will mean less income for the family. How are families going to afford that?"

"We have the technology; it's just a matter of using it. The teacher at the teaching center will see his or her class in a grid like Hollywood Squares on TV. The teacher will be able to talk to any particular student or to the whole class. It will be a lot better than being transported to school, the students will still be able to hear the laughter of the class or the questions of other students or interact with other students just as they always have. They just won't be able to poke or bully anyone. Employers will have to use the same type of technologies so their employees can also work at home. That will mean living where ever you want to and not having to worry about traffic jams, accidents, bad weather and cars that won't start. Just think how much more fun it will be to work without all the hassles we have today."

"Why haven't we done this already, Fred? It seems so obvious that the benefits far outweigh any problems?"

"Man gets caught in a routine. He gets comfortable and he is basically lazy and doesn't want to change. He will make every excuse in the world why it can't be done just so he can follow his same routine. There is always the unknown, the uncertainty. If you look back at the paths the Indians made, they established trails they always followed whether they were the best route or not and then the early settlers followed them too. In fact, some of our roads today still follow them. That is just part of man; he has a very hard time breaking his habits and thinking outside the box. If you read history, the majority of people are born to be followers and it is the leaders that force the changes. Our biggest problem is learning how to find those people who can think outside the proverbial box and who can lead. Our present form of government can't do that and you can see what is happening. Do you remember the old ad by Maypo "let Mikie try it"? Let the other person try it and see if he or she likes it. However, we are at

a crossroads today and we either change or we die. We no longer
have the luxury of time."

"Fred, I'm thinking about Freddy and Tommy. They say they
get bored at school, won't they get bored here and drive me crazy?"

"The Internet will allow the teachers to do so much more
than they can do now. They can tie in with Google World and
video's and web cams that will make the students learning
experience much more interesting and real than just reading
a book. It can be made interactive to bring students into the
programs and it will make a lot more sense to kids. Just imagine
if you could step back in time and see how mathematics was
developed in Egypt and how it was used to map out land for
fields. It will allow them to visit places instead of just reading
or talking about them. There will be new companies that form
to make videos for teachers so the student will feel that he
or she is actually at the location they are studying. Imagine
being at Carnegie Hall or in Rome or in a gondola in Venice.
The children will feel they are part of what they are studying.
Imagine the difference between reading a book or listening to
a teacher talk about an old archeology site vs. actually being
there and almost touching the artifacts and seeing where it is
on Google World. Their studies will mean so much more to
them and I doubt they will get bored if the teachers are well
trained in computer learning, the graphic arts and video training
presentations. Within five years we could have large flat panel
screens and or IMAX type screens built into every home for
teaching and entertainment. Every builder will incorporate that
into every house he builds. In fact, teaching and entertainment
will merge into one," exclaimed Fred with excitement. Just think
how dynamic our educational system could become. Wide flat
panel screens radiating vibrant colors and surround sound with
interactive videos taking kids on an exciting and exhilarating
ride through the world of knowledge. One of the worries I hear
about teaching at home is the kids need the social interaction
with other kids. But that argument doesn't hold water. There

are many children who are being home schooled now and they are perfectly well adjusted. If you ask them, they will tell you they don't miss going to school at all. If parents are worried about social interaction they can most certainly plan parties, social events and dances for their kids. We have to bring the family back so it works as a unit again. Parents can use the same fabulous educational system to stay up dated on their own profession or to train for another profession. This is the wave of the future that will allow us to move forward and keep people trained and employed for an ever changing world."

"Just think, Fred, it would allow us to unite the whole world. Why have poverty, rioting and discontent when we can train people everywhere. The common denominator is education and, therefore, jobs for all. And Fred, just think of this, if we can send electricity abroad through our fiber optic cables why couldn't we import electricity from some of the poorest nations that have tons of sun. The driest places on earth could be a gold mine of sun power feeding the world. Man can dig his way out of this hole we are in now, right Fred? We just have to be willing to change and change quickly before it is too late."

"It's up to us," replies Fred, "what are we going to do? Are we going to sit back and do nothing or are we going to look at each new day with excitement and challenge and bring forth a world man could never have imagined just a generation ago?"

"If we teach over the Internet, just think of what that means for school districts. No longer will we have good school districts and bad school districts. No longer will you have busing for the so called disadvantaged. No longer will you have to worry about bullies ruining the day for your child. Everyone will have access to the same material. I'm getting so excited about this that I have to go to the bathroom," exclaimed Susan who hurried off.

Susan returned and you could tell she had a question just waiting to escape.

"Fred, what about the cost; won't it make it impossible for many to afford?"

"The cost will be out of sight if we don't do it. The cost for land and school buildings, transportation and for teachers, I mean everyone's taxes will go out of sight, not to mention the cost to our country for not being able to retrain people fast enough for the changing times. As technology advances, the rate of change will make it mandatory that everyone is updated and retrained constantly. What our government doesn't seem to understand is if we incur debt because we are making our system more productive allowing us to reduce our costs in the longer run, then we can pay back the debt. The reason we are in debt now is we have been spending on nonproductive programs. Paying people welfare is not productive, putting them to work is, paying for a huge bureaucracy that overlaps, that duplicates and that is inefficient is not productive. There is an old Chinese adage; don't give a man a fish for dinner; give him a fishing pole so he can feed himself for life. Government is not productive. They don't make or sell anything. They create nothing except a bigger mess. The bigger our government gets the less productive we become as a nation. The more tax dollars government sucks from the productive part of the economy leaves less for expansion, for hiring qualified people, for innovation and, in the end, fewer taxes for the government. It is a vicious cycle. As everyone can see, our present form of government just doesn't work in this time and age. The only time debt works for a company or a country is, if it is young and growing or if the debt is incurred to buy equipment or software or to add talent that will make it more productive. If you pay big bonuses to management or if you put your assets in nonproductive projects your debt will eventually sink you. We are no longer a young country, this is a mature economy. If we don't change to meet this challenge we will go the way of Rome. If we don't change we won't be able to afford to keep up our infrastructure and compete with China and the rest of the world and the ball game will be over. Remember, because I think you have already forgotten, but the room we just left is on fire and we will never be able to go back. It's the new room we are now in that we have to adapt to. The question is can we adapt fast enough? The cost for Internet cameras has come way down and in mega mass production they will be affordable for all. High speed Internet and fiber optic cable will make it all feasible. We can do everything we want to over fiber optic highways. Large flat panel screens have come way down in price and the price will fall much further according to the experts. There are bottlenecks we have to fix or update like our routers and servers which even now get bogged down slowing the flow of information. Security is another problem area that needs more work. We won't be able to go forward unless our electronic highways are kept updated to keep up with the changes in technology and with the changing times."

Lacy walks in and asks, "What are you talking about?"

"Oh just chit chat honey," says Susan. "Do you have homework to do?"

"Yes, but Dad, I need a new computer, mine is just not fast enough and it doesn't have a webcam on it."

"Why do you need a camera?" questioned Susan somewhat wide eyed.

"Mom, don't you want to see who you are talking to?" exclaimed Lacy. "Mom, don't you know everything from cell phones to desk tops and laptops and many smart handheld devices will have some type of camera in them. We are going to be so interconnected and it's going to be so cool for finding cute guys."

"It's a different world," said Susan shaking her head. "Are the kids still brushing Mussy?"

"They were just a minute ago. Mussy looks like she's in heaven. She's lying on her back with her little pink tummy showing and all fours bent over at their wrist totally relaxed." Lacy bent her wrist to show Susan what she meant. "She is sooo cute. I'd be a dog if I could be guaranteed I would be with a friendly and caring family," giggled Lacy.

Susan laughed, "I think we all would. Do you have a lot of home work to do?"

"Some, but Mom, I really want a new computer, it would make things so much easier and mine is so old."

"Lacy, it is only about two and half years old."

"But Mom, that's ancient. New computers have at least two processing chips now instead of just one. That makes them faster and more efficient. They can handle multitasking better and Windows 7 will be coming out with a 64 bit operating system which should work better with dual core CPU's and in addition some computers come with a camera built in. All these advances also make it easier to collaborate with other students to solve problems. Won't you please get me a new one?"

"Well, maybe for your birthday, honey."

"But this is only April, my birthday is almost a month away," pouted Lacy.

"Oh what a tragedy," replied Susan. "Are you going to get A's this year?"

Lacy scrunched her face up. "I'm not sure about Spanish but in the rest of my classes I will."

"Good."

"Does that mean I get a new computer?" smiled Lacy.

"Lacy, if I told you, then it wouldn't be a surprise for your birthday, would it?"

"Oh foo," said Lacy as she walked out of the room.

Susan left Fred's office and went back down to the kitchen where the boys were still brushing Mussy. She was still in heaven lying on her back with the kids taking turns brushing her.

"Look Mom," said Tommy, "when I brush her tummy right here her right leg starts to run. Isn't that funny?" exclaimed an amused little boy.

Susan couldn't resist and got down on all fours next to Mussy and gave her a big kiss. "What are you doing, chasing a rabbit?" asked Susan, as if she was talking to one of her own children. Mussy just looked up at her with a face that said, 'You knit whit, they are hitting a nerve but it feels sooo good.' "Alright kids, I think it's time to put the brushes away for the night. Make sure they go back into the same drawer so you can find them tomorrow."

Later that night Susan, dressed in her nice warm flannel pajamas, wrapped herself around her husband in bed and asked, "Fred what is common sense?"

"You know it exists don't you?" asked Fred.

"Yes, of course, but why don't we know more about it?"

"Your guess is as good as mine, honey. I have no idea. What do you think it is?"

"Well, I look at it this way. We are a fantasy animal; we teach our children about the tooth fairy and we go to all lengths to get them to believe that a fat little old man with a long white beard climbs down our chimneys and leaves presents behind. There is supposed to be truth in advertising but women buy very expensive creams and lotions that claim to take wrinkles out and yet we are told by dermatologists that any cream is just a moisturizer and that they all do the same thing. Harry Potter books sell like hot cakes and yet the book is a fantasy. We have Superman and Spiderman and the Terminator who always make the bad guys pay. We love to kid ourselves about how beautiful we are; how smart we are and how young we look. Our whole life is nothing but a fantasy and the common sense part of our brain or at least in most brains is the outline of reality that keeps the other parts of our brain from making our life a silly cartoon. Another way of looking at it is common sense is the wrapper that holds all the silly putty together."

"I like that honey. That's a cute way of looking at it," said Fred.

"But everyone knows it's just silly putty," replied Susan. "Pretty smart aren't I?"

"You're beautiful and smart and I'm the luckiest man in the world."

"Oh Fred, you better watch out or I could become a tigress too," she said giving him a big sexy kiss.

Chapter Four

Jimmy's Option

Fred called Jimmy to see how his investing was going.
"Hi Jimmy it is Fred Willing. I just wanted to see how you were coming along with your investing or speculating?"

"Fred," said Jimmy in a somewhat excited voice, "I sold my option".

"You sold it? Did you make any money?"

"Yes, I doubled my money Fred. I'm so excited."

"You doubled your money?" questioned Fred. "That's great Jimmy, what are you going to do next?"

"I bought a spider call," replied Jimmy excitedly.

"You bought a call," asked Fred.

"Yes, everyone is getting a little too pessimistic, I think," replied Jimmy.

"Jimmy, people are worried about losing their jobs which means they will spend less and the economy will take a nose dive."

"Fred, look at it this way. How long can someone stay depressed? Most people get down in the dumps for only a while before they have to look to the positive side. If we always looked to the negative side we would all commit suicide," chuckled Jimmy. "Right Fred? Besides, people are always fretting over their jobs. My mother mutters to herself all the time about her job. I keep telling her there is always someone out there that wants to hire you. It's just a matter of finding the right fit. I read articles all the time about how being fired turned out to have a silver lining, forcing the employee to look for a better fit. Of course, it's always traumatic but it's not the death sentence. What it means is you have to keep your resume up to date and be networking all the time and retooling for the job you really want. It puts pressure on the employer also if he wants to keep that person. Times are changing. The pool of educated talent is growing. We have to become a very flexible society and be looking for those sectors that are in demand. We can take courses over the Internet to keep ourselves updated and retooled. But the big economic shift that will be so important is that our savings rate will have to go up and probably dramatically and good financial planning will be vital. We will have to watch every penny."

"Jimmy, if a big company like General Motors goes down the tubes it will put a great many people out of work. That will cause suppliers to close down and the ripple effect through our economy will be enormous."

"Fred, I don't look at it that way. I view it as Darwinism in the human world. Small companies get eaten by the bigger companies, big companies, with bad management, go broke and have to spit out the little pieces which are eaten by other fish. We live in a very dynamic world now. This process goes on all the time. What we really need is a bigger clean up detail that looks to eat the dead and the dying. In the case of General Motors, management was greedy and very myopic and in addition they are now being caught in a transition period where they are not producing the alternative fuel efficient cars that people need. Fred, we have a capitalistic system because it works and it works just like everything else in nature, survival of the fittest, right Fred? Do you really think our government should reward a poorly managed company by bailing them out?"

"Absolutely not," said Fred emphatically.

"In a true Darwinian world, which capitalism is molded after, GM should be allowed to go bankrupt. They would have to spit out all the little pieces that didn't fit, cut off all the fat, make wages competitive with the rest of the non-unionized auto manufacturers, retool to bring the buyers what they need and cut the prices of their cars so people can afford them."

"Jimmy, the unions gained too much power to the point GM management couldn't deal with them. The real problem, in my view, is management has always thought they were above the worker and deserved huge salaries. The truth of the matter is management can't succeed without a talented pool of skilled workers. The so called workers are just as skilled at what they do as management is supposed to be at what they do. If management got paid what the worker got paid and everyone received a bonus every five years based on the profitability of the company that would not only make a lot more sense but it would keep everyone working as a team. It would most certainly keep the unions out."

"I like that idea Fred. Think of the increase in productivity. All that money that was saved from salaries could be reinvested back into the company. The problem is our leaders in Washington are stuck in an old world philosophy with no new thinking outside the box. Everything is going to have to change and change fast or we are going to be up the creek without a paddle. Look at housing. Prices got so high people couldn't afford them. Buyers were forced to do what they really didn't want to do and that was take out huge mortgages that did not allow for anything going wrong. Now the whole economy is taking a hit for it. My generation is the one where all this garbage is being dumped. I can't imagine what our elected officials are thinking about. They show no leadership qualities, no new out of the box thinking and no work ethic. Where were they? Couldn't they see this bubble coming? They weren't even doing their job. Not only that, we elected people who don't even understand the capitalistic system. They call themselves politicians whatever that means, but they certainly don't understand how to make capitalism work in times like these to fix the problems. All they want to do is print more money and push the ever increasing debt burden off to my generation. It makes me sick to think what your generation is doing to my generation. You know my generation is being left a burnt out shell that may even collapse and it gives me a huge knot in my stomach every time I think about it. My question is why? Why are we electing people who shouldn't even be considered for dog catcher? We are entrusting our future to these people. What are we thinking about? Fred, if I sound a little emotional you would be too if you were going to inherit what my generation is going to."

"Jimmy, you are a very perceptive fifteen year old, I must say. Every American citizen should be asking the same question, why? But it is not enough to just ask why. We have to spearhead the needed change."

"But Fred, the people who call themselves politicians are not the ones we want or need. The real question is, how do we change the entire system to make it more responsive not only to the people but to the planet Earth so everyone benefits. The answer to this question defines whether we live or die. It is absolutely critical."

"There is no doubt, Jimmy; we are at a major crossroads in human history. You know, as well as everyone else that we are being funded by China and India as well as many other countries and the question is what happens when they stop? Then what? The big question in my mind is how free are we really? We are killing our own freedom. Aesop, way back in 620BC, said "Greed often overreaches itself" and we have yet to learn that over two thousand years later."

"Fred, how many times have companies tried to throw money at a problem just to see it fail? Our leaders have yet to learn that in Washington. It's not our economy as much as it is our political system that we should be worrying about. The system is out of touch with today's realities. Our system is broken and needs to be updated. Even Alan Greenspan was big enough and honest enough, which is rare in our government, to say, "I made a mistake, my philosophy was wrong". I think, what it all comes down to is, our system has become so complex that using a system originally developed at a time when we were an agricultural economy shows no common sense. It obviously needs to be updated for our times like everything else. You can stretch a rubber band just so far and then guess what? Intelligence isn't obtained at any college or university; information is obtained there and everyone has access to information today all over the world. People in the tiniest hamlets have a world of information at their fingertips. It is how we use the information that defines intelligence and that, in my mind, is what I call common sense, the highest and most critical form of human intelligence."

"Jimmy, you certainly have a very perceptive and insightful mind for your age," stated Fred. "Are you at all nervous with your call option?"

"Of course; as you pointed out in the beginning, I am speculating. It is either all or nothing. However, there is nothing worse than not following your hunch only to see it come to fruition. If I don't take the full risk, I can never hope to pay for college. If we don't take the risk as a nation and bite the bullet now and change our system as fast as a chameleon changes its colors we may not live to regret it."

"Jimmy, I have to get back to work but if I can be of help, please call me."

Fred hung up the phone with his mind spinning. He sat back in his chair and thought what a smart and perceptive young man. It is probably going to take the younger generation with the guts, drive and determination to effect the necessary changes. Our generation is to fat and complacent. Or, is it? Fred went back to work. Pessimism was rising with his clients and his Pepto Bismol was running low as the market had been going down day after day. Client tempers were rising and he had to deal with fire breathing, government hating investors who watched their nest eggs crumble.

"Fred, you have a call on line 2 and call Dean Phillips," said Mary observing Fred in a pensive pose.

Later that week as Fred got off the bus from the train station and started to walk home, the thought of Jimmy, his youth and his perception of urgency in changing our system, flashed throughout his mind. If a fifteen year old sees our problems and the need for change, why don't adults and if they do, why aren't they all "mad as hell" as Lee Iacocca points out in his book? Why aren't we all down in Washington by the millions clogging every road and every street bringing Washington to a standstill? But if we want change what are we going to change to and how? What will that new system look like?"

Chapter Five

A PLANETVATIONIST

Fred opened the door to his house to see his wife in a beautiful sexy dress. "Wow," exclaimed Fred, "what does my beautiful wife have planned for us tonight?"

"You noticed?" smiled Susan.

"How could I help but notice? I love that dress. What is the occasion?"

"Fred, I listen to the news and every day all I hear is pessimism. Whatever happened to the optimism that has made our country as strong and powerful as it is? We have turned into a country of fat bellied whiners. Think of our forefathers, who had to carve the land for homesteads; who had to fight mosquitoes, biting flies and all kinds of sickness, who had to find enough food to feed the family every day. We had Indians and the weather to cope with; we have fought wars, conquered the west, sent our children to war never to see them return and today because our bank accounts are not as cushy as they were last year, we seem to think the world is coming to an end. What has happened?"

"You got into that beautiful dress to tell me that?"

"Fred, we are going out tonight."

Oh! Where? Do we have a sitter or is Lacy going to stay home?"

"I have it all planned, all you have to do is shower and shave and we have to leave in twenty minutes."

"Oh, Ok," said Fred shrugging his shoulders.

Fred appeared twenty minutes later all ready for a fun evening.

"Are you going to tell me where we are going for dinner?"

"We are going to take a little drive. We are going to a bar down in the ghetto where I will stand a very high probability of getting raped and you, more than likely, will get stabbed or mugged."

"What," exclaimed Fred, "like hell we are?"

"Then why does our society allow it? We seem to want to stick our nose in everyone else's business around the globe when we have so many problems here at home. People are losing their jobs and their houses, they can't afford health care, the fat cats who sit around doing nothing but shuffling papers are getting paid fortunes while hardworking people who do the work are getting laid off. The disparity between pay between management and the workers, those actually doing the work, is wider than it has ever been. If management was so good we wouldn't have bankruptcies, we wouldn't have earnings misses and we wouldn't have layoffs. You would think management was irreplaceable and yet they obviously can be replaced. It's like our sports stars who get hurt and have to sit it out on the bench. It often allows someone else to show his stuff which turns out to be even better. I was listening to the radio and some stupid congressman opened his mouth and said something stupid, another said something even dumber and another wants to pour money into the black hole called Afghanistan when our country is broke and going into more debt by the minute. Don't we ever learn? We can't solve the world's problems; we can't even solve our own problems. What the hell is wrong with us? I ask you, who are we sending to Washington to represent us and why don't we have the final say in their decisions? Isn't this country supposed to be "by and for the people"? Our constitution doesn't say anything about being just for fast talking error prone handshaking egomaniacs who think they are better than everyone else."

"Susan, some people argue that Afghanistan houses terrorists and that it is necessary to control them over there rather than here," said Fred.

"Fred, no matter what you do over there, if it is putting us in bankruptcy here it is not helping us, in fact, it is making us weaker. A bankrupt country is not a strong powerful country. Our enemy is winning, not us. Take that money we spend over there and put it in defenses here at home, put people to work who pay taxes that, in my opinion, makes much more sense."

"Wow, you are really on the warpath tonight," muttered Fred.

"Fred, I am just plain sick and tired of all the shenanigans going on in this country and I think the women of this world are going to have to unite and start yelling about the stupid things men are doing. Men are only good for two things, screwing and getting into trouble with their big egos."

"God help us all," said Fred in a low muttered tone. "Now, where are we really going for dinner?" asked Fred in a more inquisitive tone.

"There's a new place in town that Sally Beasley told me about and she says they have a very good chef."

It was a quiet trip down to the restaurant with Fred very shy about discussing anything that might stir his wife's emotions.

The waiter pulled Susan's chair out for her and Fred whispered he wanted two Bloody Marys followed quickly by a signal with two fingers.

"Honey, Lacy's birthday is coming up next month, what, do you think we should get her?" asked Fred.

"Fred, are you trying to change the subject?"

"No, no, I, I ah just wanted your opinion."

"She told me she wants a new computer because it is faster and it has a camera so they can see who they are talking to. It sounds like it would be safer for her. I like the idea of being able to see the person I'm talking to or messaging to. It would be nice if everyone could see the other person, it would make the world seem more real. Everyone would feel more connected, more like we are all on the same sinking ship with the same problems."

"How is your Bloody Mary?"

"It's fine Fred. But there is only so much I can take. Everyone from the news media to people we know are feeling that we have gone astray. This is not the world we wanted to build."

"Honey, all of us have to start doing something about it. All this hot air is doing no more than heating the planet and selling newspapers. We have to force a change. But what we need to do first is formulate a plan. We need to be able to tell our government this is what we want as a majority. Then if our government doesn't change, we have a reason to demand a change."

"Sally and I are talking about starting a website. Women are very good at dredging up every little thing their husbands ever did wrong and telling them about it. If women would only do that with our government and start writing it down maybe we could come up with a plan on how to go forward."

"Honey, it is going to take everyone. We have kicked the can down the road far enough and now we have compounded our problems to the point we either all work together and come up with a new plan on how we can go forward or it is over. Our political system, as it is now set up, will not work."

Fred signaled to the waiter for two more Bloody Marys.

"Fred, are you trying to get me drunk?"

"No, I'm just trying to de-steam you."

"De-steam me?"

"Yes, I want you so de-steamed we can dance cheek to cheek and have a good time. You know, all I hear, all day long, are people complaining and uncomfortable with their finances and it's nice to just be able to relax."

"Fred, I'm sorry, but all this negativity really is getting to me. Sally called me and she was all depressed and I guess it was just contagious."

"Honey, everyone is getting depressed and it is not good. The reason we are getting depressed is that we don't see a plan to get out of this mess we are in. For our own good we all have to start working together to solve our problems. What got Sally going?"

"She feels very strongly about our environment, she is a real conservationist and planetvationist. She feels we are ruining our planet, just running it into the ground."

"I don't think I have ever heard the word planetvationist, how did you come up with that word?"

"Well; it just seemed to follow. If you want to conserve the environment you are called a conservationist, so if you want to help save the planet why wouldn't you be called a planetvationist?"

"Oh," said Fred. "Well she certainly has every right to feel that way. Many others are in the same camp with her. Did she say what got her going on that subject today?"

"Al Gore's statement that there is a seventy- five percent chance that the entire North American ice shelf will melt within five years because man is changing our climate and causing global warming is driving her crazy. Sally called me about a website she Googled and it shows the effects of different increases in ocean levels. It actually shows the water rising in the location you are looking at. So if you put in a one meter rise you can actually see what affect it will have on that particular area. You can see the effects it would have on towns, cities, bridges and, of course, roads and beaches. She tells me a rise of just one meter will change the Bahamas, the gold coast of Florida and the low lying areas along the eastern seaboard. It will force millions of people to move, she says. She is going crazy over the question of, where can we put everyone. It's really driving her up the wall."

Their young waitress, who had overheard Susan said, "You know, it really comes down to how do we go forward and survive. I mean, where are we going? My generation is going crazy because of all the stress from not knowing what is going to happen to our future. What has man been thinking about? No one has a plan except Boone Pickens and that's just for energy and he's not even part of our government. That's one reason kids are so upset with their parents' generation and this mess of a system." She blushed, "oh I'm sorry I said anything," said the waitress bashfully touching Susan's arm.

"That's alright. We all feel the same way," replied Susan. "Fred, why isn't our government listening to their constituents? The people we are electing are not listening."

"I guess we just aren't yelling loud enough. Probably the real fact of the matter is they don't know what to do. These people we elect can't think outside the box. They aren't leaders they are highly overpaid order takers. It's going to take a new vision, a new way of looking at our problems. We can't fix our problems with our old way of thinking. Einstein knew that close to eighty years ago. The system itself is broken and has to be updated."

"But what do we do?" questioned a frustrated Susan.

"Honey, you are not listening to me. We the people have to formulate a plan on how we want to go forward which encompasses every facet of our life; from business to politics to our environment to family size. We are going to be forced to do the work and we are going to have to make the tough decisions that politicians can't or won't make. Then we can tell our representatives what we want and if we don't get it, we march on Washington in such numbers that they have no choice but to change. But we have to confront the real problem which is a system designed for a different time and a different place. If we continue to send the same type of thinkers to Washington we will get the same answers. Somehow we have to have a more responsive form of government. If you work for a company and they want you out, you are lucky if you have time to clean out your desk before the door closes behind you. Why can't we do the same thing in Washington?"

"Fred, we need to list all those goals that will allow mankind to survive. Then we can tackle each one and come up with a solution as to how we want to go forward. Do you want to dance?" said a much more relaxed Susan.

Chapter Six

AT THE DINNER TABLE

S pring was unraveling its beauty and the buds on the trees were turning into a Monet pastel panorama. The sun rose higher in the sky day by day and the April days were becoming warmer. Susan mentions to Fred, "I've invited Matilda and Jimmy over for dinner on Sunday. She hardly gets out at all and I thought it would be fun to have them over."

"That's a great idea. Have you told the kids?" asked Fred.

"I told Lacy but Freddy and Tommy are at the Halls and I will tell them later."

"I hope they are behaving themselves with the girls. Did you talk to them about not being rough with the girls?" inquired Fred.

"I did, but Kathy Hall watches them carefully and she says they play well together. The worst thing she has seen was Tommy pulling Abby's hair."

"I hope she let Tommy know that he is not supposed to pull girls' hair."

"Actually, the two girls, Abby and Peggy, ganged up on Tommy and Kathy says he came out the loser."

"He'll learn," said Fred smiling. "Has Mussy been to the vet lately for a checkup and any shots that are due?"

"She's going in for her booster shot on Wednesday. She's not going to like it one bit either. I always hate doing it because then she associates getting in the car with something painful."

"There is no way around it," said Fred. "She has to have her shots. Why don't you get her a treat for afterwards Maybe that will help with your feeling of guilt and Mussy will love it."

"Fred, I don't feel guilty but it's like taking one of the kids in for a shot that you know will hurt. Every time, I take them in, I feel the shot just as much as they do."

"Do you watch as the needle goes in?" questioned Fred.

"It's like getting a shot myself. I watch until the needle almost goes in and then I turn my head and I grit my teeth. I don't know why, I just do. I can't stand to see my little babies get a needle stuck in them even if I know it is for their own good."

"The bond between a mother and her children is a psychological umbilical cord that never can be cut. Fathers don't have the same type of connection as mothers do. While we love them and watch out for them and have their best interests at heart, we still don't have the same emotional tie, in my opinion. How is our classic doing?"

"Oh Fred, I think, that is where your heart is and it is doing fine."

"No more problems with the heater?"

"No, it seems to be fine."

"That's been a really great car. It's hard to believe, but do you know that car is about fifty eight years old this year? It's over half a century old and it is still running. Why can't they make cars today like that one?"

"Fred, as much as it is going to break your heart we have to think about retiring your classic. One thing that car isn't, is fuel efficient not to mention it's very difficult to get parts for her."

"Susan, one of these days we will have to retire her; but our next car has to run on natural gas. I am waiting for our fat and happy out to lunch oil companies to put in natural gas pumps at their stations so we can get the natural gas we need to fuel our cars. As soon as I can get natural gas, I'll be the first to get a new natural gas driven car. I think as soon as they install the natural gas pumps the whole nation will change over faster than you can blink an eye. It really makes you wonder if our major oil companies are on our side. What are they thinking about? They should be leading us not trying to squeeze the last drop of profit out of their carbon killing, environmentally devastating and economy bankrupting gasoline."

"Fred, I know," replied Susan, "you don't have to go into it again. Have you written your congressmen?"

"Yes, many times."

"Fred, that reminds me, what are we doing about putting solar in?"

"That's on my 'to do' list."

"On your 'to do' list?" what are you waiting for? You've been complaining about it forever it seems to me?"

"I keep putting it off because the weather has been so cold."

"Fred, all I hear is you complain but I don't see any action on your part."

"Susan, I promise, I will get it done this summer," said Fred with a guilty grimace.

"How much money will we save by converting our cars over to natural gas?" asked Susan.

"Probably about half, I am told. But whatever it is, it is ours; dollars won't be sent abroad, it will help our deficit problem and our environment and our psychological outlook."

"Fred, people who have new cars now won't want to go out and buy another one. What are they going to do?"

"I've been told any car can be converted over and it's a fairly simple job with the cost now about two thousand dollars per car. However, once we start converting in mass, I think, the price will probably come down."

"It sounds like it's much cheaper than buying a new car," observed Susan.

"Much," replied Fred.

"I would think everyone would be converting their cars over."

"I think they will as soon as the natural gas fuel tanks are installed at gas stations. But, like everything else, we have to yell and scream to get anything done and then they move no faster than a sleep walking snail. What a system. I know some of our large corporations are trying to set a good example by converting both their cars and trucks over. Some stations on major highways in the west are installing some natural gas pumps and Boone Pickens keeps reminding everyone that time is running short."

"What will happen if we don't?"

"I don't even want to think about it. We are at a crossroads in human existence and I don't know if the world really sees it. All we have to do is make energy so expensive either because of supply or because of our environment that the result will be our economies will collapse. Europe is way ahead of us in the use of nuclear power stations and solar power to generate their electricity. We still power almost half our electric generating plants with coal which, of course, means putting carbon dioxide, CO_2, into our atmosphere. We don't know how much more CO_2 our atmosphere will take but we do know that we have put so much up there that some scientists tell us the CO_2 content of our atmosphere has never been this high. We do know that the Earth is getting hotter and since CO_2 is a greenhouse gas it would be hard to say there isn't a correlation. Everything modern man has based his life on takes electricity and right now more than half of our electricity is generated by hydrocarbons, CO_2. Just think everything from hair curlers to water pumps to refrigeration and lights and stoves and, for some, heat for their home and, of course, computers. We have trapped ourselves. The only way out is to convert to alternative energy sources in no more than a heartbeat. Our standard of living is, most certainly, going to have to take a hit. Most everyone, especially the young, takes a cushy life for granted. They have no idea how hard things can get and how fast things can change. Even our economists are way to myopic and don't see the forest for the trees. I think a car just drove up," said Fred looking out the window.

"That's probably the kids," said Susan as she looked out the window. "Yes, it is. I'll go out and thank Kathy for bringing them home."

At dinner that night, as the whole family sat around the table, Susan mentioned that Jimmy and Matilda will be coming for Sunday dinner.

"Freddy and Tommy, you know Jimmy from church. He's the fifteen year old boy who was in that horrible accident and is in a wheelchair. Tommy, please put your napkin in your lap, Freddy, no elbows on the table."

"Aren't we going to church?" ask Tommy.

"Yes, but they will come back with us after church; and I want you to be on your best behavior. Jimmy might like to play your Xbox360 hockey game. Have you played it yet?" asked Susan.

"Yes, but just a couple of times," said Freddy.

"Do you like it?" asked Lacy who was putting the dinner plate in front of Freddy?"

"There's a lot to learn. It's very realistic but you really have to get into it."

"Will you play it with me?" asked Lacy.

"Have you played NHL 08?" asked Freddy.

"No," replied Lacy.

"It's going to take you a while. You have to sit down and read everything and look at the tutorials and play around with the controls. It can get quite complex."

"You mean you really do have to get into it?" said Lacy.

"It's not something you are going to try once and be good at, if that's what you mean," said Freddy. "I think, they should make it more user friendly."

"Mom, am I serving and cleaning up tomorrow?" asked Lacy.

"It's either serve and clean up or cook. Which do you want to do?"

"Well, if I am serving, it will be hard for me to talk to Jimmy."

"You can cook if you want to."

"I don't think I'm good enough and I don't want everyone on Sunday not to like my dinner."

"You mean you don't want to do anything?" laughed Susan. "If you don't do it, who do you think will?"

"Won't you?"

"Oh thanks, let your mother do it all and then I won't have any time to be the hostess and talk to Matilda. No way. Are you serving and cleaning up or cooking?"

"Lacy grimaced, "serving" she snapped.

"Excuse me, what did you say?" asked Fred sternly.

"I'll serve, Mom," said Lacy in a more friendly tone. But I have known Jimmy for years at church and this will be the first time we have ever gotten together."

"You know what's coming up don't you?" questioned Fred.

"My birthday," smiled Lacy, knowing that her parents hadn't forgotten.

"That's right; you might want to keep that in mind before snapping at your mother."

"I'm sorry Mom, but I'm tired of serving and cleaning up."

Susan laughed, "Don't get married then."

"When I get married, my husband is going to do it."

"I wouldn't bet on it," said Susan.

"What is it with this generation?" asked Fred. "The girls don't want to learn to cook. How do they ever expect to cook for their family? Lacy, you mother is a good cook, my Mother is a good cook and my Grandmother has always taken great pride in her cooking. Everybody always tells my Mother that she is a great cook and everybody always wants to go to Grandmother's for Thanksgiving and Christmas. The girls now don't want to be home makers, they just want careers. Our whole society is teaching our future mothers the wrong thing. The most important job a mother can do is, bring her children up in the right way and in the right atmosphere of love and learning and respect for our environment. Having a career is the worst thing we should be teaching our future mothers if they want a family. She can't expect her husband to work all day long and then come home and cook dinner and clean up too."

"Fred, most mothers are working full time and it takes both husbands and wives working to make ends meet," glared Susan.

"Well, there is something wrong with our system," retorted Fred. The family is the backbone of our whole country. It's the family that has made us what we are. What's the point of getting married if you never have time to sit down and relax and enjoy each other? The dinner table is the place for the whole family to discuss the day's affairs, to pass information along, to learn, to discuss and to vent anxieties and to laugh at ourselves and each other. It helps bond us together. It serves the same purpose as a bee hive does to bees. It's not that I'm not sympathetic to couples' financial problems; after all, I deal with them all day long. But when you get married, it is a huge responsibility the couple is undertaking and, I think, if you are going to have a family, then the family comes first. If a mother can't afford to stay home and take care of her children then is that fair to the children and to the family and to society? Life is not perfect but we can see what is happening when mothers try having two careers, one at home and one at work. This whole question of mothers' responsibilities and place in society has become a very serious problem because children demand a lot of time. Unlike nature, human children take years of hard work to bring up correctly. Some women don't want children and that's fine and other women are not meant to have children. Mother Nature doesn't create all females to be good mothers and we can see that in nature too. Remember Knut the polar bear who was rejected by its own mother. Not every woman should be a mother any more than every man should be a father. No wonder there are so many divorced couples, the family structure is falling apart and our whole society is feeling the results."

"Fred, the family is important but it's the discipline that's falling apart," replied Susan. "Discipline is the key. Our schools are really falling down in their responsibility to have as part of their curriculum a course on how to discipline your children, what goes into it, how to make it successful and incorporating discipline into your own life. The problem with our society is parents don't discipline themselves let alone their children."

"It all goes back to the family and having Mom at home so she can make a loving home centered around discipline. It takes time and energy to be a Mom. You can't do a good job at it when you are exhausted yourself. Our society has somehow been completely misled into thinking that woman can have it all," said Fred. "There is only so much time in every day and we are just humans who get tired. We need our sleep and quiet time; time to relax and to renew ourselves. We need to be able to get away and get recharged."

"I think we can thank Gloria Steinem and the feminist movement for that," said Susan. These were just young girls that didn't know what they were talking about and yet women all over the world started to follow them. Talk about the blind leading the blind."

"Susan, the problem is, until a woman becomes a mother, she doesn't have any idea what it is like since she has never experienced it. How would she know? It all goes back to this crazy youth movement where the young are worshiped when it should be exactly the opposite. The older generation has the experience because they have lived through it. Why don't we listen to them?" moaned Fred.

"Dad, it's our technology. Technology is changing so fast that your generation doesn't know what our generation knows," said Lacy.

"Lacy, technology is just technology. We are human beings first and foremost and we don't change. What was true for our forefathers is also true for us when it comes to living and working as a society. Technology for the sake of technology is wrong. Technology to solve a specific problem is what we should be striving for. Look at what is happening. The family structure is disintegrating; there is no discipline in society, everyone is living for the moment, everyone is chasing money that is not worth the paper it's printed on, no one listens to the older generation, who has the experience and people are not making religion a cornerstone in their lives and our problems are mounting by the day. People, the world over, are turning to drugs, sex and violence. Is this what your dream of a better world is?" said an emotional father. "You know the men who wrote the Bible were not young inexperienced fools. They were, in fact, older, experienced and wise men who knew man always falls into the same traps; what was true then is true today when it comes to the human experience; and yet we don't see it, we think we are inventing a whole new system which is impossible. We think just because we have so called technology that we have become something other than what we originally were. Man will always be man."

There was silence for a minute with Susan breaking the silence saying, "Lacy, as this country and the world goes forward with the problems we face with energy, our environment, with our economies and with the increasing populations and the disintegration of families, jobs will be harder to get also and even harder to hold on to. There is a really interesting piece on You Tube called "Do You Know 2.0" which was originally developed for a Colorado (USA) high school staff of 150 in August of 2006. I want you to listen to that. Do you know according to the U.S. Department of Labor, one in four workers has been with their current employer less than one year, one in two workers has been with their current employer less than five years, and that the U.S. Department of Labor estimates that today's students will have ten to fourteen jobs by their thirty-eighth birthday. This all means stress levels in families will be higher, job security lower and the competition for jobs stronger."

"It doesn't sound like fun," mumbled Lacy.

"Fred, what are we doing? We have the most beautiful planet we know of even with our space probes and yet we are not only ruining it but we are not even enjoying this fabulous cornucopia of beauty and plenty," flared an angry mother.

"Do you know that in the next eight seconds more than thirty-four babies will be born that's why. Our populations are exploding and there isn't one politician that will touch the problem. Problems are not something anyone wants to face. Problems are not fun, they call for hard choices. People would much rather turn on the T.V. or radio or connect to the Internet to escape them. We are acting more like an ostrich than an intelligent animal. Do you know 'we can't solve our problems by using the same kind of thinking we used when we created them'? Einstein said that but no one listens. Man does not listen. If we are going to solve our problems and go forward, we have to be able to face reality and define what thinking outside the box means and electing those to lead us. Yes, our science and technology is increasing but for what purpose and how do we use it so we can live a natural and normal life on Earth? Clearly, what we view as intelligence must be a misnomer. Wall Street employed some of the, so called, brightest minds and yet, look at what happened. They did one stupid stunt after another which came within a hair of bringing the whole financial system down. And it wasn't only Wall Street; there was an epidemic of stupidity and greed all through our system. We have to discover what common sense is and we need to be able to test for it and find those to lead us for our own survival. It is clear to me; these are two different people with two totally different types of minds".

"We really have to transcend ourselves," observed Lacy.

"Lacy," said Fred, "Can we rise above pettiness, greed and self-interest is the big question?"

"If the world is making too many babies, why don't the girls just get spayed just like you talked about getting Mussy spayed?" asked Tommy.

"Sweetheart, it's just not that easy with people," smiled a devoted mom.

"Why? If we are thinking about doing it to Mussy and we love her," asked Tommy.

"Tommy, it's different with people," said Lacy. "You know the boys have to take just as much responsibility as the girls. Men can get a vasectomy and our drug companies are working on birth control pills for men too."

"What's a vasectomy?" asked Tommy.

"So you can't squirt your sperm into a girl," replied Lacy.

"Oh," replied Tommy. "What's sperm?"

"Sweetheart, it is the liquid you squirt into a girl that fertilizes her egg," replied a loving mother.

"Oh, you mean like a frog making tadpoles," replied Tommy.

"Yes," smiled Susan shaking her head, "like a frog making tadpoles."

Fred changed the subject. "What we really need is a master plan. I just can't believe we have been flying by the seat of our pants without one. There is not a company in this country or the world that doesn't have a game plan, a model of where they intend to go and where they want to be down the road and how they are going to get there. I really don't know what these guys in Washington are doing? How can they possibly manage without a road map of where we are going? It has been party time on our dime and they have bungled their job. If they worked for a company they would all be fired."

"Dad, I love having these discussions because we all know or at least feel there is a problem. Even my girlfriends, when they come over for dinner, like the way we can discuss the world's problems openly. Their families change the subject when, what they call, touchy subjects come up. My friends tell me their parents want to shield them but how can you shield a child or young adult from our natural biology or the world in which we live? After all, with the Internet everyone has access to everything including sex. It's the adults that have created this mess after all. Why not listen to kids and young adults for their ideas and solutions. Maybe, it's because we have these discussions that I think as openly as I do. I think our discussions help me become more aware of myself and others and the world we live in."

"I don't know why their parents would do that. If we don't face our problems, how are we going to solve them?" stated Fred. "We can't hide from our problems any longer. The whole family needs to be involved. Our children are the new generation who will inherit what the last generation leaves behind. Our children have to know because a lot of our problems won't be fixed right away and our children will have to carry on. Not only that, but our children will have to teach their children how to live and take care of Mother Earth. There is nothing as dangerous as ignorance. Anyone who is not given all the facts can't make a meaningful decision."

"Why don't I help you clear," smiled Susan, but Sunday I'm going to let you do it by yourself."

The following morning arrived with a beautiful sunny sky. "Oh Fred," said Susan, as she opened the window wider, "I can hardly wait for warmer weather," as she savored a large inhaled breath of fresh air. It's been such a cold miserable winter it seems to me."

"Me too. I hate the cold and I think once it warms up and spirits rise and emotions calm down it will help stabilize the economy."

"Spring does wonders for my mental health and my outlook on life. We are certainly in sync with the seasons. You know Fred, we never think about how much instinct we have already built in to us. The thought of spring changes our whole outlook. Don't forget Lacy's birthday is coming up. Did you buy her a computer yet?" said Susan putting her arms around Fred.

"Well, I ordered it."

"What did you get?" inquired an inquisitive mother.

"I got what she wanted with Dual Core, 350mb hard drive and 3 gigs of memory. I also got a new mini tower computer with a 30 inch screen."

"Who is going to use that?" asked Susan.

"Well, I got a little carried away but I wanted to see what a 30 inch screen would be like. I'm going to be an Indian giver and let everyone use it but also use it for work here at home."

"Oh, what fun? When are they coming and where are we going to hide them from Lacy? If she sees either one her mind will jump to the conclusion it is hers."

"As soon as I get a tracking number we will be able to check on the arrival date. You better put them in the garage and cover them up with a blanket or something. Don't make it too obvious. When I get home, you will have to take Lacy out to do something or keep her busy."

"Like what Fred?"

"Go shopping for school supplies."

"I don't think she needs school supplies," puzzled Susan.

"Well, think of something. What about new pajamas or slippers?"

"Nope, she doesn't need those either," said Susan.

"What about bones and treats for Mussy?"

"Well, that's an idea. But I think she should have enough homework to keep her busy. Did you get her a camera?"

"I bought an "add- on" because I thought it was better. It gives her HD, you know high definition pictures."

"Isn't that amazing," said Susan. Can you believe our world is changing as fast as it is?"

"You haven't seen anything yet," observed Fred. "Talk about being displaced from our roots. If technology continues to accelerate at its current pace, we will be living in some type of fantasy world run by flat panel screens and joy sticks with cameras everywhere."

"It's hard for me to keep up with it now," replied Susan. "Thank heavens the price of computers is coming down. You know, Fred, it's the miniaturization of computers that has made them so important to us. The smaller and more powerful they become the more they will be used in every facet of our lives."

"But what happens when we become obsolete? We don't change and they can," said Fred.

"It's scary," replied Susan. "They don't have to contend with emotions the way we do."

"Imagine an army of robots and drones. If people no longer fight and get hurt in war, will it be war or a very expensive video type game?" continued Fred.

"Wouldn't that be wonderful if nobody got hurt in war except our pocketbooks? We can only dream about such a day. You know Fred, when Freddy and Tommy see Lacy's new computer they will want new ones too."

"They will have to wait until their birthdays."

"Honey, can I have a new laptop with a HD camera too?"

Fred looked at Susan. "At this rate, I will have to start buying wholesale," quipped Fred. "Susan, you will have to get all your friends to get cameras first so you can see who you are talking to. It will be like having them in the same room with you especially as screens get larger. Just think what that will mean to the economy. Every time you get the urge to see a friend, instead of climbing in the car and burning fuel, you will just turn the computer on and make a phone call. That will also mean stores won't get the same amount of traffic coming through which will mean they will need cameras in their stores and on their sales people so you can walk through the store virtually and leaf through clothing or examine the product close up from the comfort of your home. So much will be purchased over the Internet."

"I bet one of these days they will have a sensor that will pick up the texture and feel of the merchandise and transfer the same feeling to the viewer" remarked Susan. "Won't that be something"?

Chapter Seven

THE BONDING

Sunday arrived with another beautiful day. "Fred, I can smell spring," observed Susan. "I can hardly wait to see the sails in the harbor with the gulls back in force. We have to start working on the boats, Fed."

"Susan, I have notes all over my calendar reminding me. Thank heavens the days are getting longer. I am going to try and leave early this Friday so I can get over to the boatyard and spend the weekend working on Blue Moon. I've got to get out right now and start work on the lawn before we go to church."

After church Matilda and Jimmy followed Fred back to the house. Matilda opened the side of her van and Jimmy was able to wheel his chair down the ramp to the ground.

"Can I help push you inside, Jimmy," asked Lacy who looked especially cute. Her square cut front blue spring dress emphasized what Mother Nature had endowed her with. Her blue dress went particularly well with her pixie type hair style that held a medium curl for her thick brown hair.

"No thanks," said Jimmy, "I can handle it O. K."

"Let's all go out to the patio," said Susan. "I have put all the patio furniture out since it is such a beautiful day; I know everyone would rather be outside."

"Susan, do you know that attendance at church is declining?" said Matilda. "You would think with all the problems we face that more people would be going to church not fewer."

"You would, I wonder why?" puzzled Susan.

"It's so much trouble, that's why," said Lacy.

"I think people just have so much to do and they don't want to take the time," said Fred.

"Susan," said Matilda, I also think with both husbands and wives working in many cases now, people have less time to do things outside the home. You know keeping a house up is no easy task. There is always something that needs to be fixed, there is always cleaning to be done and, of course, there is so much pressure in our lives, we need time just to relax and recoup ourselves."

"That's why the Internet has taken off," observed Jimmy. "You can get just the information you want when you want it. The Internet is a product of our times because we don't have as much excess time. It has and will continue to change every aspect of the world we live in. Do you know the amount of technical information is doubling every two years? For students starting a four year technical degree, this means that half of what they learned in their first year of study will be out dated by their third year of study. By 2013, a super computer will be built that exceeds the computational capabilities of the human brain we're told. I found this information on YouTube. You can find it under "Do You Know 2.0.

"But what about God, honey?" questioned Matilda.

"If we want to reach God then we will have to bring the church into our homes Mom. Just think with big flat panel screens in blazing color and surround sound it will be almost like church. Instead of passing the hat you could just fill out a form with your credit card. With cams throughout the church and on your computer you could see and hear exactly what was going on at church and others could see and hear you. In fact, you could have a Book of Psalms that enclosed a touch screen so while you sang you could see others. You could take it anywhere and you would be able to go to church anytime just by turning it on. It would be a virtual church online and you could switch between kneeling in the pew, listening to the minister or priest or Rabbi and singing or talking to friends. You could listen to a choir and organ music any time you want to. People are drawn to parties and concerts. Why not have concerts sponsored by churches throughout the world with the gospel mixed in. After all man is losing his way and he needs to be put back on the right course. Think of the millions the churches could reach and the fun and gayety they could create in the world. They could unite the world and have a constant party. We have to bring everyone together. We have to make life fun for all and at the same time remind everyone of their personal responsibilities. It could become the largest networking race man has ever seen that could even dwarf Facebook."

"Why haven't our churches done this? Our religion and our belief in a higher power have held humankind together from the beginning. It has been one of the few things that have brought and kept people together. It has been the very essence of civilization."

"Mother, our churches, our political systems, our schools, our financial systems and our businesses all have to be updated. They are all falling behind the learning curve. They don't realize with overpopulation, a changing and degraded environment and technology that we have entered into a new and very dangerous period and it will take everyone working together for our own survival."

"But, Honey, why haven't our institutions seen this already?"

"We have fallen into a rut and we need new thinking to get us out of this rut and back on the right track. Our institutions don't seem to realize how close the cliff is. If they get us much closer we are all going to fall over it."

Matilda's eyes became watery, "this world has already taken my husband and created a living nightmare for my son," murmured Matilda with tears forming in her eyes. "All our institutions seem to be letting us down. Why couldn't we see what we were doing to our beautiful little planet? Why can't we change?" There was a momentary pause, "I'm sorry for my outburst."

"Don't be," said Susan going over to Matilda and putting her arm around her. "We are all crying with you. I really don't know what our society is thinking about. I went to the grand opening of a major store not long ago and it was so jammed packed you couldn't move. Instead of everyone going in one direction they went in every direction bringing the store to almost a standstill. Management was totally out to lunch and I said to the manager why don't you paint a white arrow on the floor so that everyone would go in the same direction? He looked at me with a dumb brain dead look."

You could see the blood pressure rising in Fred. "It's absolutely critical that our society come up with a game plan on where the devil we are going," said an angered Fred. "I mean a game plan that deals with every facet of our existence. There are so many of us now that we can't just go in every direction the way man could a hundred years ago. We are flying by the seat of our pants and it is just inexcusable. We have to ask ourselves, where do we want to be in the next one hundred years and design a road map on how we are going to get there? I would respond that we first need a responsive government so we can make a world that is made for human existence; safe, prosperous and as individual as possible."

"But Dad how do we that?" exclaimed Lacy. "The only way we can achieve that is if all women in all countries are willing to limit their families to one child. Only women ultimately have the power. There is no way we can feed, educate and house more people than we have now. We can't even feed, educate and house the populations we now have," said a young woman with a worried face.

All of a sudden a little yellow fluff ball runs in with Tommy and Freddy in hot pursuit. "We took Mussy out for some exercise," exclaimed Tommy. "She ran all over even down to the water."

"I hope you didn't let her go in the water," asked Susan.

"No, Freddy caught her before she did," replied Tommy.

Mussy's little tail was wagging as she put her damp paws on Lacy's legs."

"Mussy, get down," she said, in a not very stern way, as she pet her. Mussy, being as spoiled as she was, did not pay any attention. Her little tail just kept wagging and with a little puppy bark said, "I want to sit on your lap." Lacy picked her up, gave her a kiss and put her in Jimmy's lap. Her little tail stopped wagging and she started sniffing Jimmy not sure of what to make of this new person. Jimmy started to pet her and she looked up at him as if to say, "who are you? What gives you the right to touch me? I don't know you."

Lacy smiled and left the patio only to return with a tantalizing snack for Mussy in her hand. As she handed it to Jimmy, Mussy's little eyes became glued to the tasty looking morsel.

"Here Jimmy, give this to her and she will be your friend forever."

The cutest little face licked her lips and gave a little puppy bark saying, "I can't stand it, give it to me." Jimmy moved his hand with the lip smacking morsel in it and every inch of the move was followed by a pair of the cutest little puppy eyes fixated on that tid bit. Jimmy lowered it and put the morsel in front of Mussy and it was gone. Mussy continued to look for another tasty morsel; just waiting for another one to appear. Her eyes looked everywhere. She looked up at Jimmy and with another puppy bark said "that's not the only one, is it? I want another one."

"Tommy, has Mussy had lunch yet?" asked Lacy.

"Well, I haven't fed her."

"Mom, has she been fed?"

"I don't think so."

"That's why she looks so hungry. Jimmy let's take her to the kitchen and feed her lunch."

Jimmy wheeled to the kitchen following Lacy.

"While they are feeding Mussy, I'll go in and start things rolling for dinner," said Susan. Why don't you all start moving towards the dining room in about five minutes?"

"What are we going to have?" asked Tommy.

"Something you will love," replied Susan.

"Hamburgers and French fries?" quizzed Tommy.

"Nope," replied Susan.

"Pizza?"

"Nope."

"Well, that's what I like."

"You will find out in a few minutes," replied Susan.

Tommy followed his mother into the kitchen.

"Macaroni and cheese?" quizzed Tommy again. You're not going to give me vegetables are you?"

"You like carrots and vegetable are very good for you. They help prevent you from getting colds."

"But Mom, I don't like them."

"You like carrots, don't you?"

"Only sometimes," frowned Tommy.

"Go get seated, sweetheart."

Susan pulled things out of the oven and got the dinner ready to serve. Lacy brought Tommy's plate out to him.

"What's that?" exclaimed Tommy.

"Tommy, what does your mother always ask you to do?" asked Fred.

"Put my napkin in my lap." Tommy puts his napkin in his lap and tucks it in his pants so it doesn't fall down. Susan appears from the kitchen and sits down. "Jimmy, Fred tells me you have doubled your money already. I think that is amazing. How many people can double their money in several weeks?"

"I was just lucky. I approach every trade with the view I only have a fifty-fifty chance of making money. I am part believer in the random walk theory to the extent that no one knows what tomorrow will bring. It's no different than life itself. Human life is built on emotion which is very impulsive. That's why companies have marketing departments. When you go shopping, you may go shopping for a particular item, but come home with a different item. There are an increasing number of choices as many different manufacturers compete for a piece of every market. As more and more shopping is done online we not only have more choices but we can compare prices to get, what we think, is our best value. Our world and our technology are changing so fast that yesterday may not be any indication of tomorrow. With the Internet and cell phones and laptops, new products or changes in existing products are rapidly conveyed causing yesterday's winners to become tomorrow's losers. But my overriding philosophy is my wave theory."

"What is your wave theory?" asked Lacy getting more intrigued with the conversation.

"Well, let me continue. Some say that investing for the long term is the only way to invest, and it certainly would have paid big returns to invest long term when our country was young and growing. Technology was just beginning to stir and the competition was far less than it is today. If you invested in a new technology you could expect it to last long enough to make your capital investment back and a profit. However, everyone everywhere is developing new technologies so fast now that it is much harder to recoup your investment let alone make a profit. Moreover, we need growth in our economy to make it work at all. If people don't have good paying jobs or inflation and or taxes eats up our disposable income, we can't afford to buy new things. The thread that runs through all economies today is the same thread no matter whether you are in Asia or Europe or America. That thread is our planet is a finite space with limited resources. The larger our populations become means putting more demand on our raw resources which means growth will push prices up for these dwindling resources stifling the growth we need and slowing our economies. So we are stuck. We are caught between our environmental needs, dwindling raw resources and growth. This will be true everywhere including China. I have to ask myself, why is China as well as other countries rushing to expand their economies when they won't be able to keep them up as raw resources run low or out? On top of that prices will be forced up for everything reducing disposable income."

"Fred, why hasn't man seen this and done something about it," asked Susan. "Why don't our leaders see this?"

"Our leaders are focused on the moment, on the near term. Our whole financial system has become so myopic that it is focused on the analysts' expectations on a quarterly basis. The system is killing itself. Everyone in the world is concentrating on the moment. No one is thinking about the future. It is a critical flaw in man and it will kill him if he doesn't change."

"Look what is happening all over the world, continued Jimmy. "Growth is slowing, debt in both the public and private sectors is increasing and there is no way out without uniting the world around a long term game plan. Think about this; if a person or company wants to get a loan the first thing a banker will ask is, let me see your business plan or your past earnings? Do you realize no government has a business plan and yet they are able to borrow billions and trillions of dollars? Our governments are flying completely blind with no business plan and yet they are allowed to run up huge piles of debt. Clearly, this won't work. The financial system deserves to take a big loss because they made an unwise gamble. They bet wrong. Secretary General of the United Nations, U Thant, back in 1965 said, "If we don't control our populations within the next five years it will be too late". But we didn't. Any time you don't fix a problem it only gets worse; the problem is compounded. The more people we have on this little planet just divides the pie into smaller and smaller pieces reducing incomes and reducing taxes per capita until we bankrupt ourselves. The end result is that it hurts everyone both rich and poor. What all governments are doing will not get civilization to the end result

all people want and that is a better life for all. The only solution is to unite all countries on planet Earth and establish a long term business plan or game plan. So, as I see it, from my vantage point, since I can't wait years for an investment to pay off and the future is cloudy anyway, I have to be able to understand the swings in the market. We have ruined our own system. The stock market was created so ordinary citizens could take part in the growth of our companies and our country, however, we have allowed computers and automated trading systems and huge mega funds to so unbalance the market that we have ruined our original objective. We are scaring the very money, we want to attract, away from the market. The SEC, the very core of our financial system, must be out to lunch because they did away with the long standing uptick rule which basically would help control the program trading. I'd like to know what the SEC is doing. They didn't even catch Bernie Madoff in his Ponzi scheme. In addition, our government did away with the Glass-Steagall Act which was designed to keep our banking system stable and secure. On top of everything else, people realize that we have a dysfunctional government that obviously doesn't understand and can't see the problems. Our whole political system is worthless for this time and age. Nobody is doing their job. Our short term greed has replaced long term growth as I see it. We are just starting to see the collapse of our financial ecosystem like the rest of our ecosystems. So I am forced to not only understand human psychology, which is a wave, but to also understand how these automated trading systems work. Unfortunately, I can't take that more than random walk approach which was only true for the last period B.C."

"B.C.," puzzled Susan. "I didn't know they had a stock market that long ago."

"B.C. is before computers," said Jimmy.

"Oh, how stupid of me," said Susan blushing. Well, how do you expect to make money if every trade is just a toss of the coin? That means the odds of you making money over a short period of time are probably less than fifty percent. You are playing against the odds, aren't you?"

"Well, life is a wave. The length of the wave and the height and depth of the wave are the unknowns. However, waves are influenced by momentum. If you take a look at the oceans, when there is no wind, the water is flat and when the wind blows the water curls up into waves and if it really blows the waves get higher and further apart. When it snows and we make a snowman and we roll the balls along the ground in the snow trying to make them bigger, the bigger we make them the easier they are to roll given a flat surface. There must be a law of physics that covers that but it escapes me. Human emotions are the same way. The more the media yells recession or depression the more emotions stampede and it picks up momentum; the more yelling, the bigger the ball of emotion. However, that same emotional momentum is valid for not only stocks but anything else bought or sold including houses. It even goes back to the tulip craze in the 1500's when people's emotions ran the price of tulips up to astronomical prices. But, like all bubbles and snow balls, they get so big they finally disintegrate under their own weight. It is the same reaction we find in all of nature. The tulip craze burst and left a lot of people holding the bag, no pun intended. The stock market is just built on human nature."

"Jimmy, I think the physical law you are talking about is Newton's first law, the law of inertia," said Lacy with a sweet, I know it all, smile.

"Good for you honey," smiled Susan.

"So Jimmy, how do you use that philosophy to make money?" questioned Susan. "As you know my husband is a stockbroker and he tells me all the time that the so called smartest guys who run investment funds and hedge funds are lucky if they can just equal the performance of the Standard and Poor's 500."

"First, what is intelligence?" asked Jimmy. "When we say the smartest, what do we mean; the smartest at what? Our schools teach only what they know which is self-fulfilling for the schools. We should be asking ourselves, what types of minds or intelligences are there and what types do we need for specific goals and how do we test for them? There are so many really good minds that are overlooked and wasted because they don't fit into our academic models. We have to remember, unless we understand Mother Nature completely and have a unified theory of the whole system, we are flying blind folded. And, to date, we don't have one. Why did Steve Jobs, Bill Gates, Larry Ellison and many other innovators drop out of college? I think education's greatest mission is to define the type of mind it is teaching and to fulfill its needs. A mind that cannot think outside the box is a robot. Think for a moment and ask yourself "what if" we have been following the wrong type of intelligence all these years. What if, at some point, man came to a fork in the road and he chose the wrong path to follow. The near collapse of Wall Street should be the proverbial canary in the financial goal mind that tells us maybe we are not seeing the obvious. It's like a male fiddler crab that has a great big intimidating claw. It's great for a fiddler crab because it scares off intruders. But if we watch that fiddler crab, we learn that his great big intimidating claw is almost useless. That fiddler crab is part of nature and therefore part of us. So, before I answer your question, why don't we wait and see how I do? It maybe that I can't make money, in which case my investing or speculating philosophy is worthless."

"Are you in the market now?" asked Fred.

"I bought an April 79 call on the spider for a dollar eighty, but I am very nervous about it."

"The market has rebounded this week so you must be making a little money?" quizzed Fred.

"The problem is, this market can turn in a second especially these days. People are so negative that a huge wall of worry can come crashing down at any time. That is why I am so nervous."

"If you can lose your money, why not spend it?" asked Freddy. "I have lots of things I want to buy. Mom, I want a dirt bike."

"You have a bike, Freddy, what is wrong with yours?" asked Susan.

"Nothing. But, it's not a dirt bike and my friends are all getting dirt bikes."

"We will have to see sweetheart, we have so many things we all want that we can't buy them all. I think what we all need to do is make up a budget for ourselves and prioritize everything we think we need."

"I think that is a wonderful idea," replied Fred. "This evening, I want Lacy, Freddy and Tommy all to make out a budget. You all know who Ben Franklin was and he said "beware of little expenses; a small leak will sink a great ship.""

"Can I use the computer?" asked Lacy.

"You should and there are probably lots of free canned financial or budget programs on the Internet. Two Cows is one site you might want to check out and CNET. I have Microsoft Money on mine and you can use that program if you want."

"Will you help me, Dad?" asked Tommy.

"Of course."

"My allowance isn't very much," grumped Tommy.

"Well, your expenses aren't much either?" replied Susan. "Just think of all the things we pay for. You don't have to worry about a roof over your head, the clothes you wear, the food you eat, your schooling; transportation, medical insurance in case you get sick, toys and games and on and on.. You should always be thankful for what you have because there are many children who are not as lucky. You, my little friend, are very lucky. Aristotle was a great philosopher way back in 384BC and that is before Christ, by the way, and he said "happiness depends on ourselves". Think how happy you are when you are just playing with Mussy. That is true lasting happiness. Now put a smile on that cute little face."

After dinner, Jimmy stayed with Lacy as she put on her apron to protect her beautiful blue dress and started to clear the table.

"Jimmy, what did you mean when you said, the fiddler crab is part of nature and therefore part of us?"

"Well, all of nature is interconnected. Nature didn't give different animals different parts or devise different systems that are dissimilar. The same parts are shared by all animals in slightly different forms. In other words cells are somewhat standardized and somewhat specialized. All animals have a mouth, many have teeth, all bones are made of calcium, eyes all work in basically the same way and we all react pretty much the same way to a stimulus. The human animal has been side tracked; thinking because he has a neo-cortex that he is superior to other animals. What man doesn't seem to understand is that our basic wiring overrides our neo-cortex and the same genetically passed on impulses or wiring are the same ones that we had in the very beginning. We are nature. We are of the universe."

"I think that's really profound," said Lacy. If our basic wiring overrides our neo-cortex that must mean the neo-cortex was an, add- on, of Mother Natures."

"Good observation Lacy. Guess what I saw on MSNBC's web site?"

"What?" replied Lacy, as she carried the plates into the kitchen?

"Archaeologists just uncovered a two ton dinosaur that had wings. It was two hundred and fifty million years old. Imagine a two ton bird that has to go to the bathroom in the air. Talk about a bad hair day."

"You're silly," laughed Lacy.

"Just think if a two ton bird landed on your corn field. Can you imagine each step it took would crush and decimate your crop? Or even worse, think of a whole flock of these things landing on your crop. They would wipe you out."

Lacy looked at Jimmy laughing and said "you're really silly," with a big smile and a giggle.

"I wonder what size worms they had back then?" continued Jimmy. "It would take a gigantic worm to feed this thing. Can you imagine a tug of war between a giant worm and this monster trying to get it out of the ground?"

Lacy was laughing, "Jimmy you better stop it or I will drop a plate or something. A two ton flying dinosaur," giggled Lacy. "Could it really fly?"

"It had little wings so, I am sure, it couldn't unless it could have glided off a hill," laughed Jimmy, "Can you imagine a two ton gliding dinosaur coming at you out of control? You wouldn't know which way to run."

"Oh Jimmy stop it," said Lacy laughing. The thought of it is funny, though, unless, of course, you were in the way of that dinosaur. Were dinosaurs made of the same things we are?"

"Of course, what else is there in nature that supports life? Dinosaurs had a skeleton and that skeleton was made of calcium, it moved by its muscles and muscles work the same in all living creatures, it had eyes and all eyes work on the same principles, it had a nose that breathed oxygen given off by the plants and the oxygen went into lungs like ours."

"What about its brain, did it think?"

"All animal life is wired to survive. It makes no difference whether it lived then or now. Only the outer casing, the part we see, looks different. Modern man looks upon himself as being a fabulous new inspiration of nature when in reality we are the same basic design of nature that has always existed in animal life. A crocodile, one of the oldest living creatures on earth; that lived as far back as dinosaurs, is still a crocodile no matter where you find him. He hasn't changed. He reacts the same way he did in the very beginning. That crocodile's DNA will always make it the same crocodile as it was in the very beginning. Man is no more than a branch of life that goes back to the very beginning of life with the addition of a more profound neo-cortex. Anthropologists study man to determine his primate lineage. While that may be an interesting academic question, I don't personally see it as being necessarily relevant. What I think the interesting questions are, first, primates, porpoises and elephants all have an enlarged neo-cortex and the three couldn't be more different in their appearance or in the environment in which they live, so did we all develop the neo-cortex at the same time? Clearly, the larger neo-cortex is not limited to man. Therefore, what was going on at the time of the mutation? How long did it take for this mutation to occur and was it a mutation at all? It would be very unusual for all mammals to mutate at the same time. Even more interesting is when did animals develop eyes? The development of eyes changed the course of life on Earth; moreover, it changed the basic wiring of the central processing unit or what we call the brain."

"You know, you're right, Jimmy," said Lacy thinking. "Life jumped from life with no eyes, to creatures that had eyes. I wonder how long that transition took, there had to be different stages of eye development. There must have been a long period of transformation and yet we know nothing about it."

"That's a good question Lacy. It seems inconceivable that life went from being a totally sensual creature to one being completely wired around its visual senses in one huge leap. There is a huge unexplained jump there. You would think we would find a period of transition in our fossils. While there is a fish fossil scientists uncovered they think shows different stages of eye development, scientists have not found anything, I am aware of, in the animal kingdom."

"There seems to be huge jumps in life forms where we have little data to explain why. Jimmy this is so fascinating. I think our scientists maybe going down the wrong path. But the question is," continued Lacy "how can we say that we are the same as other animals when we can look around at all the technology we have developed?"

"Lacy, we both have a basic interest in knowing more about ourselves and the human species. Let's read and study as much as we can to see what scientists have discovered. As we continue on, we will ask ourselves questions which will make us search for answers and perhaps we can pry open the door to how man developed and how man's brain works. The really big question, that may mean whether man can continue on, is can we find an answer to the question, what is common sense? What do we mean when we say thinking outside the box?"

"Jimmy, my father is adamant about defining and being able to test for what we call thinking outside the box and common sense. Are the two unrelated or are they one and the same?"

"Lacy, our discussions and research will be as much an adventure for me as it will be for you. Wouldn't it be cool if we could come up with answers to our questions?"

"Jimmy, it will be like an earth science detective mystery."

"Do you want to start now?"

"Sure. But there is so much to know over such a wide range of different fields of study that it will take a lot of time and work."

"Do you like to read about biology, nature and the human mind?"

"Yes."

"I think our common sense can help us reduce the time it will take to find our answers as well as the use of our computers."

"Jimmy that is the question we are trying to answer. What is common sense?"

"Do you think you have common sense?

"Yes."

"Do you like watching nature?"

"Yes."

"Have you always liked watching and observing nature?"

"Yes."

"Can you see a correlation between nature and man?"

"Yes."

"Can you see similar actions and reactions in the actions and reactions of different animals and man?"

"Yes."

"My hypothesis is that you do have common sense but we will find out as we explore man. To start our minds working I will ask two questions? Does technology define a species or does its ability to live in harmony with nature define it? If a species has so called technology that leads to its demise, is that an intelligent species or a mutation that went wrong?"

"What do you think?" asked Lacy.

"Let both of us take this journey together," replied Jimmy, "so we can answer that question each in our own way. Let us start by stating things we know or observed about nature that will start the thinking process. First, we know we have a basic brain, that is, we have a brain that is wired to survive. We know we have a cortex, as do other animals, as part of our CPU. I am going to use the word CPU interchangeably with brain. We know that we have a neo-cortex that Mother Nature, in her infinite wisdom, bestowed upon us. The neo-cortex is wrapped around our cortex and contains six layers. We know the size of our neo-cortex is among the largest but not the largest in mammals, however, all mammals have a neo-cortex. We know even non mammals like birds show cognition and some scientists say there is a region in a bird's brain that may serve as a neo-cortex. The African Grey parrot can mimic a large number of human phrases which shows it has a very good memory and cognition. Look at a squirrel; I have a pair of squirrels in my back yard. They have made a nest for themselves thirty feet up that can with-stand a howling wind and a tree that is swaying back and forth and a nest that can withstand a hawk attack with its long talons. Even man would have a hard time duplicating this technological feat with just leaves and sticks and his bare hands thirty feet up. In fact, I'm not sure man can even do it. Also, my bird feeder is on a steel pole stuck in the ground with a cone around it to prevent squirrels from getting to the bird feeder. There are two twine guide lines holding the pole and feeders up so snow doesn't weight it down and knock it over. I have a squirrel that tried to climb the pole to get to the bird feeder. The cone prevented the squirrel from getting to the feeders so he jumped down. I watched that squirrel and he assessed the situation and went over to the guide lines and bit through both of them. That squirrel used a very sophisticated thinking process and an understanding, a cognizance, of gravity. He thought by biting through the guide lines the feeder would fall over."

"Therefore," said Lacy, "the question is, what abilities does our brain give us over other animals and are these abilities to our advantage and, if so, to what end?

"Exactly," said Jimmy. "If we can understand our actions, that is, how the brain functions, can we change the course of our own destiny? As we ask each other questions we will start to unravel the question of why we are the way we are and the question, are we on the right path? Our answers, either right or wrong, will bring forth more questions until we piece the whole puzzle together. Are you really sure you want to take this adventure through all of human development and the human mind with me?"

"Oh yes, I find it absolutely fascinating and I want to know," said Lacy. "It will be like getting a sneak preview to our future which will be awesome. We have been fed so many wives tales and B.S about ourselves let's see if we can piece the puzzle together for ourselves."

"Then, I am going to ask you a question which I already know the answer to," replied Jimmy, "but to make sure we are all on the same page to begin with, I want you to answer this question; if all animals are wired for survival, meaning we all have a central processing unit and a central nervous system that reacts in our own self- interest; and we all feel a pin prick and we all react about the same to that pin prick, and we all display emotion in greater or lesser degrees, why wouldn't we be the same animal other than our looks? After all, we all have eyes; we have a nose, ears, lungs and legs. We all have to breathe, eat and excrete."

Lacy thought for a moment. "Essentially we are the same."

"Let me answer with a question. What makes you think we are not alike?"

"Well, I know I don't act like a cat or a dinosaur," replied Jimmy.

"When you say, act like, are you talking about our basic physical reactions or our instinctive reactions because you just pointed out our basic physical reactions are pretty much the same?"

"That's good Lacy. Let's go a step further. If I see a mouse, for example, I don't have the impulse to chase it or dine on it; why not?"

"Because our instincts are different," answered Lacy.

"What causes us to have different basic instincts?"

"Our basic instinctive wiring. Each animal species re-acts the same time and time again based on its basic instinctive wiring. Instinct is a basic molecular chemical reaction."

"We have already determined that we have our basic physical reactions and our basic instinctive wiring so the two must be different. Our basic instinctive wiring or impulse must drive our basic physical reactions? Does that make sense?" asks Jimmy.

"Yes," I would agree," replies Lacy.

"So, therefore, animals must have two impulses. There must be a basic physical impulse and an instinctive impulse. One impulse drives the motor system and the other impulse must tell the motor system how to react. Does that make sense to you?"

"Yes. It would certainly seem to follow."

"Does it make any difference where you find that species? I mean does a cat here in North America act like a cat in South America or in Asia?"

"No, it doesn't make any difference where you find that cat or even the size of the cat or type of cat. All cats act in the same way. It makes no difference where you find that species, it always reacts the same. A dog, anywhere in the world, is still a dog and will always react the same way. It makes no difference if it's a Great Dane or Chihuahua. A horse, no matter where you find it, is still a horse and will always react exactly the same way. Every time a cat sees a mouse, instinctively that cat is wired to react exactly the same way. Animals and mammals all react to their basic instinctive wiring in their central processing unit," said Lacy.

"Why do cats have sharp claws while dogs do not," asked Jimmy.

Lacy thought for a moment. "So they can catch mice," laughed Lacy.

"What word could you replace mice with?"

Lacy grimaced while she thought.

"What do mice represent?" asked Jimmy.

"Survival?" questioned Lacy.

"Exactly. Every animal is wired for survival driven by its own instincts," replied Jimmy.

"If every animal is wired for survival that means its physical characteristics have to be in sync with its basic wiring. That means body and mind have to be one. You couldn't rely on catching mice for survival and be a hippopotamus. Can you imagine a hippo tip toeing towards an unsuspecting mouse? The mouse would have to be deaf, dumb and blind," laughed Lacy. "Jimmy, do you know what this means? It means originally the way a mind was wired dictated the physical characteristics of that animal," exclaimed Lacy.

"Very good Lacy. I think as we continue along in our thinking and research we will find the same types of correlations within the mind that define the type of mind on a more individualistic basis."

"Jimmy, let me continue with my thought because, I think, it may be an important piece of the puzzle. If the mind does originally dictate the form of the body then any change in the make- up of a central processing unit would also dictate a change in the form of its body, right?"

"Lacy, it certainly follows. If you are right it would go far beyond Darwin's theory and, I think, probably make it an obsolete theory. However, since we don't have any proof yet that your hypothesis is correct, we will have to file that hypothesis in our yet to prove file. Our goal will be to come up with many hypotheses and then put them on a graph something like a scatter gram but one that is divided by epochs, physiological and biological changes and environmental changes and at the end of our research tie the epochs and the changes together to come up with our conclusion. However, I wonder if Mother Nature made some animals where their wiring and or physical characteristics worked against them which caused them to die off and become extinct?"

"Jimmy, we do find fossils of animals and even man where that particular species seems to come to a short and abrupt end. Jimmy, I want to look at something else for a moment. The first thing that happens in a fetus after insemination is the wiring starts to form. The basic wiring is in the DNA which dictates what the final outcome will be. Since all life is a product of its own DNA it follows that its DNA was already tested for survival in another living organism," observed Lacy. "I mean, life didn't pull its DNA out of a hat. So if the DNA was tested in another living thing; that obviously survived to mating, why would that DNA lead to its extinction? I mean why would certain creatures die out? And even more interesting is the question what caused so many different life forms to emerge and are they still emerging?"

"These are questions we want to answer through our research. But what we can safely say is the DNA of each species establishes a central processing unit that processes visual and sensory information in exactly the same way for each species no matter whether it lived two hundred million years ago or whether it lives today. Nothing has changed. The wiring in a crocodile is the same wiring it had two hundred million years ago. We can, therefore, safely say that the wiring in that particular species has been passed along in a genetic code that always remains the same as long as that animal mates with another of the same species."

"Now, how many other animals are going to mate with a crocodile?" giggled Lacy.

"Exactly," laughed Jimmy. "That's why a crocodile is a perfect example. Are we all together on the same page still?"

"Right on," replied Lacy. "So for millions and millions of years, life lived by its basic instinctive wiring, coded specifically for that species. But then how did different life or species form?

I mean, unless we say all animal life was created at the same time, which might indicate perhaps the creation theory, however, we know all life wasn't created at the same time, then where did new life come from?"

"Originally, fossils seem to indicate, all life emerged from the sea, which makes sense to me," replied Jimmy, "since the first form of life was a one celled animal like an amoeba and certainly couldn't have existed on dry land at that time because of the lack of soil. In fact, animals are about sixty percent water. The bones that make up our skeleton are about forty-three percent water and both water and calcium are plentiful in the sea. The brine shrimp, which lives in salt water, has a system much like humans. Did you know that?"

"I think we studied that in biology class. So once life started to flourish on Earth, there must have been a vast pool of mating going on within species and within subspecies," observed Lacy.

"Well, let's define a subspecies. I mean where did a subspecies come from" asked Jimmy? "Do you have a computer available that is connected to the Internet?"

"Yes, I have the kitchen computer I can use. I'll bring it over. Let's see, scientists tell us a subspecies often arise from a geographic separation. However, could the same species arise in more than one location on Earth at about the same time, asked Lacy? If the answer is yes, then it would be the same species just in a different location. But that response would raise more questions. If the answer is no then the original DNA of that species wouldn't change even if it moved away and became isolated, so the change would be superficial things like longer hair or a different diet. After all, planet earth is a huge mixing bowl. Life travels freely everywhere. But that would not give us a new species."

"Lacy, I want to make sure we both are using the same terminology. The zoological classifications of animals are complex, I think, so let's decide on our nomenclature so we understand what each other are saying. If we take the cat family for example, when we use the word cat, we are referring to the entire cat family, all cats. Within the cat family there are genera which is the plural of genus like the Panthera genus which includes leopards, tigers, lions and jaguars and within that genus there are the species of cats like leopards. When you talk about a subspecies, you are saying a subspecies of leopards, for example, might arise in a different location."

"Yes. Taking your example of the leopard species, there are two possibilities for a leopard showing up in a different location. Either there was a geographical separation causing the subspecies or the only other possibility would be Mother Nature gave rise to the leopard in two different locations."

"Lacy, lets continue with our example of leopards. Leopards are found in Africa and they are also found in Asia. Is the Asian leopard the same species as the African leopard?"

"Yes."

"So, while the two leopards are thousands of miles and continents apart they are still the same species."

"Yes."

"Is this an example of geographical separation or Mother Nature giving rise to the leopard in two different locations?"

"Jimmy, that's a good question. Let me see what I can find on the internet because I don't know. Let me Google leopards. O.K., the Asian leopard originated in Asia. Wow, I didn't know that. It's so much fun to learn isn't it Jimmy?"

"That is interesting Lacy. We have the same species arising on two different continents. So, if a species can arise in two different locations there must have been warm tidal pools of life not only in Africa but in other areas. Lacy, this could change our whole outlook on life on Earth."

"I wonder why Darwin didn't see this?"

"Lacy, we have so much more information at our finger tips now than ever before. For Darwin's time, his findings were new and filled a void. But today, with thousands of scientists, all over the world, all pouring out information that we have access to, giving us so much more information that it allows us to come to different conclusions. Everything man has come to rely on has to be updated. Times have changed and man is way behind the learning curve. Unless we put a total game plan together for our future we won't have a future."

"Jimmy, this is so much fun. So now returning to our definition of subspecies, we know that if a species mated with another of its species or a subspecies it would not give rise to a new species."

"That's right you can't get a new species from mating with a subspecies."

"Jimmy, I'm a little confused. We have already agreed that all cats re-act the same. It doesn't make any difference what species of cat we are talking about. Their basic instinctive wiring dictates that they all re-act the same. So even if we have mating going on between two different species or even genus their offspring would still inherit the same basic instinctive wiring. So how does Mother Nature change the wiring? I mean what did a species or genus or family or life mate with to get a different animal? Here we have all these warm salt water pools teaming with life. From these tidal pools came many different life forms from fish, to mammals to birds and insects. Darwin thought that one life form could turn into another but I don't buy that and it can't be true that evolution was totally responsible either. We have already agreed that a crocodile is a crocodile whether it lived two hundred million years ago or it lives today. It is the same DNA and it hasn't changed."

"Good observation Lacy. Let's look at what was going on at the time life first developed. We had a hot climate at least scientists tell us life evolved in tropical like conditions. Life started in the shallows where one celled animals were evolving. The one celled amoeba doesn't mate but divides in half producing two daughter cells that are identical in their genes or DNA."

"And," continued Lacy," for the most part they have one nucleus. Jimmy, that is what our cells do, they divide and each cell contains identical DNA."

"Even more interesting Lacy, "is the fact that single celled amoebas bring in food particles which are digested by enzymes. Sounds familiar doesn't it Lacy?"

"That is exactly what our bodies do Jimmy."

"Yes," continued Jimmy, "and just as interesting is the fact that the amoeba's membrane allows oxygen to pass through to the cell and carbon dioxide to pass out."

"How could anyone say our genes don't go all the way back to the very beginning of life?" questioned Lacy.

"Exactly; now we have, perhaps, made your question of how life developed into different life forms and species a little easier to explore. We know amoebas are of the protozoan family which is a diverse group of single celled animals. So, even from the very beginnings of life there were different forms or species of life. Now we can ask ourselves, how or why did different types of life form," smiled Jimmy?

"So," exclaimed an excited Lacy, "we don't even have to deal with mating."

"No." "We have taken that unknown out of the equation."

"Oh, this is so awesome," laughed Lacy. This is so fascinating, I just love it."

The kitchen door opened and Susan walks into the kitchen where Lacy and Jimmy are talking. "Well, we wondered where you two were. It looks like you have everything cleaned up and put away."

"Yes," replied Lacy. "Jimmy and I are having a very interesting discussion."

Susan looked at both Jimmy and Lacy and could tell their minds were somewhere else. "Well," said Susan, "do you two want to come in and join us on the patio?"

"Mom we will be out shortly."

"That's fine," replied Susan leaving the kitchen thinking "I wonder what they are talking about that has their minds so involved?"

"Jimmy, we better go join everyone or they will think we don't want to be with them," said Lacy.

"Do you still want to research this exploration of life and the human mind with me?" asked Jimmy.

"Oh yes, I don't want to stop now but I don't want to be rude and not go in and talk to everyone either. Let's talk on the phone at least several times a week and I will ask Mom to have you over on the weekends. Would that be OK with you?"

"Oh! Right on Lacy."

Jimmy and Lacy returned to the patio to see everyone about to take a walk. "Where are you going?" asked Lacy.

"Oh, I'm glad to see you finally joined us," replied Susan. "We are just going down to the beach and walk along the water; it is such a beautiful day. Do you want to come?"

"Jimmy, can you use your wheelchair on the sand?" asked Lacy.

"I've never tried it so I don't know, but I can try; maybe along the water where the sand is packed."

"Alright Mom, we'll come. Mom, did you know there was a two ton flying dinosaur that lived two hundred and fifty million years ago?"

"A two ton flying dinosaur," inquired Freddy.

"Lacy, you have just hit the magic word with Freddy. Dinosaurs are his favorite topic."

"Freddy can you imagine a two ton bird flying over your head?" laughed Lacy.

"How big is two tons?" asked Tommy.

"Tommy, have you ever seen an ostrich?" quizzed Lacy.

"I know what an ostrich is" exclaimed Tommy, I saw one at the zoo and sometimes they are on T.V."

"Well, a big ostrich weighs about three hundred pounds so I guess these dinosaurs were about thirteen times as big. Can you imagine something as big as thirteen ostriches flying over your head? That is a huge bird," laughed Lacy, "in fact, I can't even imagine anything that big especially flying overhead. It would be so big it would probably block the sun and create a huge shadow on the ground."

"Wow! You would have to run for cover. Could it really fly?" exclaimed Freddy.

"It had little wings Freddy," replied Jimmy, "so it would be highly unlikely. But just the thought of something that big with wings and feathers is astounding."

"Was it as big as a T. Rex?" questioned Freddy in a pensive pose of excitement.

"No, it wasn't as big but, for a bird type of dinosaur, it was huge."

"How big is a T. Rex?" returned Freddy.

"I think the largest T. Rex got as big as seven tons which would have been over three times as big as the winged dinosaur. In comparison, Freddy, the largest elephant gets to be about nine maybe even ten tons," stated Jimmy.

"Wow," exclaimed Freddy.

"How would you like to have a T. Rex chasing you?" laughed Jimmy.

"I'd slam the door in his face and lock it," exclaimed Freddy.

"Why don't we see any dinosaurs now?" asked Tommy.

"They all died out," replied Lacy.

"Why?"

"We don't really know why," replied Lacy. "Some scientists think the earth was hit by a huge meteor which sent so much ash, smoke and fire out from the collision that it destroyed everything around it for hundreds of miles and also sent so much smoke and ash up into our atmosphere that it blocked out the sun for months. It killed all the trees, plants and grass so the dinosaurs died."

"But the T. Rex only ate meat," stated Freddy.

"He would have had a lot of charbroiled dino burgers, right Freddy," smiled Fred who had been listening.

"I don't think T. Rex ate burgers Dad, he liked to kill his food," replied Freddy.

"Freddy, you are right, the T. Rex and other types of meat eating dinosaurs just ate meat," explained Lacy, "and apparently the meteor event didn't kill all dinosaurs either. After all, there were dinosaurs all over the world also. There were even dinosaurs in the Antarctic," said Lacy.

"They were in the Antarctic," exclaimed Freddy. Why didn't they freeze?"

"Way back then, when the dinosaurs lived, scientists tell us the Antarctic was warm enough so it was covered with forests. It was a very different place than it is today. Jimmy, why do you think the dinosaurs died out?" asked Lacy.

"If we look at other meteor strikes and volcanic activity which also spewed ash everywhere, it seems that the effects may be felt and seen up to five hundred miles away but we have never witnessed a meteor strike or volcano that sent enough ash up to blot out the sun for a period long enough to decimate a whole species. My guess is, since dinosaurs were spread out all over the world and we continue to find skeletons of different types of dinosaurs even in remote areas like the Antarctic; it doesn't seem plausible to me that one meteor strike would wipe out all dinosaurs on earth especially when some scientists tell us some dinosaurs lived many thousands of years after the suspected strike. There were glaciation periods that came and went that could have changed the weather enough to affect the dinosaur population. Dinosaurs first appeared about two hundred and seventy million years ago and, before the T. Rex appeared, about two hundred and five million years later, there were hundreds, if not more, different dinosaur species that had made their appearance and then left the stage. Just think how long two hundred and seventy million years is. All of man's history on planet Earth is less than roughly five hundred thousand years depending on where you draw the line for man. We can't even conceive of a time period that lasted that long. Do you realize the Earth didn't even look like it does today? Plate tectonics theory would have placed all the continents together two hundred and seventy million years ago. Over such a long period of time continents drifted apart which led to changes in weather and climates. So, to me, the cause probably was a combination of factors. But we also have to take a look at the life cycle on Earth. As I recall" said a very pensive young man in a Rodin's The Thinker pose, "life started out with single celled life about three billion eight hundred million years ago. Then about four hundred and seventy five million years ago land plants arrived, three hundred and sixty million years ago amphibians enter the stage, one hundred and sixty million years later reptiles, like dinosaurs, started to walk the planet, mammals arrived one hundred million years later, then birds arrived just fifty million years later and finally the first forms of man enter the stage just two and half million years ago. So you can see as time passed the Earth witnessed a faster and faster progression of change in life forms. It looks like the same type of progression we are seeing in our own man made technology only man's is far faster. Maybe dinosaurs were programmed to live only so long. Lacy, I'm beginning to see some of the pieces of the puzzle start to fall into place."

"What pieces, Jimmy?"

"Lacy, as we continue with our research and discussions, I want to see if you see the same pieces to the puzzle as I do."

"That's not fair. I want to know what you see."

"Maybe you will see different pieces of the puzzle or the same pieces in a different way. I don't want to taint your mind and thought with my opinion and maybe I will even change my opinion as we uncover more facts."

"Well, I guess that makes sense. You know Jimmy, when we talk of the past we think in very long time periods like thousands and millions and billions of years. Man only lives about eighty years if he is lucky so we live for only a split second in time. Whatever we see is just a very tiny time frame. We have to make a judgment about a whole film from less than one frame. It's too bad we can't go back in time and see what it was really like."

"Lacy, do you realize that if you had a radar screen that covered just several hundred million years, let's say back to the beginning of dinosaurs, the life span of a human would not even show up as a blip. In fact, if you took all of man's recorded history it still would not show up as a blip. In other words, we are not even here on Earth as far as time is concerned and yet look at the changes in our atmosphere and our seas that man has caused."

"For a life form that doesn't even show up in time we certainly have done a lot of damage," replied Lacy.

"I'd love to go back and look at the dinosaurs," remarks Freddy. Is there a way we can do that?"

"Only in science fiction," smiled Lacy.

Chapter Eight

CAN WE TALK

*M*onday came and went and that evening at the dinner table, Susan mentions to Fred, "Sally Beasley is getting fiber optic cable for her house. Do you know if it is available here yet?"

"Isn't Sally going to start a web site with you?" asked Fred.

"Yes, and I think fiber optics would allow us to use our computers as servers which means we don't have to use an outside provider."

"Do you or Sally know how to fix problems with your computers if they should occur?" asked Fred.

"No, I couldn't and I don't think Sally can, do you think we would run into problems?"

"I don't know. You can always try it and see."

"Mom, you can use a web hosting service for around ten dollars a month. They handle any problems if they happen. They have people on staff so you get twenty-four hour protection. Why wouldn't you let one of the site providers handle it?" asked Lacy.

"Well, I didn't know the cost was that reasonable. I still want to get fiber optic cable so we can combine our T.V. with the Internet."

"At school they told us the television and the computer will become one within a year or two," exclaimed Freddy with excitement. "We will be able to watch television and use our computer on the same screen and we will be able to watch television while we are working on our computer. Boy, it would be cool to have a great big giant flat panel screen with surround sound. We could Google or Yahoo or Bing things we didn't understand? Dad, can we get a big 65 inch flat panel screen?"

"Freddy, did you make out your list of the things you need and were supposed to prioritize?" asked Susan.

"Yes."

"Is a giant flat panel screen on your list?" questioned Susan.

"No," said a disappointed little boy. "Is it on yours?" asked Freddy.

"No," replied Susan.

"Why?" asked Lacy.

"It's not something that I need. We were supposed to make out lists of what we thought we needed, remember," smiled Susan. "If we can get fiber optic cable maybe Fred will splurge and get a fifty inch screen." Susan looked over at Fred with a, can we do that Fred look?

Fred looked at Susan with an, oh, no, where will this all end facial expression?

"Fred, will you call our phone company and see if we can get fiber optic cable here? Sally says they just got theirs put in."

"Susan, I hate to call phone companies. Have you tried to call ours?"

"I hate calling them to. There is nothing but menu after menu after menu until you want to pull your hair out or just hang up. I think they do it on purpose just to get us off their back. I'd like to give the CEO an ear full."

"That's why I don't want to call them. For communications companies to use such annoying archaic communications technology is just plain ludicrous. I can't tell you how many times I've gone through all their menus just to get hung up on or to get a busy signal. My blood pressure goes up just thinking about calling them. If I have a heart attack while I'm trying to call them, make sure you sue them big time for undue stress and aggravation.

Better yet, I'll buy a few shares of their stock so you can sue for inappropriate use of shareholders' funds. I'd like to know what is wrong with the old way; where you actually got to talk to a live person who could help you. I just can't imagine in these billion dollar companies, that giving employment to intelligent operators could hurt their budget. In fact, they probably would see sales go up. I think it's just another symptom of a totally myopic thinking process. The question is who are we making this planet for? Are we trying to destroy our system of a large and prosperous middle class that our whole economic system is built on? I'd like to know what these CEO's are thinking about?" said a worked up Fred. "They are really part of the problem. They are working to destroy the middle class, in my view. We have become so wrapped up in making a buck we are not only making a world not fit for man but we are destroying our own economic system."

"What raises my blood pressure," continues Susan, "is when I get an automated system and the automated voice asks for information, social security number, address, name or whatever and then when you finally get through to a live person, they ask you for the same information all over again. What good did it do to have a programmer program the automated voice to ask questions that went nowhere? We have huge companies like Microsoft and Oracle who spend billions on research so computers can talk to each other and yet companies that use computers, throughout their entire organization, seem to be oblivious to the fact that their computers do not talk to one another. It is so infuriating. Not only that, but many of our companies are getting so big that one hand doesn't know what the other is doing. I am always getting shuttled to another person or department because they are supposed to know and it turns out they don't. I spend half a day just going around in circles and getting nowhere. I really don't know how these companies make any money. They just generate ill will. Computers, I thought, were supposed to make life simpler and instead they are making life more complicated. Who are we hiring as our managers and executives? Talk about blind and brain dead," complained Susan. "Fred talk about suing, why aren't these companies sued by shareholders for incompetence?"

"If the companies are making money and growing, shareholders are happy. What shareholders don't think about is; are we destroying our whole economic system by taking our eye off the ball and focusing on just wringing every penny out of the system. We have become so myopic we are forgetting where we are going. The tail of quarterly earnings is wagging the dog so a few can get a big salary and bonus and so investors will bid the price of the company's stock up. We are cutting everything to the bone but in doing so we are ruining our middle class that feeds our economy and pays the taxes. It really goes to the very root of capitalism. The tail starts wagging the dog. We have become so focused on the near term and being able to make more money every quarter that we forget about the whole macro picture. We have made an economic ecosystem and like any ecosystem it is tightly integrated. Like any ecosystem, if you start to destroy it, the effects will be felt throughout the entire ecosystem."

"It really comes down to the fact that people don't have any common sense or they are not using what they have," commented Lacy. "What really gets me is; that no matter who you are or where you went to school or how well you did in school or your I.Q., each person individually and collectively have huge blind spots. They just plain can't see. Even if you tell them about it they still can't see. Talk about the blind leading the blind. I'm a people watcher and I find it interesting to have come to the conclusion that we are all wired differently. Some people can see some things but not all things and some people can see different things. You can see it in our music. Think of all the songs, all the pieces of music that have been written over the centuries and each one of them is different. Peoples' minds think differently. Our minds also hear or interpret music differently. Some people like some music but not all music. I can't stand hard rock but others love it. I think our life is a Greek tragedy full of hamartia and irony. The very companies that should be making voice communication easier are, in fact, making it more difficult. Those at the top either are blinded by greed or unable to see ahead. Talk about an oxymoron. If you have fiber optic cable installed, the phone company takes out your copper line so you no longer have a wired phone. What sense does that make? If your electric goes off, you are totally isolated without a phone or a computer. You are totally isolated."

"I agree with you Lacy," responded Susan. "Look at our congress. Most of them went to college and yet they don't seem to have any understanding about the issues we face in many cases. How can they be so blind? When an issue has two sides, why wouldn't you always take the side that presents the least risk to the nation? It must come down to the fact you just mentioned that we are all wired differently. If we are all wired a little differently, how do we get everyone to see the same problems or the same solutions?" asked Susan.

"Bingo, you have just hit the nail on the head," replied Fred. "How can we get everyone on the same page when everyone sees and understands the page a little differently? That's why we were meant to be a simple territorial animal so each of us could live his or her own life in small groups. Now that we have stuffed so many people on Earth we are stepping on each other, if not physically then mentally."

"As I see it," replies Lacy, "We all know intuitively there is common sense. We all know it not only exists but that some people seem to have more than others. Most of us know driving down the highway at 100 miles per hour shows no common sense. But in our upside down world, if a group, that shows no common sense, gains enough supporters, they can pass their legislation through congress forcing changes in our laws that everyone has to live by. Look at all the loud mouth bullies in this world trying to influence others when they have little or no plan for our future that makes any common sense. Our views have to be updated on how we are going to govern ourselves and survive."

"Good luck," replied Susan. "Fred, can you get your sales assistant to call the phone company?"

"I will ask her if she has time to do it, but she usually has better things to do than sit on the phone listening to menus and waiting to be cut off, hung up on or to reach the wrong department or someone who hasn't a clue."

"What a world, Fred," replied Susan shaking her head. "Lacy what do you think of Jimmy now? You have known him at church for years but have never seen him outside of church, have you? Do you have a lot in common?"

"Mom, he is very interesting, has an awesome memory and we think alike. It seems to me he has an understanding about nature and man that most grown adults don't have."

"Maybe he is a wizard," exclaims Freddy.

"He is very interesting and older than his age," replies Lacy. "Freddy, did you like him?"

"Yes, I love talking about dinosaurs."

"He is very opinionated," said Fred. "But I like him."

"Dad, I think he has every right to express his opinions. I find him very interesting and since the whole world is in a mess, certainly we need new ideas, the old ones just aren't working."

"They certainly aren't" replies Susan. "Would you like to have him over again?"

"Yes, I think it would be nice to have them over on Sundays after church. I think Matilda enjoyed it too, don't you Mom?"

"She did, she said she thoroughly enjoyed herself."

"Are you aware that in less than two weeks you will be sixteen?" asked Fred.

"I can hardly wait. I'll finally be able to drive."

"Let me clarify that a little," said a somewhat worried looking father. "You can get a learners permit and drive with either myself or your mother, but no one else. Is that understood?"

"Yes Dad."

"You are taking drivers' education at school, right?" asked Fred.

"Yes, we all are; my whole class."

"Honey, I don't want you in a car with anyone who has not been driving for at least two years. It would kill me if anything would happen to you," said Susan. "If you are driving with anyone, other than a friend's parent, I want to know ahead of time so I can call his or her parents to make sure that person is responsible and has driven for at least two years without an accident. It also goes without discussion that there is absolutely no drinking and driving. I mean not a drop. If your father or I catch you or anyone you are driving with, with liquor on their breath or in the car, you lose your license immediately for six months. I want to make sure you understand that."

"In addition," stated Fred, "I don't want you driving with any young man who you have any questions about. Not the slightest. Often girls will get into a car with someone they have an uneasy feeling about. If, for any reason, you have the slightest thought that you shouldn't get in that car, don't. Also, if you are ever out with a friend or friends who have had a drink and you don't have your own car, call me or your mother and we will come pick you up. Is that clear?"

"What about texting while driving?" asked Lacy?

"Oh my God Lacy," responded Susan, "absolutely no texting. Whoever you are thinking about driving with, you must make it clear to them there is no texting and no phone calls while driving. If you must make a phone call, pull off the road and make it."

"Lacy," said Fred, "when you are driving a car you have the ultimate responsibility to yourself, to your passengers and to those oncoming cars around you to have one hundred percent of your concentration on driving, nothing else. Your life and the lives of others depend on it. Is that perfectly clear?"

"Yes," replied Lacy. "After seeing what happened to Jimmy, I know what can happen."

"Can I drive with Lacy?" asked Freddy.

"Absolutely not" responded Susan. "Not until Lacy turns eighteen and she has driven for two years without an accident. All

I need is to have both of you in an accident together. No wonder parents' hair turns gray. I want all three of you to understand that driving is a very big privilege and with that privilege goes a big responsibility to yourself and to others. If I find, at any time, any of you are not being responsible there is going to be hell to pay."

"I can't drive, Mom, I'm too young," said Tommy.

"I know sweetheart, but when you get older and do start driving. Now do all three of you understand?"

All three nod.

"Mom, when can I get a car?" asked Lacy.

"When you turn eighteen and you have been a responsible driver. I can't emphasize enough how dangerous driving is. When people were driving a horse and carriage you couldn't get into a head on accident. Now we have these over powered cars and paved roads and super highways that allow you to go at a speed man never could have imagined and is not meant to go. You have cars whizzing by at sixty miles per hour and faster. Do you realize if you are going sixty miles per hour and the oncoming car is going sixty miles per hour that means the two cars are closing the gap between you at one hundred and seventy-six feet per second? The human cannot respond that quickly. You are traveling at about one sixth as fast as a speeding bullet. It is totally insane when you think about it."

"You know" observed Lacy, "I never thought about it like that. That's really scary; one sixth as fast as a bullet."

"Now, I want each of you to realize that the driver of that oncoming car maybe using a cell phone and not thinking about his or her driving; the driver maybe combing his or her hair, putting lipstick on, trying to drink a hot cup of coffee, having a beer, the driver maybe having a seizure or heart attack or an epileptic fit, a bee might have flown in the window and captured his or her attention, the driver maybe thinking about his wife or husband or lover, they may have had a fight or they may be so in love that the driver's attention is not where it should be. And just think what a drunk driver would see through blurry eyes closing in on you going one sixth as fast as a bullet. Kids, there are a million reasons why that oncoming car could be an unmanned missile headed right towards you. It is absolutely imperative that when you drive that you drive defensively at all times. Your mind has to be on your driving one hundred percent, you absolutely have to wear a seat belt and you have to be looking for an escape route if you see the tires of that oncoming car, or worse a truck, cross over the white line. You have to tell yourself that the oncoming car could be mentally unmanned."

"When you think about it, we must be out of our minds to allow anyone to do anything else but drive," said Lacy. "Why isn't there a very wide grass strip between oncoming cars or at the very least great big cement barriers? I can't imagine why anyone would make it legal to use a cell phone or text or anything else while you are manning that missile. It's a wonder that our roads don't turn into anything but grave sites."

"Wait, there is more kids," said Susan. "I looked these facts up on the Internet. "Do you know that every day of the year there are 112 people who die in car accidents and 6,824 more injured or maimed? Driving is unbelievably dangerous. Every year we kill and maim and injure more Americans than in all our wars combined and we have made it legal to treat our cars as our living rooms. Call it insanity but we continue to kill and maim each other every day of the year."

"Let's go back to the horse and carriage," said a worried and somewhat scared Lacy. "You know, when you think about it, it is just another example that man has no common sense. He is totally out of control. We are far exceeding our own senses when we drive a car at high speed and yet many drivers seem to pretend they are on a couch in their living room able to relax and do whatever they want to. The real question is where are our leaders? I am getting the feeling we don't have any."

"We don't," said Fred. "We are running out of control. We have stretched the rubber band as far as it can be stretched and if it doesn't start to snap back in the other direction, I think, the picture for humankind is grim."

"Dad, clearly, technology has to be controlled since much of it far exceeds the user's abilities or senses or needs. The original cars were built in Europe and went maybe six miles per hour then Henry Ford built the model T, here in this country, which went an unsafe forty miles per hour if the road didn't have potholes."

"I hope you are not suggesting that we shouldn't have technology," asked Susan.

"No Mom, but do you think going one sixth as fast as a bullet head on makes sense?"

"No, I don't. But where do you draw the line?"

"Mom, if we knew where we were headed, I mean if we had a long term game plan that had the best interests of mankind and our planet at heart, then we would know how to fit the pieces of the puzzle together to reach that goal. As it stands right now, we don't know where we are going. Everyone is going in a million different directions. Our whole infrastructure is aging, getting old and the cost to replace it or to update it is going to put a huge burden on our economy at a time when our economy is in deep trouble. If we had a plan that included maybe pneumatic tubes that transported us quickly between towns and cities and a better natural gas bus system with many different sizes of buses depending on passenger loads to get us from the tubes to the place we are going, we could use small electric or natural gas driven cars for local shopping. I mean, can't we see that we have built a system that allows for the domino effect to topple the whole economy. We are using a vehicle that costs a fortune to purchase and even more to operate; that spews out hydrocarbons that are killing our planet, that has to be parked when space is at a premium and costs a fortune and a system that kills and maims so many that our insurance and medical costs are skyrocketing out of sight. Our transportation system is out of step with the times like everything else in our world. Where are our leaders?" said an emotional Lacy.

"Lacy, I think you're right on," said Fred.

"But Fred," replied Susan; "if everyone sees things a little bit differently, how in the world are we going to bring people together to put a unified game plan together?"

"Well, we have five people here at this table of different ages, why not see what plan we can put together and if we can get everyone to agree to it?"

"First, what is the most important thing in our life? What allows everyone to clothe, house and feed themselves?" asked Fred.

"A car," replies Tommy.

"Lacy, what do you think?"

Lacy thought for a moment and replied, "A job."

"Susan, what do you think?"

"I agree a job."

"Freddy, what do you think?"

Freddy thought and said "if you don't have a job you can't buy a car."

"So you would say the answer is a job?" asked Fred.

"Yes"

"I agree also. So we have our first priority. I think everyone in our country and around the world could agree that a job is top priority," answered Fred. "After all, you can't tax someone who doesn't have any income."

"But what about our environment," asked Lacy? "If our environment goes we are dead and a job won't have any importance at all."

"That's a very good point, Lacy. So, our second priority is our environment. I doubt we would get many if anybody in our country or anywhere else who wouldn't agree. Do we all agree?" asked Fred.

"Dad, if we depend on our environment to live," thought Freddy, "why wouldn't that come first?"

Everyone thought for a moment and Lacy says "Dad, I think Freddy is right. If our environment goes then everything else collapses."

"So our first goal should be our environment and our second goal should be jobs. Well, in the last couple of minutes we have put together the beginnings of a game plan that, we think, everyone would agree on. Tomorrow, before dinner, I want all of us to think about the third priority," instructed Fred.

Later, after Lacy cleared the table, washed and put away, the phone rang.

"Lacy, it's Jimmy" shouted Susan from down stairs.

"Jimmy, I'm glad you called. Dad wants us to put together a plan that everyone can agree on as a nation that would allow us to move forward. What are those goals that we would all vote for? I'm afraid I started this because I said everyone is wired a little bit differently and, therefore, how can everyone see the same problems."

"Wow," replied Jimmy, "talk about a complex issue."

"It doesn't seem to be that complex. At dinner we came up with the first goal, which is our environment and the second goal which is jobs. Now we have to come up with the third goal. What do you think?"

"Lacy, you can't create jobs without a strong economy. So, by jobs as your second goal, you must be implying a strong economy and that hinges on whether you have a government that is functional and one we all believe in and one that sees the problems and also the solutions. Today, our government is dysfunctional; a government we have lost faith in and one that can't see the problems. So, you see, your question really goes right back to the core of our system. This is not a problem you can fix by just changing the faces in an election."

"What is the problem then," asked Lacy.

"Lacy, there are many problems but if we limit the discussion to just jobs and, therefore, the economy, the problem, as I see it, on a near term basis is we have priced ourselves out of the world markets with a dysfunctional system. We have made it so expensive to do business in this country that we have forced our companies to move abroad taking their jobs with them. Because our wages have exceeded our productivity, prices have had to go up. Since, a government doesn't make or sell anything it is not productive and relies on taxing those who are productive for its existence. Obviously, the larger the government gets the less productive the nation becomes. We also give yearly salary raises in our businesses without any correlation to increases in productivity adding to the problem. Obviously, by increasing wages we put upward pressure on prices. So, the end result of rising salaries does not work for our own benefit. Our system is totally dysfunctional. The difference in wages between what workers make and what management makes is wider than it has ever been. The system is top heavy. Management, by and large, does not increase the company's productivity anywhere near enough to justify what they now get paid. Management, in order to make their company more profitable, allowing them to pay higher salaries, is forced to cut its workforce in many cases, creating more and more unemployed. Ask yourself, could I run a company without any employees? The answer is obviously no. So, it follows, therefore, that a company is a team. Why shouldn't all team members be paid the same with five year bonuses based on the profitability of the company? Wouldn't that make more sense? The tax laws could be modified so bonuses could be treated as long term capital gains instead of income. After all, the less you payout to team members the more productive the company becomes because the more you can reinvest in the company. It also means being able to take a longer term view instead of quarter to quarter or year to year. We have taken our eye off the ball. The goal should be employment not greed and a more holistic approach to our whole economy."

"I don't know Jimmy. Don't companies have to pay higher wages to attract the people they need to be competitive not only here but globally? After all, talent will go to the highest bidder won't it?"

"Lacy, as I see it, we compete on three different levels. We compete on a technology level, on a price level and on a productivity level and all three are closely tied together. Our global system competes on all three levels. It really is like the tail wagging the dog. The tail of competition demands all three. However, we already pay high salaries to management and to our engineers and we are still falling behind. So, I would say, higher salaries have not translated into better technology or better management."

"I think the reason we are falling behind is due to our dysfunctional government. If we had a thirty year game plan, a business plan then, I think, we would see both capital and talent quickly follow. Our own government is causing our demise, I think," said Lacy.

"I think you are right on a shorter term horizon. Longer term, the truth of the matter is, we live on a tiny planet and we are using up our raw resources on our planet Earth and our growth will become more and more limited because of it. The combination of more people, limited and dwindling resources and technology that allows companies to use fewer and fewer workers will lead us into a depression that we will not be able to get out of using our present thinking. So, our whole economic system is wrong for the times in my view. It worked when we were a young country and growing quickly but now that we are a mature country it calls for a completely different type of system."

"Jimmy isn't that scary? Just the thought that we are on the wrong road makes me sick. Where have our politicians been? It looks like everyone that is supposed to know where we are going has had their head in the sand. Do you see a way we can fix it?"

"Lacy, are you sure you want to keep going because it looks like it is going to get us really upset?"

"What choice do we have, Jimmy? We can't bury our head in the sand too and pretend everything is cool."

"Lacy, it is man's willingness and ability to come together to make the needed changes that ultimately determines the answer. We are not the only ones in this mess. Europe is in much the same mess. Many of their banks are caught up in this sub-prime mess also. Greed has dented the capitalistic system everywhere. The cracks in the structure of the capitalistic system are getting more

profound as our debt burdens increase. The human mind looks
at the near term, not the long term and the mind looks at the
symptoms to problems rather than the actual problems and their
solutions."

"Why?" questioned Lacy.

"Don't forget, Lacy, what we determined in our study of
amoebas. Life was and always will be reactive, born in those warm
tidal pools a billion years ago. We are part of life on Earth and
therefore reactive. Our wiring will never change. We live for the
moment, for the near term. Our cellular system was built for
defense, to react to a present danger. All our senses are made to
react to the moment not to look for the cause. That's why man
almost always reacts to the symptoms. What Mother Nature
devised is really a very simple design in a complex form. She took
a single cell which divides into two different cells both carrying
the same DNA so no matter how many cells she put together they
all worked exactly like the one cell it came from. We are no more
than a conglomeration of cells all acting in unison with some cells
specializing for a particular reactive function. All animals attack
the immediate cause which comes from their visual or sensual
perception."

"Why hasn't man seen this and devised a system to safeguard
us from our own blindness? How do we start to fix this mess?"
quizzed Lacy.

"Lacy, we need a much better understanding of ourselves
and our place in nature. We have placed the value of business
and technology above instead of behind our understanding of
the world in which we live and of ourselves. Man is way behind
the learning curve. He has been critically side tracked by his own
greed and ego and our priorities have been rearranged due to
his greed. All of our man made systems have been developed to
revolve around business, technology and growth and yet we don't
even have a business plan or a road map. Our system is a free for
all that is totally blind to the effects it will have on the world
around us. How can you reach your destination without a road

map and what is our destination? It is clear our political system has not been guiding us and leading the way. The structure of our government makes it truly dysfunctional. The very first thing we need to do to get us back on the right path is develop a business plan, a model of where we are going for the next thirty to fifty years with ten year interim plans and we really need to do that on a global basis as one unified planet. A beauty contest for president of a country is ridiculous."

"What I want to know is where has our parents' generation been? Why haven't they seen what we are beginning to see?"

"That's a good question Lacy. Our parents' generation has had more college graduates than ever before. They have had more information to work with than ever before too. How could they not see the trap they were setting for Mother Earth and for us?"

"Jimmy, it doesn't make sense unless either it was their greed or they just let it happen by doing nothing to prevent it. Maybe they just got swept along in a type of tsunami tide and they didn't do anything to change it."

"Lacy we mimic our parents. Mother Nature programs all animals in the same way. Our parents' generation was programmed to follow their parents. We are a robotic animal and unless we can change we won't have a chance. Our generation has no choice now. We have to change to meet the challenges of our times."

"Obviously, Mother Nature never intended for us to change. Mother Nature programmed all animals to always react in the same way which means we are a product of our original cell or cells."

"Right Lacy. We have been wired to react in the same fashion from the very beginning."

"But look at bacteria, they are constantly changing and mutating to meet the chemicals around them."

"Our bodies are constantly reacting also Lacy but to a far lesser degree and when you consider that man has perhaps ten times the number of bacterial cells as he has human cells in his

body it becomes obvious to me that bacteria were the first living organisms on earth and make life, as we know it, possible on Earth. Their cell structure is a chemical structure that breaks down and recycles everything."

"So the way they react must revolve around the chemicals around them. That means they are far more free form than animal life; they are a constant chemical reaction machine. That means they don't have a defined structure like mans' cells and, therefore, can change to meet whatever chemicals they encounter."

"Lacy, are you starting to see the answer to your question, how did different life form and evolve?"

"Jimmy it is amazing how everything is tied together. It just took huge periods of time to make it all work and come together."

"We are beginning to see that man lives for such a short period of time, really just an instant in time and that he reacts to those short time periods without any association with his very long past or to the future. He is really an alien in his own world."

"How can we turn a reactive animal into a thinking one?" asked Lacy.

"Do you have a solution to your question Lacy?"

"I guess that is our goal Jimmy. If we knew the answer to that maybe we could solve all our problems."

"Perhaps the answer to your question is also tied into why we have good and evil or greed and sacrifice? If we all thought everything through instead of just reacting then we would be a different animal. If we could only see around the bend in the road but man has a hard time seeing past the end of his nose."

Lacy giggled. "Jimmy, I know there is an answer but I can't quite put my finger on it. I have a feeling that it is a Noah's ark problem and solution; a question of twos."

"That would really be pulling the rabbit out of the hat Lacy, "chuckled Jimmy. "But until we figure your question out we have to create a system that revolves around our reactive nature. That means our election process should only be based on answering two questions. What are the problems the candidate sees and what are his solutions? But it does our country no good to have a congress that is not on the same page with the president. I would do away with the congress and hand much of their work back to the states. After all, there are fifty states and only one federal government. If we handed the congress back to the states, we could divide their work load by fifty. You would also do away with the inherent conflict between states needs or wants versus the country's needs. The way I see it, Washington would set the outline and goals for the nation as a whole and the states would carry out those goals tailored for each particular state. Do you realize that when our present form of government was enacted we were only thirteen colonies and our population was approximately two and a half million people? We are now fifty states with a population of three hundred million. Our federal government was only supposed to give us a working outline of what is permissible and what isn't. It was never meant or designed to micro manage a whole complex economy. In fact, our founders could never have dreamed of the complexity we have today. Just think, they rode to work on horse back to their farming operation, or saw mill or little store or the pier where ships, that in many cases were less than one hundred feet, were docked that carried goods from abroad. Paul Revere didn't pick up the phone or pull out his laptop to send an email. He had to saddle his horse, no matter what the weather, and ride to get a message through. It was a completely different world. We have to have a structural change in our political system that not only updates our political system for the new times but brings everyone in sync with the president who we elected to solve the problems he outlined in his election platform."

"But our present political system has checks and balances so the president is held in check," observed Lacy.

"But Lacy, we the people, are that checks and balances now, not some middleman group that works at a snail's pace and is enormously inefficient and costly working for its own self interests. The system originally only had to think about thirteen colonies and a simple agricultural economy. The congress was elected to serve the people, they were not paid, and the people trusted them. The time and place is far different now than it was at the time when our present system was first enacted. Our technologies connect us like never before so why would we cling to an old outdated system? We live in an entirely different world now. Most of us don't live on farms anymore; we are not isolated without telephones, computers, cell phones, televisions, tablets, radios, newspapers, or the internet. Today bears no resemblance to the time when our present system was born. Why in the world would we keep a system that no longer works? We should be electing a president on his ability to see the problems and who also sees the solutions. Think for a moment, each candidate for president would give us a list of the problems he sees and the solutions to those problems. Then we could have experts in each problem area the candidate lists; debate the pros and the cons to his solutions. We would pick the candidate that, we think, has the best solutions."

"Jimmy, no one is going to like the solutions and there are probably no perfect solutions to our problems anyway."

"But Lacy, we have pulled the rubber band back as far as it can go and we are forced to find solutions or it is over. I am hoping and betting that man will change when he realizes that his very survival depends on reaching solutions to his problems no matter whether he likes them or not. After all, problems are problems because we don't want to face them. It would follow, therefore, that we won't like the solutions. The candidate we elect to be president has to give us his written agenda and it is up to us to make sure he sticks to it. We would all review his progress on a quarterly basis and with our Press, on top of everything Washington, you can be sure the president's actions would be closely followed. If he deviates from his written agenda then he is either fired or put back on track. If circumstances change mandating a change in his plan he could always give the pros and cons to the needed changes and we could all vote yes or no on them over the Internet. That means we need a responsive system giving us the right to demand that he stick to his agenda or that he be fired literally on the spot and that could be done through a Board of Review. Companies do it, why should the president of our country be any different? He is supposed to be carrying out our wishes not his. I also believe there should be an incentive for the president so we get the best with those abilities we need. Let's use a compensation plan that is better than any company's compensation plan to bring about the changes we need. Why not give him a percentage of the increase in gross national product he achieves tied to the reduction in our national debt over a four year period? The compensation formula would also have to include the health of our environment and our population problems also. Lacy, Mom just walked in to work on my legs, let's continue tomorrow."

"As much as I get knots in my stomach, I find this so interesting, Jimmy. I really do want to see where we are going. Call me. I'm usually finished cleaning up by seven."

"Mom usually comes in about seven thirty to exercise my legs, so up to seven thirty is fine. You can call me too."

The following evening at dinner, Fred opens the discussion with "have you all thought about what our third goal should be?"

"Dad," said Lacy, "I was talking to Jimmy and he thinks our discussion is superficial. He says we can't fix the problems by just changing the faces in Washington."

"Lacy, Jimmy is an exceptionally observant and intuitive person especially for his age. I think Freddy called him a wizard and I am beginning to agree. He has already tripled his money. I think you will find, however, that we will all end up in the same place at the end of our discussion. Both of us are taking a little different route to get there. Our group is looking at the obvious; those things that we emotionally know are good for our survival. We started our list with the environment and jobs, however, when we start asking ourselves, at the end of determining what our political platform should entail, why don't we have jobs, then we have to drill down to determine the answer.

For example, why don't we have enough jobs? Many people will say because there are too many regulations, others will say education or reeducation; still others will say infrastructure or capital investment and research and development. I would say taxes. Others would say we have to throw more money at the problem with a stimulus program. These are all symptoms of the problem. What is the real problem, you ask? The real problem is a dysfunctional and unresponsive government which really is blind to both business and our environment and doesn't see the solutions to our problems. We, the people, have a better idea of what the problems are than does the government. There seems to be a total disconnect between what the people know and what our government seems to see. Our government has become our problem not the solution. We need a structural change to update our government. Why even have political parties in this day and age when it's a dysfunctional system? The two parties just fight like school yard bullies and waste tax payers' money and if they are even able to come to a conclusion it is so watered down that it's not worth the paper it's written on. With our current technology everyone is tuned into what's going on and with a fabulous news media that lets us know almost blow by blow what's going on, why do we need a two party system that is asleep at the switch? Times are totally different now. Unless we can update our political system making it much faster and responsive, we won't survive. We know the same thinking that got us into this mess is not the same thinking that will get us out of our mess. Is that close to Jimmy's conclusion, Lacy?"

"Yes," Lacy said with a smile.

"What is our third goal?" asked Fred. "Tommy did you think about our third goal?"

"A good police force."

"Good answer, Tommy". Tommy smiled.

"Lacy what do you think our third goal should be?"

"I think Tommy is right except I would include a strong military."

"Susan?"

"I agree with both Tommy and Lacy."

"Freddy?"

"I agree with everyone."

"Good," said Fred, "we have three important goals everyone can agree on. I want everyone to think of our fourth goal for tomorrow."

WHAT'S HAPPENING TO OUR BEEF?

"Mom, will you help me clean up tonight so I can talk to Jimmy. We have the best discussions."

"Lacy, I have had to go through a bunch of newspapers and cut out the coupons I think I will use, make out our menus for a week, drive to the store, read tons of labels to make sure we are getting the most nutritious foods and make sure I don't get anything with trans fats, with hydrogenated anything, no high fructose corn syrup, no hormone additives, no red dyes, nothing with high sodium which is salt, I mean what they put in our food is just horrible. Then I had to drive home, bring it all inside, unpack and put everything away, then, I no sooner get that all done than I had to start cooking. You mean you don't want to clean up because you want to talk on the phone? Lacy I am pooped tonight."

"Alright Mom, but why do the food manufacturers put so much stuff in our food that is not natural and which may not be good for us."

"Dieticians tell us that food manufacturers use all these additives because it's cheap, it helps prolong the shelf life of their products and it creates something that people will eat."

"You mean because it looks good or tastes good?" quizzes Freddy.

"That's right sweetheart, it has nothing to do with nutrition. In fact, much of what is in a grocery store is not, what I would call, nutritious for you."

"Why do they carry it Mom, if it's not nutritious?" asked Tommy.

"The grocery stores are trying to cater to everyone's taste buds and make a profit. I guess they feel they are not everyone's mother and can't tell people what is good for them. If people want to eat stuff that's not good for them then it's up to the person to make that choice."

"But what gets me," pipes Fred, "is, those of us who watch what we eat and eat nutritious foods and stay healthy have to pay for all those who don't and who get over weight and have all kinds of medical problems. My insurance bill is out of sight and yet we rarely have to use the medical system. It just doesn't make any sense."

"I'm beginning to think our whole system doesn't make any sense," observed Lacy. "We just can't be all things to all people. We can't have medical insurance if everyone isn't on the same playing field. At some point insurance will just become so expensive that we won't have any for anyone. In fact, studies show our cost of health care will reach a trillion dollars within the next few years. We have to face reality that we can't afford it. It will really bankrupt our already bankrupt country."

"There is going to have to be a tax on non-nutritious foods," pipes Susan. "I think you are right Lacy, we just can't be all things to all people. While we want freedom we have to ask ourselves freedom to do what? If a person does something that is not in the best interest of society shouldn't that person be penalized in the form of a tax? I mean how can we expect society to continue to pay for others' indiscretions?"

"Mom, what does indiscretion mean?" asked Freddy.

"Lack of judgment."

"Oh."

"What happens if I want to buy some bubble gum?" questions Tommy.

"Bubble gum isn't good for you," replies Freddy.

"But I don't have bubble gum very often. How can that hurt me?"

"Well, when you do buy bubble gum you would have to pay a tax," replied Freddy.

"What happens if I don't have enough money for the tax?"

"Then you wouldn't get any bubble gum," retorts Freddy.

"Mom, our government needs revenue to pay for health care and I think a tax on non-nutritious food would be a good way. I think we could use the same thinking on our environment also. Everything that is manufactured that is not returned to the company to be recycled would be taxed. After all, the health of our planet is more important than even our own health," reflected Lacy.

"I agree Lacy. But instead of a tax, I would put a heavy deposit on everything which you would get back when you returned it to the store for recycling. If it can't be recycled it can't be made. We just manufacture things without any plan for it when it wears out or how to recylce the packaging it comes in. I believe I read a review of a Harvard study that indicated eighty percent of the goods we produce are not really needed for our survival, just to be thrown away. Our planet can't take any more rubbish without ruining Mother Nature's system completely and, therefore, our own health. But returning to my previous thought, I just don't understand why food companies continue to put additives like red dye in our food. Red dye causes Tommy to go bonkers; his system just can't take it. I was talking to our doctor and he says lots of kids have a bad reaction to red dye and many other additives that are put in our food. So I ask, why do the food manufacturers continue to put things in our food that cause bad reactions in some people? I think what would work for us is, for all grocery stores to have specific isles in the store where they only have all natural nutritious foods. In the other isles they can have whatever they want. Let the people decide what they want to eat."

"Mom," replies Lacy, "why not have grocery stores get a weekly list of what a family wants over the internet, the computer sums up all like items for everyone and places the orders. That way there is no waste for the grocery store and we get exactly what we want."

"That certainly makes a lot of sense Lacy," replies Fred. "You could have an order form on the store's website and you could just electronically mark the items you wanted. I just don't understand why we are not updating all our systems for our times. What good is it to have technology and not use it for our benefit? All these outdated views and systems occur throughout every facet of our society and yet man either doesn't see them or doesn't do anything about them. I don't know how we expect to go forward in an increasingly complex and crowded world and survive."

"Something else bothers me," said Susan. "I read recently that genetically modified food is not turning out to be the great panacea they thought it was going to be. The pests, they thought they could control, turn out to be doing their own modifications through mutation and no sooner do the scientists come up with another product than the bugs mutate so they are resistant to the toxins the scientists just bio engineered."

"Trying to fool Mother Nature just won't work in the long run," replies Lacy. "Jimmy and I are researching life from the beginning of life and what we have come up with makes these life science companies look like they don't understand our environment at all. Whatever products these companies develop will only work for short periods of time and at great expense. Just read any agricultural magazine and farmers tell you they have to put more and more herbicides and pesticides on to control the weeds and bugs. In some cases they are using double doses. I hate to think what all that stuff is doing to us. Any time you cause a change in one part of the natural system, no matter how small, Mother Nature will counter act to bring the system back into

balance. It works beautifully if just left alone. It is man that is out of balance, not nature. Our populations are out of control. That's the problem. Dad is right. The human always sees the symptoms but rarely the causes. We are working under the wrong assumption, that we can control nature. Furthermore, because our whole system is so interconnected, if you disrupt this balance that has taken three billion years to evolve, the outcome will not only be devastating to us but to the planet and I know that for a fact. Again, it is just common sense. Why is the environment so interconnected? Because it takes all the little interactions that go on every second that makes our system work, if it didn't work we would have a different system, one that may well be deadly for us. The human animal is so blind. We just don't realize how blind we really are. It's like our visual senses and the color spectrum. We can see some colors in the color spectrum but not all. The colors we can't see are still there but we just can't see them. Another example is dust mites or pollen that we can't see but ask anyone with an allergy and they will be glad to tell you the effects they have on their system. If we can only see some things then we don't have all the information and our thinking may well be faulty."

"Why can't I see them?" asked Freddy. "I have 20-20 vision."

"Freddy, there are two reasons; but before I go into a scientific reason, look at it this way. An ant has eyes also but do you think it sees what you see? When we have ants in the kitchen on the counter we dispose of the ants and wash the counter top. However, the ants come right back. Now, you have to ask yourself, why would the ants come back after I have washed the counter top; there isn't anything there that I can see. To an ant, however, they must see something we can't. Now on a more scientific level, first, the cones in our retina only pick up certain wavelengths so you can only see certain wavelengths. Secondly, our wiring dictates what we actually see. The eye itself is a collector and collects light in the form of photons which are light particles. It also collects information such as the shape and size and color and depth of our surroundings. This information is then transferred through the optic nerve to the visual cortex which interprets the information. What each of us sees both visually and mentally depends on our own individual wiring and how the mind interprets that information. Mom's body is not a cookie cutter and, therefore, each of us is wired a little differently based on our own electrochemical make up, so each of us may see things differently. Our wiring will let us see something's but not all things. All of us have huge blind spots but, for some reason, man has never realized this or, at least, completely over looked it. We can see the difference in our own wiring in many different ways. Take a baseball player, for example. The wiring in some baseball players allows for an almost exact picture of a ball coming at them at high speed which is then transferred to the mind and then into mechanical action. We call it eye hand coordination. Many people do not have the wiring that allows them to hit an oncoming ball and when they swing they miss the ball. It is not because they don't see the ball but because their wiring ether is not relaying the correct information to the mind or the mind misinterprets it."

"How do you know it's not in the muscle coordination Lacy?"

"Mom, just take a ball on a string and hang it up. Take a baseball bat and try to hit the ball. If you can hit the ball squarely your eye hand coordination is fine. But that doesn't mean you can hit a thrown ball."

"I tried that" exclaimed Freddy "and I can hit the ball."

"Then you have good eye hand coordination. Man, instead of using any common sense has rushed headlong into an environment he has yet to understand with a mind he knows very little about," replied Lacy.

"What have you and Jimmy discovered?" asked Susan.

"We are reading everything we can get our hands on that has anything to do with our environment and life. But, more importantly, we are using our common sense to put the pieces together. Once we have assembled all the pieces we will see how they all fit together and then we will draw our conclusions.

However, while we are on the subject of food; Jimmy and I have uncovered what, we think, is a very dangerous trend."

"That sounds very scientific," replied Susan. "So you won't really know the final answer until you have completed all your research and fit all the pieces together?"

"Correct," replied Lacy.

"What trend are you talking about?" asked Fred.

"There has been an explosion in the raising of beef and pork and it is worldwide. Everyone, for some reason, thinks eating meat is healthy for you. People want to upgrade their diets to include more meat. Maybe it's all the hamburger chains but the population of cattle has exploded."

"Why is that dangerous?" asked Susan.

"Well the FAO or Food and Agricultural Organization study tells us we are putting more carbon dioxide, methane and nitrous oxides from the raising of livestock into our atmosphere than we are from all our cars, buses and trucks or from industry. These are greenhouse gases which are being blamed for the warming of the Earth. These gases are not helping our ozone levels either which helps shield us from ultra-violet rays from the sun. Everything is interconnected in nature. We are warming the oceans due to our climate change caused by greenhouse gases. The warmer the oceans get, the less CO_2 they can absorb until they can no longer hold any more and they start to release some of the CO_2, back into the atmosphere. It is a chain reaction that feeds on the same cycle; pollution to distribution in our atmosphere causing the entrapment of more heat, causing the warming of the seas that causes the release of more CO_2, causing more greenhouse gases which cause more warming. It is a vicious cycle. So you can see the warmer our Earth becomes the faster our seas release the CO_2 they are holding which could cause our ecosystems to collapse far quicker than we thought."

"Lacy, it is very scary and I don't know why all countries are not up in arms about it. I can't image what our own government is thinking about. Perhaps the reason is some people don't accept the fact that greenhouse gases are causing the planet to warm. They say it is an increase in solar activity from our Sun," said Fred.

"Dad, scientists tell us that solar activity has not increased over the past ten years but our planet is setting new heat records almost yearly. I think common sense would tell you that when we dump thirty-six billion tons of pollutants into our atmosphere every year there is going to be a reaction and that figure comes from the United Nations. Scientists tell us we have more CO_2 and other pollutants in our atmosphere than at any time in Earth's history. There is no way that much pollution can be good for life on Earth. The same thing holds true with our oceans. We can't continue to dump all the plastics and human waste into our oceans without it causing a change. I think all of us can agree that anytime we create an imbalance in nature we are asking for trouble in huge doses. We know that sooner or later any system, that is not balanced, will either re-balance itself or self-destruct. But wait, that is not our only problem with our desire to eat meat. What are the two raw resources that man depends on that are in short supply?" asked Lacy.

"I know one," exclaims Freddy.

"Which one Freddy?" asks Lacy?

"Fresh water".

"You're right, Freddy. Do you know the other?"

"It must be oil because Mom and Dad are always talking about it."

"Yes and the livestock industry use huge quantities of both. It takes well over ten times the amount of energy to produce livestock over an equivalent amount of grain. On top of that, about half of our fresh water is used in raising our livestock for food. That equates to approximately 2400 gallons of water to make one pound of meat according to the United Nations; to produce one pound of grain takes only twenty-five gallons. We are using over ninety times the amount of a very precious and dwindling resource in order to have a burger or stake. Moreover, we are ruining our rain forests by cutting them down for pasture to raise these animals. In the process we are causing the extinction of species that could lead to better cures for man not to mention the fact we are destroying a warehouse for CO2. Our hunger for meat is not only killing our planet but it is killing us slowly by using up our fresh water supply. On top of that, we are cutting down our oxygen giving trees and plants in the rain forest.

We all have to ask ourselves also, is this morally right? To raise animals in livestock yards in an inhumane way to fatten them up for slaughter, in an industrial type setting, packed together like sardines in a can, stuffed with hormones and antibiotics to finally have their throats cut while they are still alive? Do you know our pigs, cattle and turkeys are being fed Ractopamine to fatten them up and it makes them so sick they go lame; they can't walk? Our slaughter houses are allowed to use these lame animals. They must have to drag them in for slaughter. Can you imagine that? What is this doing to us? Some countries won't even buy our meat because of the chemicals we use. In addition the dung from these animals is full of the same antibiotics. When it falls to the ground it dissolves into the ground and, therefore, into our ground water and is assimilated by other living organisms. At this rate it won't be long before our antibiotics won't do us any good because the bad guys will be immune to them. Just think every time you chomp down on a burger or a piece of meat of all the bad things you are putting into your internal health system. You are destroying your health."

"Did you have to tell me that?" said Freddy. "I love burgers and now you ruined it for me. That's gross."

You could see Tommy listening. "Why are they so mean to our animals?" asked Tommy with a long face.

"Sweetheart, it breaks my heart too. Man is just out of control," replied Susan.

"And it's not particularly good for you either," said Fred. "I read an article by the National Cancer Institute that said red meat is the cause for many of our diseases including heart disease and cancer. Other than burgers for the boys once in a while, we eat very little red meat. Susan, lets only have red meat twice a month and then only if it comes from a local farm that treats its animals in a humane way with no chemicals. If the boys want meat they can have chicken or turkey and let's get our chickens and turkeys locally also from a farmer who doesn't stuff them full of chemicals. But let's reduce eating red meat," stated Fred.

"Tommy, did I just see you slip some food to Mussy?" asked Susan.

"Mom, she stuck her little nose up under the table cloth and told me she was hungry."

"Sweetheart, has Mussy had her dinner yet?"

"I haven't fed her."

"Freddy, did you feed Mussy yet?"

"No".

"Would you both, please get up and feed her, then come back for desert."

Five minutes later the boys came back into the dining room.

"Was she hungry?" asked Susan.

"You should have seen her Mom. We put her bowl down and she dove right in like she hadn't eaten in a week," exclaimed Tommy.

"Don't forget kids, she is a growing puppy and she needs lots of nutrition throughout the day," mentions Fred. "Before we leave the table, I want everyone to realize what a fabulous agricultural and distribution system we have. Just think of what it was like for most of man's existence on this planet. Just think if you couldn't go to a grocery store to get whatever you felt like whenever you wanted. For all of man's time on Earth, except for the last few seconds in time, we had to take long walks perhaps taking all day to find the berries, nuts, seeds, fruits and vegetables we needed to survive. Meat was a luxury because without electricity and refrigeration, whatever you killed had to be eaten right away or salted and dried. Imagine being hungry and not being able to go to the kitchen to get something to eat. If it was raining or miserable outside you still had to go out or go hungry. It is no wonder so many people are overweight today. The human evolved over hundreds of thousands of years from being a hunter gatherer not a lounge lizard that slithered into the kitchen to stock up on goodies before going back to sit in front of the television. So kids, I want you to realize how lucky you are to have an agricultural system with a distribution system that can get fruits, vegetables, nuts, seeds or whatever from anywhere in this country to your grocery shelves within a week or less. We have a fabulous bounty of nutritional food that Mother Nature bestowed on our planet, so do not eat anything that did not come directly from nature, that way you don't have to worry about additives, trans- fats, and hormones or hydrogenated anything that is not good for you."

"Fred," retorted Susan. "The kids love their bite-size shredded wheat and that is a processed food which is all natural and good for you, so not all processed foods are bad. But kids, the more all natural foods you eat the more you are getting the nutrients that our Mother Earth meant you to have. Remember, you are what you eat. If you eat processed foods make sure you read the label first."

"But Mom, I can't read a label."

"Tommy, I will make a list of those words you have to look out for and we can go to the grocery store and start reading labels so you will know."

"Can I come too," questions Freddy.

"Of course, I will take both of you."

Chapter Ten

LACY'S BIRTHDAY PARTY

"Fred, the men just pulled in with the tent," said Susan over the phone.

"Susan, they know where to set it up, just make sure the whole patio is covered. It could rain tomorrow and I want Lacy's sixteenth to go as planned. How many people are coming?"

"Unless someone shows that hasn't already replied there will be twenty-five not including the adults."

"How many adults are coming?"

"Of course Matilda who is bringing Jimmy, Sally and Hank Beasley, Freda and George Partridge and Tina Mulberry but Dick is out of town. Tina will be driving her two girls, Domino and Dede or maybe they will be driving her."

"So, all together we will have thirty-one not including our family."

"Yes, that is what I am planning on."

"I hope you have hired someone to help you. That is far too many people to do it alone. You will be a nervous wreck not to mention completely exhausted."

"Fred, I have. Tina told me about a couple and I hired them. They both cook and then she and I will serve."

"I hope it won't be too crowded."

"Fred, I think we will be fine. Please stop worrying; I have the spacing for the tables all figured out."

"Susan, are you going to have a little dance floor?"

"Yes, and we have a little band coming that Lacy knows."

"Are you going to have a bar?"

"Fred, what are you talking about? Certainly not for this age group."

"Not that type of bar Susan, a health bar. This is a great time to teach kids how really tasty a combination of fruit and vegetables juices can be. If I can get them to taste a carrot, apple and lemon juice they will see how absolutely delicious Mother Nature is."

"I thought you had lost it for a minute Fred. I was ready to come down there and bang you over the head with one of my pans. But that is a good idea. I will set up a little bar with our juicer and lots of fresh fruits and vegetables. Will you be the bar tender? I don't know if I can get anyone at the last minute."

"Sure, I don't mind."

The following day arrived amid raised emotions. "Fred, it looks like the clouds are lifting observed Susan looking out her bedroom window. Oh, I hope we have a dry day."

"Susan, we have the tent, why worry?"

"I know Fed, but it would make it nicer if it wasn't raining. I think I see a little blue on the horizon."

"Relax; I think you've done a great job. The tent fits the patio, the tables and chairs fit nicely, the health bar is all set up, the flagstone is all washed off and looks good, the dance floor fits nicely, what more is there to do?"

"Fred, I have to blow the balloons up with helium so they float to the top of the tent. Do you think the napkins go with the table cloth?"

"Yes honey, it all looks great."

"When are you going to give Lacy her present?" asked Susan.

"After the party, later tonight. I really don't want to make a big deal out of a present. This world has become too crass; we really need to get our priorities straight. I would much rather we emphasize the things that are really important like friendship and love and camaraderie."

"Fred, kids these days are very materialistic. It's what they have that seems to impress them. You and I may feel presents are not the important thing, but kids look at it differently."

"Susan, not all kids feel that way and I blame parents and our whole economic "shove it in their face" thinking. Man has made everything to materialistic, in my view."

"Fred, we don't need to go into that today. I want you to promise me no deep discussions at the party."

"I don't think I'll have a chance behind the health bar," mumbled Fred.

"Good," quickly replied Susan. I'm going down and start getting breakfast ready, Fred. I've decided to have French toast with cinnamon and nutmeg and waffles this morning. The kids love them."

"That sounds good. Now you are making me hungry. Do you want some help?"

"I can always use help and since today is Lacy's birthday, I thought I'd let her off the hook for one day."

"Good morning birthday girl," smiled Fred as he walked into the tent and over to her, kissing her on the forehead. Can you believe you are now sixteen?"

"No, I can't. It went so fast now that I look back. I'm going to be old before I know it at this rate."

"Imagine how fast it goes for parents," said Susan walking into the tent also. "It was just yesterday I was bringing you home from the hospital all seven pounds two ounces of you."

In ran the kids with Mussy. "Mom, this looks nice," said Freddy, "we should just leave the tent up all the time. I like having all this extra room to run around in and Mussy does too."

"Mom," said Tommy, "Is Freddy and me coming to Lacy's birthday party?"

"Of course, sweetheart. I want you to be dressed in your nice clothes so you and Freddy can show Lacy's friends out to the tent when they arrive."

"How is Jimmy going to get down that step from the house to the tent?" asked Tommy.

There was a moment of silence when everyone looked at each other. "Lacy, can Jimmy handle that step?" inquired Susan.

"Maybe, but a ramp would be easier. He may be able to get down but getting up would be difficult."

"I knew there was something I had forgotten. I always forget something. Fred, can you make a ramp in your shop quickly?" asked Susan.

"The simple answer is yes. But I have to figure out how I am going to make it. You can't have the end of the ramp sticking up because the wheelchair couldn't handle it and people would trip. After breakfast I'll draw up a couple of designs to see how much lumber I'll need."

"You could have a wedge as the ramp so it won't stick up," observed Freddy.

"Freddy that is a very good idea," replied Fred. We could put a rubber mat both on top so people won't slip and under the wedge so the whole thing doesn't move. After breakfast do you want to go shopping with me?"

"I guess, but Tommy and I have to take Mussy out for her daily exercise."

"That's fine Freddy that will probably be more fun anyway than going shopping on a Saturday."

That evening the guests started to arrive. Freddy and Tommy were both dressed the same in a white shirt, grey flannel pants and a blue blazer. "Freddy and Tommy, I want you to say hi to all the guests and then show them out to the tent," said Susan softly.

"O.K. Mom," both replied.

Tina arrives and is greeted by Freddy.

"Hi, I'm Freddy; do you want me to show you where the tent is?"

"Freddy, I am waiting for my two daughters."

"Where are they?" asked Freddy.

"I let them park my car for me."

"Oh".

Domino and Dede come in after parking the car in their knee length spring pastel colored party dresses. "Freddy," said Tina, "do you remember Domino and Dede?"

Freddy looked up at the girls. "Yes, I've seen them before, I think. Didn't they go sailing with us last summer?"

"That was two summers ago, Freddy. They have grown, haven't they?"

"No wonder they look different," replied Freddy looking up at them.

Matilda and Jimmy arrive to be greeted by Freddy and Tommy, Tina and her girls.

"Where's Lacy," inquired Jimmy.

"She's out in the tent, I'll take you out," exclaimed Tommy, "We even made a ramp for you so you can get up and down." Matilda followed behind as they all walked down the hall and down the ramp into the tent.

Fred was wearing an apron as he stood behind the bar which had a sign Mother Nature's best, try it, you'll love it. Susan comes down the ramp wheeling a cart of nutritious munchies and is greeted by everyone.

"I just love the way you have arranged everything," remarked Matilda

"It is just lovely," mentions Tina.

Susan was full of smiles. "Fred came up with the idea of the health bar so the kids could taste different concoctions of fruit and vegetable juices. I think it is a wonderful idea. Have you ever had a beet, apple and lemon juice or a pineapple peach or a pineapple apple?" asked Susan.

Matilda and Tina looked at each other. "No," smiled both Matilda and Tina.

More guests came in and the tent filled with laughter and greetings. Sally and Hank Beasley arrived right behind Freda and

George Partridge and their oldest children who were all at that stage of learning to drive. Freddy and Tommy showed them into the tent where Fred was peddling a sample of his juices.

"Jimmy try this and tell me what you think," asked Fred.

"What is it? Asked Jimmy.

"It is part carrot, part apple and part lemon and I call it my carrotapplelemon juice," chuckled Fred. "It's good, really, just trying it. It is good for your hair, nails, skin and just about everything else."

Jimmy smelled the cup and then took a little taste. "Boy that really is good. Did you put any sugar in or anything else?"

"Nothing, it is all from Mother Nature's kitchen. Do you think it's delicious?"

"Yes, I do," smiled Jimmy. "Do you have any more?"

"I'll make you more after I convince others to try it too." Fred went over to a table, picked up a fork and tapped the side of an empty glass that made a sound like a bell loud enough for everyone in the tent to take notice. "For those of you who don't know who I am, I am Lacy's father. It is hard for me to believe our little blue eyed, seven pound two ounce baby is now five feet six and sixteen and about to embark on the greatest adventure of her life. It will be fraught with grave dangers and demanding challenges, with hardships and triumphs, with despair and euphoria. This is a celebration for all of us to realize that time never stands still. If there is one thing that will keep you and your body in top shape and working its best, it's eating the right foods. I have the most nutritious, the most natural and the most delicious drink that I want all of you to try. It is great for every cell in your body. It will make your hair shine; your nails glow, your skin look youthful and it will also do wonders for your mind. Just come over to the health bar and I will make you something so good you will want more. However, I am limiting each person to one cup until everyone has had one."

There was a rush to the bar. Fred handed out small paper cups of his nectar as fast as he could. He realized he needed two or more juicers and more hands. Even the adults came over for a glass. The nectar of the God's he told everyone.

"Fred, you sound like an advertisement on T.V.," said Sally.

"Have you tried some?" asked Fred.

"Not yet."

"Here Sally, try this and tell me what you think."

Sally raised the glass to taste the nectar of the Gods.

"Fred isn't that amazing how good that is and, to think, in all my life I have never tasted anything like it."

"See what you have been missing. It certainly beats any alcoholic drink and your body loves it," mentions Fred.

"You sound like you are against alcoholic drinks, Fred," smiled Sally.

"Why would anyone drink something that is known to kill tons of brain cells with every sip?"

"Fred, I've seen you drink," retorts Sally.

"Everything in moderation Sally," smiled Fred. "I have an alcoholic drink only on occasion and the next day I always regret it unless it was wine."

Lacy is a very cordial host as she moves about her friends talking, laughing and, oh yes, some flirting with the boys. The girls radiated their beauty and showed their assets to the best of their ability. You could tell that many of them had not worn high heels enough to be comfortable in them. However, the girls stayed in one group and the boys in another. "Domino" said Lacy, "what are you planning for this summer?"

"Lacy, I've been looking for a job but I haven't found anything yet."

"I know, I've been talking to Caroline and she says jobs are really hard to come by this year. It's the economy. We are going into our senior year and you would think we could find something."

"I've tried everything Lacy and my parents want me to get a job so they can save more for my college tuition coming up in about a year and a half. I sure hope the economy hurries up and straightens itself out."

"I know I hear a lot of my friends telling me the same thing. It's our government; they let this sub-prime mess happen. These people, we elect, are supposed to know what they are doing and it turns out they don't. Our government needs to be restructured."

"Lacy, my parents are furious at our government. They were planning on getting a home loan to help pay for my college and now it doesn't look like they will be able to. All my friends are talking about the mess our generation is inheriting. We are not going to be able to maintain the same standard of living as we have now. I just can't believe that my parent's generation could have let this happen. I mean the greed, the complete misuse of our environment, a government that is asleep at the wheel; what was that generation thinking about?" said Domino.

"It's not a good situation Domino, the whole thing could collapse and for what, so they could have a big car, a bigger house and a big family and pretend that everything would work out. Their generation even produced a movie called Wall Street with Michael Douglas who actually said "greed is good" can you believe that? Greed is not only not good, it is our worst enemy."

"I hate to say this Lacy, but parents turn out to be just big irresponsible kids living for the moment. What I don't get is, parents will do anything to protect their children and yet when it involves their children's future they just don't see it. Why would you protect your children near term but trash their future. Does that make any sense?"

Lacy grimaced, thinking about the amoeba, a blind reactive organism living for the moment. It all fits together, maybe we have eyes to help us see the dangers of the moment but we are still blind to the future, she thought to herself. "Domino our generation is going to have to do a better job. I don't know how we are going to change our government's structure but we're going to have to in order to survive. We can't go on with a government that takes forever to do anything, fights like a bunch of rowdy kids, can't see the problems and costs a fortune."

Susan makes the rounds among the guests and whispers in Lacy's ear that dinner is about ready to be served and to tell everyone to find their name card on the tables. "Lacy, I have a seating chart with everyone's name and their table number. The seating chart is on table one. Ask everyone to check the chart and find their table and then go to that table and find their seat," whispered Susan.

As the word spread that dinner was about to be served, the guests moved to find their seat. Susan had arranged the seating so all the boys wouldn't be at the same tables. She had interlaced the sexes and placed Jimmy next to Lacy. Tommy and Freddy were seated at the adult table with their parents.

"Mom, what kind of soup is this?" asked Tommy.

"Honey, put your napkin in your lap," whispers Susan who was sitting next to George two seats down from Tommy.

"Oh!" mumbled Tommy. "Mom, what's this?" asked Tommy again.

"Try it and see," said Freddy who was sitting next to Tommy.

Tommy bent over to smell it. "It smells like potatoes."

"Well, then that is what it is," replies Freddy bending over towards Tommy.

"Oh!"

Fred was sitting the closest to the next table and could hear their conversation.

Jack Partridge was saying, "Lacy, are you going to get your own car next year?"

"Dad says I have to have two years of accident free driving before he will consider getting one for me."

"Caroline, is your family getting you a car next year," continued Jack.

"I'm getting something that is energy efficient. I'm hoping those snails in Washington adopt the Boone Pickens plan so I can get a car that runs on natural gas. But my family won't help me unless I get all A's next year."

"Betsy, are you getting a car next year?" asked Caroline

"We already have three cars so it really doesn't make sense to buy another one. I can always use a family car. But, I think, you're right, we need to get off all this imported oil and change to natural gas which is ours. It seems like a no brainier and I just don't understand why it is taking so long for our congress to back it. We have no energy plan at all now. I'd like to know why we have these people in Washington. I think they are doing more harm than good."

"You sound like our family," said Lacy. "You should hear my Dad on this subject, but please don't get him going or you will never hear the end."

"Jack, are you getting a car next year?" asked Caroline.

"I want one but I got some C's and it doesn't look very promising."

"Why not get a job and get a used one?" asked Betsy.

"I'm not the best student and I have to work hard just to get a B so working too wouldn't work for me."

"Have you started looking at colleges yet?" continued Betsy.

"No, I have a C+ B- average so this year is really going to be important. I have to bring my grade average up to at least a B. Have you been looking Betsy?"

"Yes," said Betsy with a smile. "School comes easily for me and I am thinking about Dartmouth, U Conn and a school down south probably UVA."

"Jimmy, have you been looking at colleges yet?" asked Caroline.

"I'm a tire kicker," smiled Jimmy. My grades are not the best either. I know it's important but school, for some reason, just isn't presented in a way that makes it interesting to me. I think it is because our world has so many problems and we are learning the same old stuff that got us into this mess." Jimmy thought for a moment, "you know Caroline, college is like our congress. Both are a mirror of each other. You learn the same old stuff in college, we aren't taught to think outside the box, therefore, we choose our representatives on how well they parrot information

back to us the way they did on tests in college. That is not intelligence, at least not the type we need. That type of mind is a robot. Instead of being able to define the problems and come up with solutions they look in their old books and rehash the past. The whole system is self-perpetuating. The problem is we have to use the knowledge we have gained but use it in a way that gives us a different solution. In other words, we have to take the facts and use our common sense to fit the pieces together to solve the problems. That means we have to determine what common sense is and be able to test for it. If we don't change our entire system we won't survive or if we, at least, don't learn how to define different types of minds for specific jobs so the right people with the right minds are in the right jobs."

"Jimmy, you can't do that. Everyone has a right to do whatever he or she wants to," replied Betsy.

"Betsy," replied Jimmy, "if you are in a dark cave that has a cliff with no return, would you follow someone with a light or would you follow someone who is analyzing the dimensions of the cave? If you were working for a company that was on the edge of bankruptcy would you bring in a new CEO who said, "I will continue on the same path while I analyze the problems" or would you bring in a CEO who said, "These are your problems and these are the solutions?"

Betsy frowned. "But what you are suggesting goes against what we think of as freedom. No one would go for that."

"Betsy, if your company was about to go under and you were about to be out on the street selling apples, wouldn't you want to try something different?"

"But what would I try?"

"As I just said, you would bring in someone who could see the problems and who also could see the solutions. Then you would ask him or her for a detailed outline step by step of the path he or she would take to fix the problems and you would watch that person to make sure he or she kept to the game plan. The same would apply to our elected officials instead of a nonsensical beauty contest that is a total waste of time and money."

"But Jimmy, if we were to change our whole system that would cause a huge disruption."

"Betsy, what do you think is worse, a controlled disruption or falling into an abyss that we can't get out of?"

"Jimmy, this is all hypothetical. We don't even know how to define a mind. We only know who is good at math and who has a good memory and we can determine who has an aggressive personality."

"That's what Jimmy and I are trying to come up with?" interjected Lacy.

"Lacy, you and Jimmy think you can come up with a way to define different types of minds?" quizzed Betsy.

"I don't know if we can, but that is our goal. We are researching life back to the very beginnings of life. We are looking at every aspect of life, every element; every biorhythm to see if all the pieces can be assembled that will lead to a conclusive conclusion."

"Wow, that is a huge undertaking, isn't it?" asked Betsy.

"But it is so much fun to uncover facts that I had never thought about or didn't know about. It's also like getting a sneak preview into our future," replied Lacy. "Our big problem comes if we find the answers we are searching for. Since all of us see things a little bit differently, we have to be able to present our findings in a way that makes sense to most everyone."

"Lacy, people can't think that differently if you explain it to them," said Betsy.

"Betsy, you are so wrong, I hate to say it. If you line a group of people up, let's say fifty people, and you tell the first person something and ask that person to pass it to the next person and so on until the last person is told and then ask the last person what the information was that he or she received, that information will be so distorted that you wouldn't even recognize it. And moreover, all these people speak the same language. Imagine if you didn't even speak the same language?" replied Lacy.

"But if you talk to a person directly certainly that person will understand you," said Betsy.

"Betsy, Jimmy called MIT and was fortunate enough to talk to a professor about the differences in people's wiring. The professor told Jimmy that everyone is wired a little bit differently and in many cases one person can't see what the other person sees at all. The professor continued by saying that even among his fellow professors, who teach the same subject matter, that they all can't see what another professor may see even if that professor can prove he is correct."

"Well Lacy, then how do we communicate?" asked Caroline

"That is probably one of the reasons we developed mathematics, so people could understand what someone else was saying. If we want to be as exact as we can be, we would all communicate through mathematics. However, even math is not perfect. You are taking a thought and turning it into defined symbols that can be manipulated which may or may not hold true. Even mathematics can lead you astray. The second most effective way to communicate is through music. There is nothing that can move a person's emotions and communicate a thought like music. The third way to communicate is through hand signals or facial expressions and the fourth and least effective way to communicate is through language. Our language is so vague and can mean or be interpreted so differently that other than remarking on the weather, it is like passing signals on a defective tom-tom. Just think how many times a friend has said something that you misinterpreted and that hurt your feelings or that created a question within your mind. It happens frequently in our personal lives and it also happens in business and in education and even in the scientific community."

"But then how do you get everyone on the same page so we all understand and feelings aren't hurt?" remarked Caroline.

"The difference between mathematics and speech is, one is specific and allows no emotion; the other is less specific with emotions added. In many cases, speech describes how you feel in a general way and may not call for an answer. When you make a statement like I've had a horrible day it doesn't call for an answer. Speech is many things. It maybe just venting anxiety, or maybe you are just lonely and need to talk, usually conveying little information or, you may be angry and want to give someone a piece of your mind. When we are talking, the way we are now, we may use different words to describe the same thing. So, it is within the context of our conversation that we translate the words we use. It is within this translation that we may become unclear. When we are emotionally upset we try to communicate our emotions and in doing so we often use different words which, for the most part, are very general, maybe inexact, and maybe even totally incorrect. So Caroline, to boil this all down, the only way to communicate is, keep it short and simple and make sure the context in which you are wrapping your words is clear so it doesn't leave any doors open."

"Lacy, you know we probably haven't really advanced much more than our ancestors when a hand signal and a grunt said it all."

"Exactly, Caroline, it's only our technologies that take us out of our past. Every dog, for example, in the whole canine community knows how the other dog is feeling. Their communication leaves no doubt about their meaning. You don't see any dogs scratching their heads wondering what the other dog is talking about. They know exactly and while dogs have been on this planet longer than man you would think man would have learned from them."

Jimmy continued Lacy's thought. "Man hasn't learned that simplicity is the key. Any time you make something complex the wider you open Pandora's box of problems."

The band started to play "Dance Me If You Can" by the Cheetah Girls. You could see the boys starting to look around thinking, I wonder if I should ask a girl to dance? The girls were way a head of the boys and had already determined who they wanted to dance with. Caroline looked over at Billy, who hadn't said a word all evening, and smiled a smile that no one could misinterpret. Billy gave a weak smile in return and you could see him become a little tense. I wonder if she wants to dance with me? She is cute. I better have desert first, he said to himself.

Indeed, it was a hard decision, to dance or to have that big piece of cherry pie with vanilla ice cream. Fred and Susan walked hand in hand up to the little dance floor to be the first to dance to the song DOT by Chilly Gonzales. It didn't take long before one by one the boys asked the girls to dance or was it the girls asking the boys; it is often hard to tell who was actually the motivating force. The right smile with the right hint from the girls often brought forth the right response. The little dance floor filled and Susan and Fred decided to cede to the younger generation.

As the night went on Lacy was asked to dance and Jimmy was left alone with sadness in his eyes. You could see the emotional effect on his face as the table became empty and he was left to watch Lacy on the dance floor. Matilda watched her son and it was obvious what he was thinking. She watched as he tried to get up, but in vain. He tried again but with no success. Her heart sank and she got up and walked over to him and sat down. You could see her jaw tighten. "Honey, we will have to work harder to see if we can't retrain your nerves and muscles"

"Mom, it is so hard. All I want is to be normal," whispered Jimmy with water in his eyes.

Matilda's heart throbbed with sadness to see what had happened to her handsome son who could pass for a young Brad Pitt "We have to work harder, honey. Life is not easy for anyone. It is a struggle from the day we take our first breath. The only time we truly fail is when we give up or we don't change to meet the new challenge."

"Mom, I may never be able to stand," said Jimmy emotionally.

"With God as our strength you will," returned Matilda with her jaw taught with determination.

The band stopped to take a break and the kids returned to their seats. Matilda put her hand on her son's shoulder and said "you will" as she rose to return to her table. Fred could over hear Matilda and was emotionally affected by her determination and Jimmy's emotion. Fred leaned over to Matilda, once she was seated, and asked "can Jimmy move his upper legs?"

"Yes," she replied. "It's his lower legs that don't communicate with his upper legs. The spinal cord or peripheral nervous system wasn't cut but somehow it was injured enough so the neurons don't communicate."

"Matilda, I don't know much about the spinal cord do you know how it all works?" asked Fred.

"It's very complex, Fred, but as I understand it the central nervous system runs through the center of your vertebrae which is a hard calcium bone all the way down to just above your anal region. By the way Fred, the vertebrae is a real piece of work. It is a bone that is allowed to bend and twist by being divided by cushions or discs between vertebrae sections and then all held together by ligaments and muscles. Just think of the flexibility of the vertebrae allowing you to bend over and touch your toes or to twist and turn when playing a sport. The spinal cord is very territorial and by that, I mean, certain sides of the spinal cord control different bodily reactions. Not only does the injury involve the position of the injury around the spinal cord but it also depends on the location of the injury along the whole spinal column."

"So to injure the spinal cord you first have to penetrate the backbone or the bone we call the vertebrae?" inquired Fred.

"That is the strange thing, Fred, the vertebrae, which protects the spinal cord, doesn't have to be broken or cut or pierced to have the spinal cord damaged. Any sudden blow to your body can, if it jars a disc, causing it to touch the spinal cord, cause a trauma that causes a disconnect between neurons. Jimmy's injury is in the L3 area which is the lumbar region, third disc down. The electrical impulses of the spinal cord are like a high speed elevator that goes up and down on the spinal track. When there is an injury, or even apparently a bruising, it may stop the elevator from going past the damaged area. Apparently, the spinal cord is extremely sensitive and fragile; anything that touches, jars, bruises or worse can cause the elevator to shut down. I can't imagine that society would allow anything but one hundred percent concentration when we drive. The human skeleton is way too fragile and easy to damage to drive with anything less."

"Matilda, are there any signs that the lower leg is getting any electrical impulses or is there a complete disconnect?"

"No, here is another strange thing, the electrical impulses don't allow Jimmy to move his lower legs, however, when I message and work his lower legs he does feel it."

"Matilda, as I understand it, our skin is a sensor that sends electrical impulses to the central nervous system or spinal cord so if Jimmy can feel your touch then electrical impulses are getting through."

"Fred, there has to be more than one type of electrical impulse. There must be two, a sensual impulse and a motor impulse. It is the motor impulse that is not getting through to his lower legs."

"What has the doctor recommended to try to stimulate his lower legs?" asked Fred.

"The only thing we know, at this point, is for a therapist to work his legs manually to keep his muscles strong and flexible as possible. If they become weak then they won't be able to support him and there won't be any chance for recovery and, besides that, it would not be good for his overall health."

"Can he get a brace?" asked Fred.

"We haven't gotten that far yet. Right now we are focusing on his therapy, however, from what I have been told; a brace is far from the answer. I know it is not the answer that Jimmy wants."

The evening passed quickly and the band played the last song of the night. Susan had already put the two boys to bed since it was way past their bedtime. Mussy had jumped up on Tommy's bed, as she always did, and curled herself up at the bottom by Tommy's feet. Lacy, Susan and Fred said goodnight to the last guest.

"That was so much fun," said Lacy to her parents. "I'm sorry I couldn't have danced with Jimmy, I was very uncomfortable leaving him. There has to be a way he can become more mobile, that chair is just too confining. I know he will never be able to dance a fast dance but even if we could just dance a slow dance it would make me feel better."

"Lacy, it's not like having a cold that you can just get over," said Susan.

"I talked to Matilda and she explained the problem more in depth to me and it has given me an idea. It may not work but if we don't try we will never know," explained Fred. "In retrospect, when we look back on our lives, it's those things we didn't do or didn't try that we regret the most."

"What is it?" exclaimed Lacy.

"Let me put my game plan together and I will tell you tomorrow."

Chapter Eleven

WHAT IS FREEDOM?

*T*he following day was greeted with a rising sun and a
bustle of noise emanating from down stairs.

"What's that noise, Fred?" questioned Susan.

"I don't know, I better go down and find out," said a still
sleepy Fred.

Fred pulled himself out of bed, put his robe on and went
down stairs. The noise was coming from the tent.

"What are you two doing?" asked Fred as he entered the tent
where two little boys were pulling all the chairs to one side.

"Dad, we're clearing the tent so Mussy can run around,"
exclaimed Tommy.

"Look at all this room," shouted Freddy with excitement from
the far side of the patio trying to move a table.

"I don't want you straining yourselves," said Fred.

"We won't," replied Freddy, a little red in the face as he moved
the table.

Fred went back upstairs to let the boys and Mussy have fun
playing in their new temporary room.

"What's all that noise?" asked Susan.

"The kids are moving the chairs and tables off to the side of
the tent so they can play with Mussy. I don't think they can hurt
anything."

"Fred, it's only six fifteen in the morning."

"Susan, they must have been thinking about this all night."

"They must have planned it last night at the party," said Susan.

An hour later Fred and Susan went down stairs to start breakfast. All the tables and chairs and health bar had been moved over to the side making the tent look roomier than it had. The canvas door in the tent was open and the boys and Mussy were not in sight.

"Oh no, Fred," grimaced Susan, "they must have gone outside. Will you please go out and get them. Tell them breakfast will be ready in a few minutes."

"I wonder where they went?" questioned Fred, who went through the tent door to find the kids. Fred looked around and no kids. Oh God, he said to himself, what are they up to? Fred looked in the garage, no kids; he looked in his workshop, no kids. Fred walked all the way down to the water and looked up and down the beach, no kids. "Oh my God," thought Fred, "where the devil did they go?"

Fred raced back to the house to call the police. "Honey, I can't find the kids. I'm going to call the police."

"Fred, the kids are in their rooms taking their beds apart so they can take them down to the tent. They want to be able to sleep out there with Mussy."

"Oh no, those beds are heavy and so are the mattresses, but thank God they are alright," said Fred wiping his brow.

"Well Fred, now you know what I have to go through three hundred and sixty five days a year. Being a good mom is the hardest job in the world. You think your job is hard, try mine. Are you going to let the kids take their beds down, Fred?"

"I guess, what do you think?"

"Other than the work you are going to have to do to get the beds down and back up, I can't see why not. The kids can't do it by themselves. They will trip and fall down the stairs and we will really have a mess. But you have to tell them they can't go outside with Mussy unless they tell us first." replies Susan.

The noise wakes Lacy who liked to sleep late especially on a Sunday morning. She slips her robe on and wanders downstairs to the kitchen.

"What's all the noise?" asked Lacy.

"The kids moved all the tables and chairs off to the side of the tent so they could play out there," replied Susan. "Now they are in the process of bringing their beds down so they can sleep out there with Mussy."

"Isn't it a little chilly out there?" questioned Lacy.

"I looked at the thermometer and it is fifty-five degrees. The forecast calls for a high in the upper sixties today. If it gets to chilly out there tonight, I will just get them to sleep in their sleeping bags. The kids are so excited about sleeping out there that they don't even notice the temperature anyway, Lacy."

"What are we having for breakfast?"

"Scrambled eggs, whole wheat toast with olive oil and shredded wheat with fruit."

"Oh, where's Dad? I want to see if he put his game plan together for Jimmy."

"He's up with the kids helping them to take their beds apart so they can bring them downstairs."

Lacy goes up stairs to talk to Fred. "Dad, have you put your game plan together for Jimmy?"

"Lacy, I still have to get a question answered before I can."

"What question?"

"Can't you see I'm busy with the kids?" said Fred a little red in the face himself from having hauled the two mattresses downstairs and now on his knees trying to get a bed apart. "When we get back from Church, we will sit down with Matilda and Jimmy and see if my idea will work."

"O.K.," mumbled Lacy and she turned to go back downstairs."

"Mom, do you know what Dad's game plan is?"

"I think he is still putting it together."

"He should ask me if he has a question. I've been reading a lot about Jimmy's type of problem. Did you know that man has been faced with spinal cord injuries almost from the very beginning? There are written spinal cord cases dating back to Egypt in approximately 1700 BC and that is before Christ. Of course, they didn't know what to do and the person died. Then we have accounts of spinal cord injuries by Hippocrates in Greece between 460 and 377 BC. As you know, Hippocrates is thought of as the father of western medicine. I think, even today, doctors take the Hippocratic Oath."

"I'm not sure if they take the Hippocratic Oath, Lacy, or the hypocritical oath these days. As far as I am concerned, you have to watch doctors as close as you have to watch anybody else."

"Mom, doctors are just practitioners. They go to school, learn what has already been done and then parrot it back in their practice. Look how long it has taken doctors to change the way they think about breast cancer. They used the same thinking they used thousands of years ago until recently; if a part of you is diseased just cut it off. It's only been very recently that doctors now try and use micro surgery to just take the tumor out without taking the whole breast off. Anyway, Hippocrates tried traction on injuries of the spinal cord when his patient wasn't paralyzed. Can you imagine being put on a traction machine and stretched when your back was probably killing you? But what Hippocrates did realize was the mind and body is one and that you had to approach the body holistically which was a huge break through from thinking the Gods were taking revenge for something the person did."

"Lacy, just think, of all the people who were really brutalized and tortured in the name of medicine, back then. We have to be so thankful we live today."

"Unless, of course, you had taken thalidomide when you were pregnant," replied Lacy. "Even today there are over a million people a year who have to be admitted to a hospital because of a bad reaction from drugs that have been prescribed by doctors. Mom, there is no doubt that medicine has come a long way but, here again, man is looking at the moment rather than the long term. If man unbalances nature by keeping everyone alive, at some point, mother nature is going to re balance us which means it is going to be a real mess, huge populations will die off from starvation at the very least if we don't ruin all our ecosystems first at least that is what the United Nations sees happening. It is typical man all over again. He doesn't look at the long term consequences. He doesn't understand nature and he doesn't live within the confines of nature even though he is of nature and part of it. That is so mystifying to me."

"Lacy, I hope you are not saying that we shouldn't have medicine."

"Mom, we need a complete plan of where we are going. We need to know how many people our little planet can support on a sustainable basis. We don't want people starving, we don't want people out in the cold freezing, and we don't want little children in poverty without any future do we? The human, I think, is a loving, feeling creature and he doesn't want to see people suffer. We have a tiny little planet that can support only so much life. Medicine is great as long as the end result is not to unbalance our tiny planet causing grave hardships on everyone. We have to come to the realization that Mother Nature rules and we can't go outside her laws".

"Lacy, people want freedom to do what they want."

"Mom, do they want to see little children starving? Do they want to watch as our ecosystems collapse with a sure end to the human species? The United Nations sees huge populations starving to death. We have to rethink our old ways and update them for a different world. But getting back to our original discussion, it wasn't until approximately 200 AD that a Roman doctor, Galen, came up with the idea that there must be a central nervous system that controls the whole body. Then about five hundred years later, Paulus of Aegina, realized that bone fragments from the discs could be surgically removed to help the patient recover. It wasn't until 1200 years after Paulus of Aegina, that man developed sterilization and antiseptics so doctors could operate without the high risk of disease killing his patient. It took us almost as long to develop sterilization as it did for us to get from Hippocrates in 377 BC to the point we had a text book with illustrations of the spinal cord in 1543 AD and now we are about 467 years after that famous text book was published and we still don't completely understand the spinal cord. In fact, we still don't have much more than a superficial knowledge."

"It's amazing, Lacy, how complex our system is. It is an absolute wonder we know as much as we do about it."

"But Mom, think of the immense amount of time and money we are spending on trying to understand this system of ours and how little we still know."

"What does this have to do with your Father's game plan?" asked Susan.

"Well, we have to know what has been tried before and we need an appreciation of how much time man has put into understanding the spinal cord. Even today, doctors really only know that exercise is an important part of recovery and keeping the rest of the body functioning and that was known a thousand years ago. We have mobility aids today but as far as understanding our circuitry and being able to rewire ourselves we have barely scratched the surface. There is always hope for the future but we really haven't gotten very far, it seems to me."

"Lacy, will you go up and tell the boys and your father to come down for breakfast."

Fred and the boys are bringing a bed down the stairs. Actually, Fred was bringing the bed down the stairs and the two boys were supervising.

"Dad," said Lacy, Mom says breakfast is ready."

"O.K." puffs Fred.

"Freddy and Tommy have you fed Mussy yet?" asks Lacy.

"No, but we will. We want to set the bed up out in the tent first," exclaimed Tommy.

"Tommy, you have to have breakfast now, you can set the bed up after breakfast."

"Oh," replied a disappointed little boy.

"Dad, now that we are sitting down can't you tell me your game plan?"

"Lacy, first I have to find out from Matilda whether Jimmy has any bone fragments or broken vertebrae that exercise might disturb and that could cause more damage."

"Dad, Jimmy has had a number of x-rays taken and they don't show anything broken or any bone fragments loose moving around. That's what is so mystifying. What happened must have been a compression of the spinal column in the accident or a bruising of the spinal cord in some way."

"Lacy, to make absolutely sure, I have to talk to Matilda and probably Jimmy's doctor. Matilda tells me the spinal column is extremely sensitive. The last thing we need is to further complicate matters for him. Thank God he was wearing his seat belt. The worst place to have a compression in the spinal column is the neck. If he hadn't been wearing his seat belt there is a good chance he might be paralyzed from the neck all the way down."

"Dad, something is wrong not only with our driving laws but with the design of our cars. If we are going one sixth as fast as a bullet towards each other when our speed is sixty miles per hour our laws should mandate we do nothing other than have one hundred percent of our concentration on our driving. But also, why not have an inner and outer body to a car. An inner capsule made of light weight high strength carbon fiber that encapsulates us, the inner capsule could be suspended by magnetism or springs giving us two phases of shock suppression. Even better, sensors could adjust the cars' speed and distance from cars around us. With our technology today there is no reason to have crashes at all. Here is another example of man not updating his systems for the times. We would much rather design another cell phone when we already have a ton of them to choose from. We are still using old outdated designs when times, technology and speeds are far different than they were. Our whole infrastructure needs to be redesigned and updated."

"Lacy, man has a hard time thinking outside the box; you find it in our government, our businesses, our law, our medical system, we find it everywhere throughout society. We would much rather put a patch on something or kick the can down the road rather than pin point the problem and fix it. The truth of the matter is the human animal does not like to change especially when it comes to how he makes his living. We really have become a nation of whiners not doers. In fact, there are so many whiners that we now have professional whiners who get paid very big bucks to whine. These whiners have reached such status that we call them anchors and personalities, commentators and analysts; they whine to the whiners but they very seldom have any solutions and very little ever gets changed. In fact, God forbid anything should get solved which would mean they couldn't whine about it anymore. If there is one human trait that will do man in, it is his inability to pin point the problem, face it head on and solve it fast enough. He wants to address the symptoms instead of fixing the problem."

"Dad, I think it's a highly contagious disease that started in our congress. What is the point of just talking about a problem? They say talk is cheap. I guess that is why we just talk so we have enough money to fritter away on unimportant things. Jimmy is always telling me if you don't find the problem and fix it, the problem will only get worse until there is a cataclysmic breakdown."

"Jimmy is right," replies Fred.

"I want everyone to finish up so we can get ready for church," interrupts Susan.

"Mom, Freddy and me want to put our beds together now."

"Sweetheart, you can do it when we get back from church. You have all day to put your beds together and play with Mussy in the tent."

Later that morning everyone arrives back from church to Fred's house with Lacy anxious to know what her father's game plan is for Jimmy.

"Matilda," says Lacy, "Dad has an idea that might help Jimmy but he needs to get some information from you to make sure his idea will work."

"Fred, what's your idea?" asks Matilda.

"Matilda, I have this idea, that may not be earth shattering, but it just may help Jimmy. However, I need to know if there is any reason that exercise could move a bone fragment or dislodge anything or move a disc that could cause further complications for Jimmy."

"Fred, I have to know more about your idea, however, we have had X-rays and MRI's and they show no bone fragments, broken bones or anything else that could move and cause further damage."

"Isn't that strange, Matilda. It's hard to understand why his lower legs are paralyzed when there seems to be nothing causing it."

"Fred, the spinal cord is extremely sensitive. You not only have the spinal cord which is enclosed in our vertebrae but you have the peripheral nervous system that extends out from the vertebrae connecting your internal organs like the heart and skin and all the other nerves in your body. But the peripheral nervous system, which is vital to the central nervous system, is not protected. It's a system that, to me, doesn't make a lot of sense. Why is part of the nervous system protected behind bone and the rest unprotected?"

"Matilda, the only way it makes any sense to me is, instead of bone protecting our peripheral nervous system we were given muscle. Mother Nature, in her consummate wisdom, couldn't make an animal that couldn't move, that didn't have the flexibility to run, climb trees, swim and protect itself. So the only way was to encase the central nervous system in segmented calcium bone to give the animal some rigidity, so it had a central support system. That central support system could protect a jelly like central nervous system that could instruct the cells, in a conglomeration of cells, how to react. She tied the segmented vertebrae together with ligaments and tendons to give it flexibility. From that central support system Mother Nature attached legs with the use of tendons and muscles. Muscles hold the whole vertebrae systems together. They not only hold the whole skeleton together but muscles protect and support all the vital organs of the body also. Muscles make the whole vertebrae system possible. Without muscles the animal world would not exist. Don't forget, it took about three billion years for Mother Nature to come up with this solution. We can't begin to imagine how long three billion years is. Anyway, Matilda, my idea works around what man has already figured out and that is to exercise and build muscle to keep the body functioning the way it is supposed to. If you don't keep your muscles in good shape your whole system is affected including the heart, respiratory system and even our bowels. Our muscles are not just for looking good or lifting things but to protect our vital organs and to make our own vertebrae system work. The worst thing man can do to himself is become a lounge lizard or to sit in a chair all day. It's no wonder that our medical costs are soaring. It has been estimated that our medical costs for our sedentary life style will exceed one trillion dollars shortly. We can't afford it and it will break our economy. Here again our medical system is addressing the symptoms and not the cause. The obvious solution is for man to exercise daily or he will bring an end to himself. Unless we start addressing the problems and not the symptoms we don't have a chance. Jimmy, do you have any pains at all?"

"Not really," replied Jimmy. "I did in the beginning but what pain I had has gone away."

"What about bowel movements, do you have any problem there?" asked Fred.

"Mom is always asking me about that but I seem to be the way I have always been."

"Jimmy, I think, you are a very lucky person."

"That's what the doctor says," replies Jimmy.

"So Fred, what is your idea?" asks Matilda.

"Matilda, we have an exercise room here and everyone uses it. I even have the kids on a little workout program of cardio. What I want to do is put a track in the ceiling so I can hang a ceiling lift that will enable Jimmy to be able to move around the whole room to all the different types of exercise equipment. It will allow him to stand up and he will be able to try and use the treadmill. He will have to wear a harness so the lift can lift him but, I am hoping, we can not only strengthen his muscles but maybe we can retrain the leg nerves."

"I love that," smiled Matilda, "that is so nice of you Fred. It sounds like a good workable program that we can hope will help him."

"Jimmy, what do you think? Would you like to try this for six months?" asked Fred.

"What can I say, I'm speechless. When would I come over and how would I get here?"

"Why don't you and Lacy figure out a schedule; maybe two or three times a week and then on the weekends. Somehow you would have to work it in with your physical therapy program too; maybe physical therapy three times a week and four days here or four days at physical therapy and three days here. You should talk to your doctor and see what he thinks. Susan, would you be willing to work around your schedule so that we can get Jimmy over and back since Matilda works during the day?"

"Fred, neither of our cars is made for a wheelchair. We could buy a van" smiled Susan.

"I really don't want to buy another car until the U.S. is converted over to natural gas."

"You could buy a used van and convert it to natural gas. Didn't you tell me the cost for conversion is about two thousand dollars and then you could use either gasoline or natural gas?"

"Yes, but the problem is Exxon and the other energy companies are sitting on their fat tails not adding natural gas pumps to their stations. Talk about people who are blind as a bat when it comes to our country, our budget deficit and our environment. We all need to call them and give them a piece of our mind."

"Maybe we could lease one," chirped Lacy.

"Lacy, that is a wonderful idea," gleefully replied Susan. "In fact, I saw an ad in the paper that said $160 a month with no down payment."

"Susan, that is for a regular minivan with no way to get a wheelchair up into the van."

"Fred, I was looking for something on Amazon.com and by accident I came across a lightweight ramp made just for that. It actually rolls up so even Lacy or me could pick it up and put it in the van."

"Do you know how much weight it will support?" asked Fred.

"I think it said up to one thousand pounds, more than enough for what we need it for."

"Well, that's the answer Susan. You and Lacy are so smart," smiled Fred. "Lacy, why don't you and Jimmy work out a schedule, Jimmy can review it with his doctor and tomorrow I'll call a contractor, I know, to get this lift installed. You will also have to look on the internet for harnesses for the disabled. There are many types but what we want is a lightweight small foot print harness. We want to make Jimmy as free as possible to do bench presses; curls, abs, pull downs, and incline and decline exercises and also use the treadmill. If you don't find anything you like, design your own and we will get it made. But you have to show it to Jimmy's doctor for approval."

"Jimmy, let's start looking on the Internet to get ideas for the right harness," suggested Lacy.

"Lacy, before you run off, we have to set the table for lunch."

"Where are we going to have lunch? The boys are on the patio which is now the tent and their playroom."

"Fred, are both the boys beds down in the tent now?" asked Susan.

"Yes, down and set up but the kids still have to make them up."

"You mean I have to make them up Fred. Will you and Lacy bring the patio table out and if you have to move the beds to one side you will just have to explain to the kids that they can move them back to where ever they want after lunch. Fred, also roll the side of the tent up so we can get some of this beautiful spring day in the tent."

At lunch Fred mentions "Matilda, we have been trying to put together a plan that everyone or most everyone would vote for. Our goal is to unify our country and maybe even the world. Lacy says we are all wired a little bit differently and ,therefore, how do we put a plan together that most people would vote for and that would enable us to move forward. So far, the five of us have been able to agree on three major goals; our environment, jobs and a strong military and police force. Our family became tied up in Lacy's birthday party so we haven't continued our discussion. Maybe it would be fun to see if the seven of us could agree on our fourth goal. Tommy, do you have any ideas for our fourth goal?" quizzed Fred.

"I forgot what I was thinking," said a little boy with a big plate of macaroni and cheese in front of him confusing the issue. "Mom, will you pass the salt."

"Tommy, I already put salt on and it doesn't need any more." "Oh."

"Lacy, do you want to start us off?"

"Well, everyone wants freedom, so I will say freedom.

"Susan, what do you think?"

"Gee, Fred, that covers so much. That's tough," thought Susan. "I think I've previously said freedom to do what? If we mean by freedom, we don't want to be slaves, then I would have to agree. However, we know we don't have the freedom to shoot or stab anyone, we know we don't have the freedom to slander someone, kids know they don't have the freedom to pull girl's hair or to scratch anyone, so the question really is, where does freedom step on someone else's rights? Should we allow personal freedoms to overstep on societies rights? Does making a living mean we have the freedom to stomp on the word honesty? Does freedom allow us to mislead someone just to make a buck? Do the words democracy and capitalism give us the freedom to step outside the laws of Mother Nature? Should we have the freedom to over populate when it endangers all of mankind and even the word freedom itself? Clearly, the word freedom is ambiguous."

"Mom, what does ambiguous mean?" asks Freddy.

"Unclear, easily misinterpreted."

"Oh".

"Fred, I would have to say limited freedom, freedom to live our lives as we want without stepping on the rights of others."

"Freddy, do you think freedom should be our next goal?" asked Fred.

Freddy thought for a moment. "I guess, but I was watching Judge Judy on TV and we don't even have the freedom to be stupid or it will cost you. Mom, you are always telling Tommy and me not to do something so we don't have freedom."

"Sweetheart, I love you and I don't want you to get hurt that's why I tell you not to do some things," explained Susan.

"Well, if you love us and are looking out for our own good then why don't we tell others not to do something when they are doing something stupid and that is not good for them?"

There was a moment of silence before Susan said "because other people don't like to be told when they are doing something stupid."

"That doesn't make any sense. I don't think I understand what freedom is," scowled Freddy.

"Do you want to pass on this one?" asked Fred.

"Yes," replied Freddy.

"Jimmy, do you think freedom should be our fourth goal?" asked Fred.

"Fred, freedom is what the whole world wants, however, we all know "Idle hands are the Devil's Tools" a proverb used since Chaucer's Tale of Melibee in 1386. For centuries we have known that freedom is not only a physical need but also a mental need.

When we are being productive, whether it is planting a field or writing a play or working in a store, we feel good. We have to feel we are accomplishing something and that we are moving forward. Our minds have to be kept busy. Today, with our technologies that allow us to have global mass visual and oral communications, the whole world now compares themselves to everyone else. It's like a family where if one child gets something the other child wants it too. It is just human nature. So, we have stumbled into unifying the whole world unfortunately around the idea of materialistic freedom. If he has it, why can't I have it? The problem is we have to look ahead, down the road, around the bend in time to realize that the industrialized world makes up only about 19% of the world's population. With less than twenty percent of the world's population we have polluted our air and our water, we have put ourselves on the brink of ruining our oceans and atmosphere and we are causing a dramatic change in our weather. We have to realize that much of everything that is made is made from Earth's nonrenewable raw resources like oil and water. Since this is a finite tiny little planet there are only so much of the needed resources available on Mother Earth. We are already tightening our energy supplies to the point we are causing prices to go up, reducing our disposable income with the result of hurting our economies and our own freedom. Not only have we boxed ourselves in around oil which can hold us hostage to an increasingly hostile world, since so much of our oil is imported, but it also limits our freedom. Since the industrialized world has trapped itself with debt, our economies will now only work if there is growth. How can we grow when we have limited resources remaining and a population that is out of control? It is clear that we are not only killing our own freedom but we have convinced the world, at just the wrong time that freedom is found in materialism. Now, the only way out is to limit the birth rate, turn our focus away from using our raw resources to reclaiming them, recycling everything, purifying our air and our water and allowing our oceans to regenerate by sharply limiting the food we take from them. We are going to be forced to live a simpler life style with less freedom. Debt is the world's worst enemy and there are only two ways out of it, either, we grow our way out or we write it all off and those that made a bad bet take a big loss; isn't that the way the game is played? No one listened to Polonius in Shakespeare's Hamlet or Mr. Micawber in Dickens's David Copperfield. Since we can't continue to grow our way out with limited raw resources, we will be forced to write all debt off around the globe and then we will only be able to buy what we can afford. We are about to take a big step back just to survive and with it our vision of freedom. If we eliminate debt and we limit our birthrate to only one child per family, I think, we can survive without growth. This will obviously be very disrupting with the result of limiting our freedom drastically but what other choice do we have? Even many economists realize we can only continue to kick the can down the road to be able to continue on. But the more we kick the can the more we compound our problems. Our whole economy and many world economies right now are teetering on insolvency with only low interest rates keeping them from crashing. The lower the interest rates, the farther you can kick the can on a very temporary basis and our Federal Reserve Chief, Ben Bernanke, knows this. We can't inflate our way out because a large portion of the population is on fixed income or unemployed or making a low wage not to mention the cost of a country's debt would soar forcing them into bankruptcy. An economic system is a manmade ecosystem. If you fool with it the ecosystem will react somewhere else. For every action there is an equal and opposite reaction. We can see what is happening in Europe with austerity becoming a bad word politically. People can only take so much. Economists often work in a vacuum. They don't see the human side to their flawed alchemy. Man almost always looks at the symptoms and not the causes. The only way to fix a problem is to meet the problem head on and take the necessary medicine which means, in this case, wiping all debt, both personal debt and public debt, off the books and starting over. This doesn't include Social Security which was paid for from work already completed and should not be considered debt. Social Security is the past savings of hard working people. There is no other alternative, either we voluntarily start over or our governments will be forced into bankruptcy and we will get the same outcome. Our huge debt, here in this country, will reduce our growth, that's our GNP or gross national product, by over a full percent every year and it just compounds. It is just a matter of time before we have to pay the piper and our vaults and goodwill will be empty. If interest rates go up, watch out below. I get myself so upset when I think about these problems my generation is inheriting. How could mankind be so thoughtless, so blind to the future they are handing to their own children? Once we start over we can revert back to the gold standard so all countries can again trade with each other. However, this time all countries have to set a limit to the debt a country can incur in relation to the gold it holds, let's say fifty percent.

"Fred, what has man been thinking about?" asked an emotional Susan.

"Susan, it has been man's greed and ego; thinking he knows what he doesn't know. Man does not listen."

"Let me continue, we can't continue to grow our populations when our resources are declining and also maintain our standard of living. The obvious result of growing populations and declining resources will be escalating prices that will kill our economies not to mention our environment and our own freedom. Moreover, we are piling more people on this planet at an exponential rate. Our own freedom is killing us. Man misuses his freedom. We are going to have to update our idea of what freedom means. So, in short, we have trapped ourselves and the only way out is in reducing our own freedom drastically. Fred, to answer your question, our type of freedom is only a mirage in time. Time always marches on, it never stands still. It's like our government that needs to be updated for a different time and place with different circumstances. Our whole perception of freedom has to change and be updated with the times also. It is very sad but man has not faced his problems. I really get sick to my stomach when I think about this and it makes me want to scream at everyone for robbing my generation by plundering our Mother Earth. It makes me cry inside when I see what my generation is going to have to contend with. I mean it really sucks. Man is at the ultimate turning point in his survival. We are either going to face reality or it's all over. This is our last chance. Susan said she would vote for "limited freedom," I would say, freedom to live within the laws of nature and within the 'Bill of Rights' without involuntary servitude".

"What's involuntary servitude?" asked Freddy.

"It means slavery, being forced to work against your will, and our 13th amendment prohibits it," replied Jimmy.

"I don't think anyone wants to work," returns Freddy.

"You are probably right, Freddy, but there is a difference between getting paid a fair salary and complaining about it versus being forced to work when you can't quit if you don't like it."

"Well, what's a wage slave then?" said a pensive little boy.

"Where did you hear that?" asked Jimmy.

"It was on a TV show," replied Freddy.

"A wage slave is the feeling of being trapped in a job solely to get paid. If you are in debt, you feel as if you are trapped and you can't quit. But you have the right to quit, you have the right to look for another job and you have the right to start your own company. If you have a good idea and raise capital from others then you are a capitalist. Capitalism has been what has made our country so innovative and rich. The problem with capitalism is everyone wants a piece of it including our own government. Our dysfunctional government has put us in debt and wants to fund this debt by overtaxing the goose that laid the golden egg. We are killing our own success and freedom every way we can."

"But if we are running low on raw resources how can capitalism work?' ask Freddy.

"Freddy, you are amazing for eight years old and I am glad you have been listening to our conversation because capitalism performs two vital functions. The first is, to see what has to be done and to raise the needed capital. The second function of capitalism is to direct the limited resources available to fixing the problem."

"Why is our country having so many problems if capitalism is so great?" asked Freddy.

"Capitalism is not a perfect system. There are no perfect systems, all human systems change with time, however, as we go forward with dwindling resources there has to be a way to allocate those resources to those areas most vital to our survival. I am sure you have heard on TV that capitalism is flawed and it is. In many cases capitalism is excessively greedy almost to the point of killing itself like the current sub-prime crises. However, the basic premise of raising capital and directing the necessary resources for good ideas is what we have to uphold. If we need to raise taxes then we should direct those taxes to those areas of capitalism we don't want or agree with. Taxes, instead of being our worst enemy, should be used as the policeman directing traffic. Where do we want our limited resources to go? Obviously, we don't want to tax those areas that are vital to our survival like alternative energy. However, for unnecessary financial manipulation like take overs that only line the pockets of a few, we need to increase those taxes. Today we have so much capital that we are awash in it and it really doesn't know where to go. We can see it piling on like a football game causing unnecessary roughness, it runs to the latest new fad or piles into futures contracts whipping prices around like a yo-yo. Our policemen directing traffic at the IRS are asleep like everyone else. With so much pessimism and uncertainty, due to an ineffective and dysfunctional government, that can't see the problems or the solutions, we have nothing more from them than more regulations that clouds our future even more. We need a business plan for our government but instead of a game plan for the next thirty or fifty years we are flying by the seat of our pants allowing every zephyr to change our views. If we want to survive then we have to update the structure of our government to reflect our needs for the critical times ahead of us."

"Oh," said a pensive little boy".

"So Jimmy, you and Susan want to redefine our definition of freedom. Susan says "limited freedom" so we can live our lives as we want without stepping on the rights of others. You want to define freedom as "living within the laws of nature and within our Bill of Rights without involuntary servitude. Matilda, do you think freedom should be our fourth goal?"

"Fred, how can we have freedom when the human animal has no common sense? We allow drivers to drive at speeds faster than they can react, we allow drivers to impair their ability to react by taking their concentration off their driving by talking on cell phones, by texting, or putting lipstick on, by combing their hair and drinking hot coffee and by eating. We are allowed to treat our most dangerous activity that has taken many more lives than all our wars combined, as if we were sitting at the swimming pool or in our living room or bathroom. We have the most beautiful planet in the universe and yet we are allowed to trash it. We fill our oceans with trash and we fill our atmosphere with pollution and we wonder why our environment is collapsing. The problem with man is he misuses his freedom. Man can make something but then he will do everything to tear it down. He can't seem to control himself. He will contort it, stretch it to its max or find a way to circumvent or ruin what he has already made. Man is not only destroying Mother Earth but he is destroying himself. Man is as blind as a bat."

"So you don't think we should have freedom?" asked Fred.

"Fred, my problem comes when I ask myself if I want to be a slave to another human who is as blind as everyone else. We were born free; it is a natural gift of life like love for a child or a puppy. We want the best for our children; we will work at something we dislike to give them something better. We will cry our hearts out if something happens to them and so we are caught between our greed for a better life for ourselves and our children and the fundamental freedom that Mother Nature bestows on us at birth. If only man had the common sense and the discipline to place the necessary limits on his own freedom so we could stay within the limits of Mother Nature, we could have it all. So Fred, I am caught between my dreams and reality. I can't vote against freedom but I would have to agree with both my son and with Susan that we have to redefine what freedom really means if we are to survive. Fred, what is your view on freedom?"

"Matilda, to me freedom is really no different than a garden. If you don't take care of it the garden will get run over with weeds. If we had total freedom we would be in chaos and many people feel we are getting closer all the time. If we had common sense, I would also vote for common sense freedom but, since, we don't, I have no other choice, since we don't want chaos, to say limited freedom that will allow us to survive. Lacy, you started this discussion off, what do you think?"

"Dad, I hear everyone saying we are out of control. It is so obvious we need a structural change in our government and in governments around the world that it is a no brainier. We really have to ask ourselves, is our idea of freedom working for us? It is so upsetting to see our beautiful little planet go downhill as fast as it is. Don't forget, man has barely stepped onto Mother Earth and in a blink of an eye we are close to ruining it and killing ourselves. I feel like Jimmy does, that I just want to burst into tears and yell as loud as I can at man for his stupidity and blindness. Certainly, if we don't change and change quickly it's all over. Our own freedom is killing us. We are our own worst enemy. We need to unite the whole planet under one common environmental law whether we like it or not. I think there should be one body of scientists, with all countries represented on that governing body, that sets the environmental and population laws and freedoms for the whole planet based on our own survival. We have started a revolution with the Internet, which can be seen all over the world, and now we have to fulfill its destiny and unite the planet with one nonpolitical scientific body that we all agree to follow. If our social sites, like Facebook, have any real reason to be it is to unite the world behind our own survival. If any country disregards the laws of this body they will be highly fined and boycotted. No one can buy or sell anything to them. We have to isolate them so they realize it is in their own best interest to live by the laws established by this body."

"But Lacy, countries can't even agree on limiting greenhouse gases let alone population," replied Susan.

"Mother, everyone has to ask themselves one simple question. Do we want to survive or do we want to die? There are no ifs ands or buts. We can't even handle the populations we have today. Talk to any scientist and he or she will tell you our ecosystems and our man made systems can't change fast enough to handle our growing populations even here in one of the most developed countries. We don't have the time to play stupid human egocentric games and continue to kick the can down the road only to compound our problems further and it is my generation where everything is getting dumped. Your generation has caused this mess and now you are dumping it on your children. Jimmy is right, it sucks. What you are doing is not fair or right," said an emotional young girl. "What has your generation been thinking about?" said Lacy with watery eyes. We need to ask for everyone's help everywhere on our little planet. After all, we are all on the same sinking ship together."

"Lacy do you want to start clearing so we can have desert?" questioned an unsettled mother with a tear in her eye and a sad look.

"What are we going to have for desert?" asked Tommy.

"We still have some cherry pie and ice cream left over from Lacy's party. Does that sound good?"

"Cherry pie is my favorite; can I have two scoops of ice cream?"

"Tommy, where are you going to put it all?"

"I always have room for something I like," replied Tommy.

"Sweetheart, everyone has to have desert first and we will just have to see if there is enough left over. Fred, I must say, that was a very eye opening topic. It is clear that the word freedom doesn't mean we can do what we want."

"Susan, the question is how would we bring everyone together with freedom as one of our goals? On the surface it seemed so simple."

"That's why our founders had to add the Ten Amendments to our Constitution outlining our freedoms," replied Jimmy. "It was clear then as it is now that people see freedom differently and, therefore, our freedoms had to be defined. The world looks at us as being free when in reality we are not only limited in our freedom by our own laws but also by the laws of Mother Nature. The problems we are having today are in part because we are trying to contort and circumvent the meaning of our original laws without understanding their consequences and forgetting that the overriding laws that govern everything are the laws of Mother Nature. Also, all of us have to realize that the word freedom is very time sensitive. Mankind's very first objective has to be and always will be survival. Freedom plays no part in survival. It is only when we have achieved a world that allows us to survive that we can think of freedom. Today, our very existence hangs on a very thin thread that is getting thinner by the day. The two most valuable assets man can have are the two he lacks, common sense and discipline."

"Jimmy, we just have to discover what common sense is. It is vital to whether we live or die," stated Lacy.

"Have you been reading and learning as much as you can?" asked Jimmy.

"Everything."

"Lacy, even if you can discover what common sense is; how are you going to prove it to the world?" asked Susan.

"We will have a simple test that everyone will understand."

"Don't forget Lacy," chimed Jimmy, "there are two parts man is lacking. Even if we can test for common sense how will man use it? The reason we are in the mess we are in now is due to greed and self-interest. Do you think those who are sick with greed will listen to common sense unless we impose very heavy taxes on them? Since growth and debt are our worst enemies now, our technology and energies have to be channeled to those areas that will allow us to survive. We may be able to test for common sense but the second part is discipline and that can only be taught at home from the earliest of ages and in our schools and colleges and universities around the world. One without the other will get us nowhere. Perhaps the biggest error man has ever made is in his lack of understanding in the importance of discipline both personal and as a society. We can see how important it is in nature. All animal groups have discipline and discipline is taught at the earliest of ages. Each member of that group knows his or her place in it and what is expected. For some really off the wall reason, man came to the conclusion that discipline was bad or wrong or not needed. It has been one of our biggest mistakes. The Bible teaches discipline but no one listens."

"Jimmy, it's because we are wired to act individually. Discipline is not part of our wiring and it will take everyone to focus on how important discipline is to our own survival and make a real effort to teach their children about the importance of discipline. It will not be easy because it goes back to our idea of freedom which we have just determined does not mean we are free of responsibility or from the laws of nature."

"Lacy you can see what happens when our human system breaks down" chimes Susan. "A system developed over hundreds of thousands of years based on tight knit families that taught and disciplined their children and who believed in God. You can see what happens when our families disintegrate, when we are not disciplined and when we forget about the importance of religion. The result is our whole system breaks down and becomes centered on greed. Our family system was used for centuries because it worked. The system we have today is breaking down because it does not work, but no one wanted to listen. Everyone thought they were smarter than their ancestors. Everyone thought they were disconnected from their past because of all the technology we have developed. In reality, they have no idea of the interaction of so many human variables that had been established over time that allowed us to survive. Now we have a real mess and we have compounded our problems and now our own survival hangs in the balance. Lacy, do you want to start to clear?"

"Mom, I didn't get my second scoop of ice cream," mentions Tommy.

"Do you really have room in your tummy for more?" quizzed Susan.

"I think so, but I am pretty full," replies Tommy.

"Sweetheart, I think you have had enough. Remember, your eyes are usually bigger than your tummy. There is only a little bit left anyway. Maybe later, O.K.?

"O.K."

Chapter Twelve

A CRUISE THROUGH THE
MEDITERRANEAN

Jimmy stays with Lacy as she clears the table. "Jimmy, all this talk of survival really has me worried. It really gets me upset. Are we totally losing it? Why can't man just come together and solve his problems so we can get over this hump?"

"Lacy, adults are acting more like children than adults these days. I don't really understand it myself. Man has always had obstacles to overcome but today he seems to be out of touch with his past and his struggles from the very beginning of time. It may be, some of our problems, like over population, have always been handled by Mother Nature. We have never had to cope with over population before on such a grand scale. If we just all acted like the adults we are supposed to be and realized that everyone thinks a little differently and sees things a little differently even in the same family and that we have many different religions with different beliefs now. We all have to realize that we are on the same ship together and it is in everyone's best interest to come together to solve our problems before the ship sinks."

"Jimmy, I think technology is overloading our minds to the point we just can't handle any more. We either tune our problems out or we don't want to even listen. I think the very technology that is supposed to save us will end up killing us indirectly. Our minds will become so over loaded they will completely shut down. Even Pope Benedict XVI of the Catholic Church said about the same thing recently. It's going to take cool heads on everyone's part to come up with solutions before it is too late."

"Lacy, it is only man who stands in his own way. There is no reason we can't solve this problem of over population, however, since it is a holistic problem that affects everyone everywhere we need to have a round table discussion by all those representatives of all our religious groups combined with all the Earth's top environmental scientists to hash out the number of people our little planet can support on a sustainable basis. The United Nations would be a perfect place to hold this meeting. You can be sure every religious group wants the best for its followers and would be willing to sit down to see how they can best meet the needs of their followers. It is time to unite the Planet Earth around our survival and to create a world we can all live in."

"I don't think it will be easy trying to satisfy so many people, Jimmy. Everyone has different views."

"Lacy, nothing is easy but it is in the best interest of everyone to solve this problem. Just because we have different views doesn't mean that everyone can't act in the best interest of our beautiful little planet. After all, let's face it. If the Earth's ecosystems collapse everyone will suffer. All life will collapse. It is not in any ones best interest to have that happen. Also, look at our problem this way; in a company that has thousands of employees, many who come from many different backgrounds, with many different faiths, and many different races of different colors, all are able to work together for the common good of the company. Why should it be any different for our planet Earth? We all have to work together for our common good and for survival. Look at husbands and wives. Even if both don't agree on everything it doesn't mean they can't live together happily."

"Jimmy, do you think we would have had overpopulation without all the medical advances, drugs, hospitals and doctors we have today?"

"First Lacy, let's take a look at what causes over population. The number one ingredient is food. All animal life is held in check by the availability of food."

"And we know we always have had plenty of food thanks to Mother Nature," answered Lacy.

"Right, so the next deterrent was disease. But if we look at the plains of Africa or our own West where there were huge herds of animals, disease was overcome by the animals' ability to reproduce in such numbers that disease was not an overriding factor. In fact, it would have culled the weak and injured making a stronger herd."

"The next deterrent would have been predators," continued Lacy.

"Or weather," replied Jimmy. "The important point is Mother Nature had it worked out so no matter what the deterrents were there was always a natural balance. Lacy, can I use the kitchen computer? I want to check something."

"Let me clear the table and I'll bring it over. What do you want to look up?"

"I want to see how many people were on our planet at about the time of Christ. Let's see, experts tell us that in 1 AD there were approximately one hundred and fifty million to two hundred million people on Earth. Lacy, where did all those people come from? We are talking over 2000 years ago. My mind can't even comprehend that many people that long ago. Do you realize in all our cities in the United States today combined with the suburbs, we only have maybe a third more people than we had back 2000 years ago. Of course, it was spread out more in different countries."

"So Jimmy, we have packed more than the world's total population that existed in 1AD into the United States of today. And to think, we now only comprise four percent of the world's total population. No wonder our ecosystems are having a very difficult time. We are in a race against ourselves. Jimmy, let me use the computer for a moment because I want to see how all those people were spread out. Let's see, approximately sixty-five percent of the entire worlds' population lived in Asia. That means more than one hundred million people lived in Asia. Good heavens that is a huge number of people. We think of 1 AD as being ancient but there were about one hundred million people just in Asia. It's hard for my mind to grasp that many people that long ago also."

"Lacy, they didn't even have high rise buildings the way we have today, so they must have been spread out and that many people would have covered large areas. They must have had a thriving trading business going on with that many people not to mention advanced agriculture."

"It is amazing," observed Lacy." It is hard for my mind to grasp that thousands of years ago there were already so many people that they numbered in the tens of millions. I guess it is because we live for such a short time and we only understand what we see today. Jimmy, man is very myopic and we really can't see either back or ahead in our own little world. When you realize that man has been on Earth for roughly five hundred thousand years and it's only in the last two hundred years that population has really become a problem. Two hundred years isn't even a blip on the radar screen of time."

"We have pulled the rubber band back as far as it can go, Lacy. We have kicked the can down the road until there is no other place to kick it. What gets me so upset is, man can't see his own demise or, I would think, he would have done something about it. We have known for years that our populations were out of control and we did nothing to solve the problem. If your neck was stuck in a guillotine and someone came along who was wearing extra thick dark sunglasses and started playing with the pin holding that very heavy sharp blade that dangled ten feet over your neck, don't you think you would be a little nervous?"

"It makes me so mad, Jimmy. It really makes me very sad also to realize that man could not see what happens in nature and associate it with his own species. But the problem we face now is that our Mother Earth has been divided into many different countries all working for their own self- interest instead of being united as one planet and working together. Jimmy, we just have to unite the whole planet around the common good of all. Man can make beautiful things and beautiful music and develop symmetrical mathematics and yet he can't or doesn't see he is part of nature and, therefore, under the same laws as nature. Jimmy, man must be living in a fantasy world. He is a total dichotomy in nature."

"Perhaps that dichotomy gives us our imagination, Lacy. Maybe there is a switch in our mind that gives us imagination but in doing so it cut off our ability to live within reality. Anyway, let's get back to I AD and continue with our exploration of what we call the ancient world."

"Jimmy, most of the early population in Asia was in China and that population was right along the Pacific Rim next to water. I wonder how far back agricultural cultivation began there. Unless they all ate fish all day every day they would have had to have agriculture to support that many people."

"Lacy, historians tell us the birth place of agriculture was the Fertile Crescent which has been called the cradle of civilization. Looking at a map, the Fertile Crescent was around the far eastern side of the Mediterranean. The Fertile Crescent included parts of Egypt around the Nile over to what are now Israel, Jordan, Lebanon and the West Bank. It followed the Tigris and Euphrates rivers down through Iraq to the Persian Gulf."

"So the birth place of agriculture was in the far eastern portion of the Mediterranean."

"Right Lacy."

"I'm not sure that makes sense to me, Jimmy."

"Why not?"

"Well, let's continue on with our discussion and maybe my understanding will become clearer. If we are talking about approximately one hundred million people in Asia and, by the way, some scientists put the number higher, they all couldn't possibly fit into the Fertile Crescent area. And, in fact, population experts tell us most of the world's population was in China which is thousands of miles away from the Fertile Crescent. I have to ask myself, where did all those people come from in China?"

"I'm beginning to see what you mean Lacy. If scientists are right, our populations have been growing proportionally to the size of the population. That would mean that man had to have a big head start in China."

"Jimmy, why did China populate at a faster rate than other areas? I think, I recall that the oldest fossil of man found in China dates back one hundred and thirty-nine thousand years ago which is younger than the fossil in East Africa that dates back one hundred and sixty thousand years ago. However, it could mean we just haven't uncovered all the fossils in China. After all, in one hundred and thirty-nine thousand years a lot can happen geologically."

"Or it could mean China produced more food. But if agriculture started in the far eastern Mediterranean region that means China and India didn't have a head start at least with agriculture."

"It's very puzzling," pondered Lacy. "There are so many unanswered questions. It must have to do with the size of the land mass but still there was plenty of land mass to fill in Europe. Both India and China produce rice. Maybe rice is the common thread. With rice and a large land area they must have grown at a faster pace than anyone else."

"Lacy, rice is not a complete protein. If you combine rice with fish or rice with beans or with soy then you have a complete protein you can live on."

"That means the Chinese had to have agriculture at an early stage. With sixty-five percent of the world's population they had to have extensive agricultural and also fishing operations over a wide area because you can't pack one hundred million people or more into a small area."

"Lacy, let's take a look at European populations to see what they were doing at about this time. If the scientists are right and we grew proportionately to the size of our population then all populations were growing at about the same rate proportionately. That means the base from which the Chinese population came either had to be much larger to begin with or the birthrate had to be higher than anywhere else making the scientists incorrect in their observation. Let's see what Europe was doing that may account for China's larger population."

"Jimmy, I'm going to use Dad's laptop so we both can work. Wait for a minute until I get it. Let's see, Damascus, Syria and Byblos, Lebanon claim to be the two oldest continuously inhabited cites in Europe. Through carbon dating they date back to between seven and nine thousand years BC. However, they really didn't become cities for another six or seven thousand years."

"Being at the far end of the Mediterranean in the Fertile Crescent area, we can be sure they were on the trade route which helped them grow. Edessa, Greece dates back to the six century BC as does Kavala, Greece both on the trade route around the Mediterranean," observed Jimmy.

"The cities of Mangalia Romania and Constanta, Romania are on the Black Sea. Both cities date back to about the sixth century BC also," continued Lacy. "That means they must have been on the same trade route. Their returning ships would have had to go up the Dardanelles, known then as the Hellespont, into the Sea of Marmara and through the Bosphorus into the Black Sea. They must have stopped at Istanbul, first Byzantium then Constantinople, for supplies and to trade. Naples, Italy and Athens, Greece date way back also and both were on the same trade route. So the early cites of Europe were all tied together by trade. This is so interesting, Jimmy. They had ships and traded along the Mediterranean for thousands of years and we think we are so modern. This was where all the money was and with it entertainment, restaurants and a place to make a living. So it would be interesting to take a look at their currency."

"Rome in I AD had a population, Lacy; check this out, one million people in Rome. It would have been like New York without the skyscrapers. They had ships that sailed all over the Mediterranean and Black Sea, they had an army and they had roads, some paved and currency. Here we are today, two thousand years later with much the same."

"Except we have so many people that we have to pack them into skyscrapers and high rise buildings," laughs Lacy. "But population figures are somewhat fuzzy and range over a wide range of estimates. In Rome, for example, in approximately two hundred twenty BC we have census figures taken so the Romans knew how many people they had and how many young men were available for their army. At that time the census shows four million people. That is four times your one million and many years earlier. But we don't know the area each covered. Was it just the city of Rome or was it the city and suburban areas and how did they define what area was included in their census. It also may mean they experienced a large loss of life due to wars or disease. In any case, there were still a lot of people."

"Lacy, even Athens in the fifth century BC had about half a million people and Greece had as many as three million. I can't believe this. Europe was a hot spot for humanity. It wasn't really all that different from what we have today. They had roads connecting different cities and states, instead of getting into a car you would have climbed into your cart or wagon or onto your horse."

"Except they didn't have over two hundred and fifty million cars spewing out hydrocarbons killing their environment and producing smog and ruining their atmosphere," replied Lacy, "and that is just in the U.S... Go to YouTube and search under world populations because there is a world globe showing the increase in populations since I AD to the present. It is really scary."

"Well listen to this Lacy, researchers have found pollution in glaciers coming from early metal factories in Greece and Italy. Human caused pollution started long ago."

"Jimmy, to buy all these goods being produced they needed a good currency. I want to look at that."

"Aren't we getting a little off the topic of population?" questioned Jimmy.

"I don't think so. We were wondering why China seemed to be growing its population faster. It's clear that Europe wasn't doing badly either growing its population. But China's populations continued to grow at a faster rate than Europe's if we look at today's world populations. So our question is why?"

"There were probably two reasons," responded Jimmy. "The first we already said was probably land mass. Europe was a smaller land mass and started to feel overpopulation at a much earlier age. Lacy, I think what you are leading up to is Europe became tied to materialism at a much earlier time and people started wanting things so they cut back on their family size."

"That makes sense to me, Jimmy, and would, perhaps, explain why China's population grew faster. However, China and India had the Silk Road which was a major trade route also which tied into the trade routes of the Mediterranean. It is absolutely amazing how quickly man established his own economic ecosystem throughout such a large area and this is over two thousand years ago which we think of as ancient."

"It is amazing, Lacy. Business seems to always carry on no matter what governments do. But does that mean the Europeans were more materialistic than the Chinese or Indians?"

"Maybe not," replied Lacy. The European system was based on trade around the ports of the Mediterranean. They had an easy way, not only to travel and transport goods to widely spread out populations, but they also had an easy means of communicating over a large area versus slow caravans on the Silk Road and because they had this great distribution system they probably changed from an all agricultural base to more of an industrial base much earlier. They began to specialize which freed more people to produce items for sale. The more wealth they got from their trade the more education they wanted and the more they traveled. The more they traveled the worldlier and more connected they became. You know people are so funny. We all are so interested in what someone else is doing and it hasn't changed. Talk about a snoopy animal."

"Human kind loves gossip even if it's not true," replied Jimmy. "Our snoopy trait was one of the reasons trade was so successful. We wanted to know what someone else had. Our snoopy trait led to new products being imported and exported. It also led to larger economies being able to support more people. With more wealth they could afford more medical attention. Don't forget the medical knowledge at this time was scanty at best, recalled Jimmy. Hippocrates (460 to 370 BC) who lived somewhat earlier began to set down in writing a system for clinical medicine. However, if you read about some of his practices they were brutal. I doubt people were lined up outside his door."

"They probably had to be dragged in," giggled Lacy "if the practitioners of that day followed Hippocrates work. But what the lack of medical help did mean was there was more of a balance between nature and man. While populations were growing they were still not getting out of hand with the balance of nature the way we are today."

"However, Lacy, even then there were a good many references to overpopulation and this is two thousand years ago. While the populations were still in balance with Mother Nature, man was seeking and moving to new areas. If one area became over populated he moved to another. I mean population spread out to all the many Greek islands and even to Mesopotamia, which lay to the north of Greece which had a population of a million people or more. It is just unbelievable that we are talking two thousand years ago. This was going on all over Europe. Where have we been putting everyone since? We don't have that luxury today of moving to a new unpopulated location unless you want to go to Siberia or Alaska. Every place is over populated and polluted. We are even taking our farmlands and turning them in to housing and roads and shopping centers. It is really scary to realize we are reducing the ability of our planet to feed us and to make the oxygen we breathe at the same time we are pouring more people onto it. It is hard to believe we can be as blind as we are to our own demise. If man realized there was over population thousands of years ago, why didn't he do something about it?"

"Jimmy, you can be sure they left population control up to Mother Nature. Populations went up and down depending on disease, weather and wars and because medicine and diseases were not understood they just let the natural course of events occur. Also, the more people a country had meant the more men they had for their armies."

"So what's changed Lacy? Our systems still work about the same after 2000 years. This is what Cicero said in 55 BC. 'The budget should be balanced, the Treasury should be refilled, public debt should be reduced, the arrogance of officialdom should be tempered and controlled, and the assistance to foreign lands should be curtailed, lest Rome become bankrupt. People must again learn to work instead of living on public assistance.' Talk about times not changing. It is clear that man doesn't learn. He repeats his same mistakes over and over and over but he never learns. Man is not an intelligent animal just a reactive animal. We have just been changing the technology and our costumes but the human wiring hasn't changed."

"Then how have we come to have all this technology?" quizzed Lacy.

"Lacy, that is a question we have to answer. How does the human mind work? On one hand we have technology but on the other hand man never learns. It is so confusing. Man has misled himself because of his blindness. But let's come back to how the human mind works. Let's continue with our study of populations. We still haven't answered the question where did all that population in China come from in the beginning if populations were growing proportionately. Even if we say they were populating faster than Europe, how fast can you populate to become sixty-five percent of the entire world population at that time?"

"Jimmy, I already answered that question in my mind. North and South America had very few inhabitants, Australia only had the aborigines and New Zealand didn't have a population scientists tell us. That leaves Europe, Africa and Asia as having the vast majority of the world population. If we take a range of the estimated population at that time, one hundred and fifty million people to over two hundred and fifty million and say sixty-five percent were in Asia that would have been approximately one hundred million people to one hundred and sixty million people. Most of the Asian population was in China along the Pacific Rim. The remaining thirty-five percent would have been spread between Africa and Europe. Alexandra, in Egypt, was the largest city on the African continent followed by Carthage, we are told, and, while I don't have any figures on the population of Alexandra around 1AD, we are told it was the largest city in the world even larger than Rome. That would mean a range of guesstimates from about one million people to two and a half million people. I am guessing that the rest of Africa would be another million to two million people so, just as a rough guess, taking an average, maybe Africa accounted for three million to four million people. That would leave approximately fifty million in Europe. So basically, India and China would equal twice the family size of Europe. India's women are known to have six children so that would mean the average size of a European family would have been three. Even if I am off in my estimated population in Africa by another million or two, the figures would still work out to be about the same. To me, that explains it."

"Good Lacy, but I am still puzzled. Scientists and historians say man evolved in Africa. Even Darwin thought man evolved in Africa. However, if we agree that the wiring in a crocodile has been the same over the last two hundred million years or more and we agree the wiring in a species remains the same throughout its existence; then let's take a look at man based on his wiring. African people seem to be a tribe oriented people with great rhythm. The Europeans are more trade oriented, more city builders and the Chinese more inventive and resourceful. The three groups look nothing like the other. Then let's ask ourselves, if there was enough food in Africa why would people leave? Granted there are always the explorer types in every population. But most people would rather stay in the general area where they were born given enough food. As families grew they would naturally spread out. But why would they travel thousands of miles to live a different life style? We know the Cro-Magnon man looked like Europeans not like Africans or Asians and, in fact, fossil remains of the Cro-Magnon man were found in southern France in a town called Les Eyzies not in Africa. If Cro-Magnon man was not of African descent, my next question is, how can we be so sure all human life evolved in Africa?"

"But Jimmy, scientists use DNA testing and they are positive that early man came from Africa."

"I know it is very confusing to me."

"Jimmy, we learned that in the Leopard species there was the African leopard and the Asian leopard and they were the same species but originating on different continents."

"Good Lacy, so are you thinking if leopards could originate in two different areas so could man?"

"Why not; if life started in warm tidal pools and we think these pools existed in more than one location why couldn't man have evolved in more than one location?"

"That brings us back to China. We have to ask ourselves, why would the population of China, which is thousands of miles away, have a population larger than Europe when Europe is much closer to Africa? If agriculture started or at least thrived on the far eastern end of the Mediterranean then how can we account for a base population in China, thousands of miles away, to have gotten to be bigger than Europe? Unless there was a huge migration out of Africa or Europe to China, and we don't know of any, then the only answer, that makes sense to me, is man actually arose in different areas not just in Africa. After all, when you are dealing with fossils and tens of thousands of years it would be easy for Mother Nature to develop man in different locations where fossils are not easily found or that we have not uncovered. We have observed before, that to make an historical projection based on just one frame or even less of a whole film is very difficult. After all, life on Earth, jumped from being totally sensual to having eyes which must have taken at least a million years and yet man has not uncovered any fossils showing that very important change. Using DNA opens up a lot of questions as to the interpretation of data and how it all fits together over extremely long periods of time."

"Jimmy, people can always be wrong, even scientists. Let's continue with our investigation of populations in Europe. As we continue our analysis of life and we plot all our hypotheses maybe it will all come together."

"OK, let's look at currencies and maybe that will give us a better understanding of the economics of the time which would give us an insight into populations and the flow of goods and people."

Chapter Thirteen

THE HARNESS

The door to the kitchen suddenly swings open and in comes Tommy and Freddy with Susan close behind. "What's going on?" asked a surprised Lacy.

"Your father is all upset," replied Susan.

"About what?" asks Lacy?

"I'll let Tommy tell you."

"Tommy, what in the world is going on?"

"Well, we were down at the water and Freddy picked up a stick and threw it in the water."

"And Dad got upset about that?"

"No, he got upset because Mussy ran into the water to get it."

"Didn't you have her on a leash?" quizzed Lacy.

"Yes, but she just went zoom and she pulled it out of my hand."

"Tommy didn't realize how strong Mussy is getting now, Lacy. She is growing faster than Tommy and she is not as little as she used to be. Time marches on and sometimes we don't realize how fast it is moving, right sweetheart."

"Mom, she is so fast, she just went zoom, so it's not my fault."

"Tommy, she was reacting to her natural instincts," replied Lacy. "Freddy, you can't throw anything in front of Mussy unless you want her to chase it. Where is Mussy now?"

"She is outside with Dad," replies Susan. "Tommy, grab some paper towels and Freddy you get a bath towel so we can dry her off."

"Mom, we have to put Mussy in dog school," remarks Freddy. "She is growing faster than me and Tommy and we have to be able to tell her what to do."

"Why don't we all discuss it at dinner? You know we all have to be involved with her training. You just can't drop her off and let a trainer do it," said Susan.

"Why Mom?" asked Tommy.

"Sweetheart let's get her dried off first so your father doesn't have a fit and then we will discuss it at dinner. Lacy, have you and Jimmy decided on a harness yet?"

"No, but we will do that now."

Tommy brings a kitchen chair over and climbs up to grab more than enough paper towels while Freddy goes into the laundry to get a bath towel. Lacy types disabled lifting harness into Google. There were pages of subject matter relevant to the lifting of the disabled. "Jimmy, you got to see this," giggled Lacy. "It's a site about disabled dogs that have to be retrained and look at this, it's a Basset Hound with four booties on and neoprene panties with a long strap attached to them so its owner can lift its rear end to help it walk. I think that's a riot."

"Lacy, I don't think I'm going to be wearing four booties and neoprene panties," smiled Jimmy.

"I just thought it was funny. Alright, I'll go to another site, what do you think about this type of harness?"

"It looks too bulky. I need complete freedom of movement."

"What about this type?"

"Lacy, it's made for standing up but what happens when I lie down? If I am doing bench presses or incline or decline presses, my back will be flat against the bench and it will be uncomfortable. We may have to design our own because it doesn't look like many people are using the type of harness we want for working out. Let's write down what we want and we can make a diagram to make it easy for someone making it to understand."

"Jimmy, we will probably have to make one and then try it out. After you try it, you will have a better idea if it's what you want. Let's make our first design. What's your idea?"

"All I need is one inch wide nylon or polyester webbing material rated for about three hundred pounds. While I am only one hundred and sixty-five pounds I want to have an added measure of safety. You will have to measure my chest because I want it to go around my back, under my arms and clip together in the front. That way I can easily undo it if I want to take it off. That should give me enough freedom to do all the exercises I want to. It has to have a loop of the same material in the back that the lift can attach to."

"I will have to drive Mom down to a fabric store and get the webbing. Once we have the webbing we can put it around you and see how tight or how lose you want it. Getting the loop right where you want it in the back will be the trickiest. Also, in the front, where it clips together, we will have to put webbing underneath the clip or buckle so it doesn't dig into you. Lift your arms and I will put this tape measure around you to get an idea how much material we need. Jimmy you have a forty inch chest."

"How soon do you think you can get down to the store?"

"Well, Mom wants to get her new van this week so I don't know what day but certainly sometime this week."

"Do you have a sewing machine that will work with heavy duty webbing?"

"I don't know. We have a sewing machine but I never use it."

"Lacy, we should take a class on how to use a sewing machine. I think it would come in handy."

"Jimmy, I think we have enough going on without taking another class on something."

"Do you think your Mom could see if her sewing machine will work with thick webbing? If we could work up a complete sample harness and try it out, then we would know for sure if it will work before we take it to a professional for the final sewing."

"I'll find out but if our sewing machine can't do it maybe we can rent one. Once we get the original made and tested I'll ask Dad, since he is into boating and, I think, has a friend who works at a sail loft. If he does, once we have it ready for the final sewing, I'll run it over to him. Do you care what color the webbing is? I found some here on line and it comes in red, blue, green and many other colors."

"Maybe blue, what do you think, Lacy?"

"Blue is fine but red would be easier to find, red sticks out and , if you are like me, I'm always misplacing things or throwing something on top of other things."

"You mean you're messy."

"I am not messy, Jimmy. I just forget to hang things up."

"Alright, make it red and does the fabric store have buckles too?"

"I'm sure they must but if they don't we can go on line and get what we want."

The kitchen door swings open again and Matilda sticks her head in. "Jimmy, I think we should think about going. I still have to cook dinner."

A week passed quickly with Susan joyous with her new minivan after living with Fred's beloved antique for years. Lacy had driven her mother to the fabric store in the new van, amid a continuous recording of "please be careful, you have to drive extra carefully Lacy, watch your speed, stay way back from the car ahead of you," and picked up more than enough red one inch wide webbing to make Jimmy's harness. Fred had contacted a company with a worldwide reputation for ceiling lifts for the disabled on Monday and they had referred him to a certified dealer in his area. The dealer assured Fred the track and lift could be installed within a week. The track would allow Jimmy to reach any part of the exercise room. The lift came with a remote control so Jimmy could keep the control in his pocket if he wanted to move the lift out of the way when he was doing his exercises. The lift and track could also be set up to enable Jimmy to get to the bathroom alone. Fred was excited and could hardly wait to see it installed. When Fred arrived home Friday evening Lacy informed him that the dealer had called and said he would install the lift and track system on Saturday.

"Dad, I am so excited, we have to pick Jimmy up tomorrow so we can make his harness while they are installing the system."

"I want to be here, Lacy, when the installer comes. You better ask your mother."

"Mom, the lift system is coming tomorrow and Jimmy has to come over so we can make his harness. Can we go pick him up?"

"Can't Matilda bring him over?"

"I guess, but I want to drive over and get some practice."

What time, Lacy, and have you called Jimmy to see if he can?"

"I'll call him in a minute and Mom, will your sewing machine sew the webbing we got. I mean if we put two pieces together will your machine handle that?"

"We can try it; if it can't then you will have to sew it by hand. Have you used a thimble before?"

Lacy grimaced, "I don't think so."

"Lacy, you should think about taking a sewing class. You will be surprised how handy it is to be able to sew and use a sewing machine."

"I should get you and Jimmy together," replied Lacy.

"What do you mean?" asked Susan.

"That's what Jimmy said; he thought it would be useful if we took a sewing class."

"He's right you know. You wouldn't have to rely on me to mend you clothes or alter your dresses or slacks."

"It takes to much time. Jimmy and I will be busy working out not to mention our school work."

"Lacy, this is not a course in nuclear physics. Many places, that sell sewing machines, give you a free class. You can also call one of our local community colleges that gives sewing classes in the summer or evening when you are not in school. Any school that gives adult classes at night probably has a sewing class and, of course, you can look on-line."

"Maybe this summer Mom. I'll go call Jimmy."

"Jimmy, I'm all excited, I got what we need for your harness and the lift and track are going to be installed tomorrow. Isn't that cool? You have to come over tomorrow morning so we can make your harness."

"Wow, this is really awesome Lacy. What time do you think you will be here and what about the ramp?"

"The ramp came yesterday. Everything is new so this will be the first test to see how everything works. I'll leave here at ten so figure I'll be there about twenty minutes later."

"Your Mom is coming, isn't she?"

"Yes, for six months. After six months and for another six months I can only drive with my parents and Tommy and Freddy, but, I know, that will never happen. Mom has already said she doesn't want the boys in the car with me until I turn eighteen. So for a whole year I have to hear, Lacy, watch your speed, don't tailgate, drive defensively, keep both hands on the wheel, check your back and side mirrors so you know where other cars are at all times. I can't drive by myself for one year and that is if I don't have any accidents."

"Remember, your Mom has your best interests at heart."

"I know, but I do learn, I don't need to hear it over and over."

"Lacy, she knows repetition will always stay with you. Until you die, every time you get behind the wheel of a car you will always hear her."

"How do you know?"

"Lacy, it's just human nature. It is like your Mom telling you to look both ways before you cross the street. How many times did you hear, look both ways before you cross the street, when you were growing up. Now, every time you are about to cross the road you look both ways automatically. Even when you are driving and before you pull out into an intersection you look both ways.

It works the same way in nature. Whether you are just learning to waddle or to walk on all fours or to fly your Mom is always giving directions. All animal young are great mimics; it is just part of their survival kit. Everything you learn growing up stays with you. That's why a good family life style is so important when you are growing up."

"You know, Jimmy, that is something our schools should have as a short course in their continuing education classes."

"You mean a refresher type of course to get Moms and Dads refreshed on the needs of their children."

"Yes. With all the stress and strain that everyone is under today and with over worked parents free classes should be available to keep parents updated and mindful that even with their busy work schedules the most important duties of parents are to bring their children up in a manner that gives them a good outlook on education, Mother Nature and life and also to remind them how important discipline is."

"If "Do You Know 2.0" is right Lacy, the pressures families will feel, as we go forward, will continue to increase. The more people we pile on planet Earth the more stress there will be for survival and for having enough time and money to raise a family. We don't want poverty, we don't want little kids starving, and we don't want our children not having a good home life or not having a good education so mankind will be under great pressure to limit their families' size. The more people we bring onto this planet the more strain there will be on our natural resources also, forcing prices up so fewer people can have them, not to mention trying to find good jobs that will become increasingly difficult to find demanding higher and higher degrees of education."

"It sounds like a pressure cooker, Jimmy. It makes me so mad that man hasn't done anything about this problem. Man doesn't seem to understand how fast things are changing. At this rate, I don't think I want to have any children."

"I think, as the pressure increases for jobs and as everything gets more expensive, a lot of people are going to decide not to have a family too. Life has always been a big gamble. Having the personal discipline to say no is so important. Life has always been hard. There has never been perfection and there never will be. It has always been a struggle for survival. We are only kidding ourselves thinking technology is the answer. One of our many problems is we are making life so complex we are leaving a lot of people either overloaded or behind. We are creating two worlds. It is like Wall Street and the subprime mess. Wall Street didn't fully understand what they had created. Man is doing the same thing with technology. We are creating something we don't fully understand."

"You mean Jimmy, the consequences of our technology. We have to remember that life doesn't revolve around technology but technology is supposed to revolve around life. We are forgetting to establish a goal for the future. We need a road map of where we are going."

"Lacy, the faster we chase technology the more we rely on it to solve our problems, the more complex we make our lives and the deeper the hole we dig trying to get back to a balanced system which, we all know, is fundamental to survival."

"So we come right back to the basics of survival," observes Lacy. "No matter what period of time we look at the two ingredients most important to man are the two he lacks, discipline and common sense. But what is common sense, Jimmy? We have to answer that question."

"Lacy, I am beginning to understand there are two types of common sense. One is a combination of maturity and experience which we call wisdom. What many call common sense is really wisdom which is built on information we have obtained through living. To be able to look ahead we have to be able to look back. In designing our future we have to know the traps man always steps into."

"Jimmy, I never thought I'd being saying this but by listening to the youth generation without any real experience means we are listening to a void, a future built on wishful thinking, a fantasy land that doesn't exist in nature," replied Lacy.

"Unfortunately, man from the very beginning has fallen into the trap of chasing illusions, of chasing symptoms rather than being able to see the core problems. There has to be something to build on, in this case, knowledge, to be able to understand ourselves and the world we live in. If you think about it, it just makes common sense. If you have a computer it is no more than a hunk of junk unless it is programmed. Without programming it has no idea what to do. It is the same in nature. That is why the young of all animals and probably of most living creatures mimic their parents. Their parents are programming them so they know what to do. When you couple mimicry with instinctive wiring you have a recipe for survival. Humans who are programmed with the wrong information by their parents, like hate and greed and disrespect for our environment and in addition were not born with the same instinctive wiring as animals are getting a formula for failure."

"Jimmy, when is your birthday?"

"I'll be sixteen next month. Why?"

"We are young and, I think, we have common sense."

"Lacy, we have the second type of common sense which is fundamental common sense which only some are born with from what I can see. I believe intuitive or instinctive common sense comes from two things. Probably the most important is, a person's wiring and the second is, his or her ability to observe nature. It maybe the two go hand in hand. One follows the other. We know a person's wiring is the key to his knowledge because there are many examples throughout time where mere children have had a deeper understand and knowledge than adults on certain topics or categories. In school there are kids, you know, who don't have to do any work. It is so frustrating because they get A's in school with little or no work while the rest of us have to work hard just to get a B. The A team is born with a particular type of wiring that our educational system caters to and is built upon. Our schools have no idea about any other type of intelligence."

"Jimmy, we have child prodigies who have the voice and also the emotional understanding and maturity of much older seasoned opera stars. There is no way, by the time you are only eight or ten years old, to have learned what it usually takes a life time to learn. There is no doubt that it is our wiring, our molecular make up that endows us with certain abilities that others may only acquire over time and I think it is vital to find out how it works which, I think, will lead to the test we are searching for."

"However Lacy, if you are not that fortunate to have been given that type of wiring, that allows you to see at an early age, then it is a life time of learning, of making mistakes, of getting your fingers burned before you can look back to be able to see ahead. However, it is apparent many people never seem to learn at all, therefore, we can substitute wisdom for common sense in only some cases."

"So the further we get from nature, the less common sense is gained and the hole we dig gets deeper," pondered Lacy.

"The understanding of nature in relation to our own survival is what is so vital. But ones wiring or DNA is the real key. The probability of a certain type of wiring is what all of nature is based on or what we call survival of the fittest. Nature makes a certain percentage of life with faulty wiring so others can eat and survive. In nature the three ingredients to survival are health, a keen instinctive sense and just plain luck or timing. Humanity wants to treat all people as if their wiring was equal which is not found anywhere else in nature."

"So some of us are born with a tool kit that instructs us on how to begin; in our case it is common sense."

"Lacy, all of us have our strengths defined by our wiring. The tool kit, you are referring to, is already in our wiring. We are born with it; but it has to be programmed. As we continue our investigation of the human mind we will discover how it actually works. It doesn't seem to take a lot of programming to program someone with a specific type of wiring. A little programming

seems to trigger a chain reaction in the mind so everything starts to fall into place."

"If youth needs years of learning and experience to learn what will work, why has the world decided to follow youth?" Jimmy.

"Lacy, your question really involves two questions. Why do we follow youth and why does man want to follow anyone? It all goes back to the tidal pools a billion years ago. It was a physical world, a reactive world. The cellular systems that arose were made to live for only a short time. The only reason life continued on was due to its ability to over reproduce. Whatever the life form, it had to produce more offspring than predators could kill. All life forms were built on the same formula. Look at the crab family, for example, that dates back one hundred and fifty million years or more. Crabs will lay as many as a million eggs and out of a million eggs maybe two will survive. The human animal can't fly, or swim very well, or run very fast, we don't have the type of teeth to pierce tough hide like a lion's, we don't have a nice fur coat to guard against the elements, so nature gave us the ability to mate literally around the clock, seven days a week, three hundred and sixty-five days a year."

"Jimmy, if you couple that with man's ability to subdue his predators you have a formula for over population. So, even without doctors and hospitals we would still have overpopulated. Boy, did we fool Mother Nature. I wonder why she didn't see that flaw."

"Don't forget, it's not nice to fool Mother Nature," smiled Jimmy, "but your observation is probably right. It just would have taken longer. However, the wiring in man dictates his need to kill his enemies so whether we call them doctors or not, we would have learned to subdue our microscopic enemies also. Remember, we have had tribal medicine men that go way back in human history probably almost to the very beginning of communal living."

"So, from the very beginnings of life, life's function was to re procreate at a rate far greater than replacement needs," replied Lacy.

"Mother Nature's goal has always been to have all forms of life carried on from one generation to the next. Because life didn't live very long and had to protect itself the two things that were important were youth and strength. Here we are a billion years later with exactly the same instinctive wiring. The wiring in all animals evolved from those early tidal pools. It has always worked the same. Nature does not change. Everything in the human world is based on youth because the wiring dictates that youth re procreates quickly before it dies. The human economic system is based on the male wanting to please the female so she is willing to mate. Mating means offspring; which means shelter, clothes, food and much more; which creates an economy. The males' job has always been to provide the necessary necessities of life so he ended up monetizing the human life cycle all centered upon youth. The second part of the question of why we want to follow anyone is not as clear. On the one hand we are independent; we work for our own self-interest. On the other hand we want to follow a leader. Talk about two opposite goals. Man is a real dichotomy in nature."

"Maybe that's why our political system won't work. We are being pulled in different directions. If you couple that with greed and self- interest and ego our political system doesn't stand a chance of working."

"Lacy, it worked in the beginning when we all felt we were on the same ship. We all had a higher mission of making something new work. It really came down to survival. There wasn't the level of greed and self- interest originally so everyone worked together. Youth followed the teachings of their parents and they expected to be disciplined if they did something wrong. Religion played a much more important role which held everyone together. Today we are doing almost the opposite and it isn't working. We are living in much more of a world of hope and dreams and not within reality."

"And Jimmy if you are born with wiring that allows you to always live close to a fantasy world of hope and of dreams you may never learn to see reality."

"Or maybe some don't want to see reality. Lacy, our cells reacted to a world of shadows from the diffusion of photons or light waves through water. We originally reacted sensually to our surroundings. Light and dark permeated our cell and eventually, although, we haven't discovered any fossils, as we became a multicellular organism some of our cells began to develop into receptors for light. Cells are reactive and they are constantly reacting to a change in not only their surroundings of light and dark but to their chemical surroundings. So your previous observation that eyes were an add-on is correct."

"Jimmy, you mean this is what your common sense tells you what happened since we don't have any fossils."

"Lacy, I think, common sense is associated with logic; by taking the building blocks of knowledge that we know are correct and then associating with them our hypothesis that lies outside those building blocks to come to a conclusion. The second step is to test the conclusion to prove that it holds true. Look at clouds in the sky. We know that clouds are formed by water droplets and we know there are different types of clouds some of which produce rain. Through this basic knowledge of clouds we can come to a hypothesis that certain types of clouds produce electricity. By watching clouds we can prove our hypothesis when there is a lightning storm."

"Jimmy, I think you just explained what thinking outside the box means. So when we say thinking outside the box we mean associating what we know with something we don't know but we think follows and then testing to see if it really does follow. Jimmy, I am so excited, I have to tell Dad we think we know what thinking outside the box means. So thinking outside the box is part of common sense. Jimmy, I am euphoric, we really are beginning to put the pieces together."

"Lacy, I think you left something out. In the process of developing a hypothesis there are the elements of imagination and creativity and in ones' ability to recall or associate that creativity with the natural world around him or her. Developing the hypothesis calls for thinking broadly. Schools can teach logic or at least test for it, that one thing follows another. However, what is lacking in our educational system is the understanding of what thinking broadly means and which goes into being able to think outside the box. I think, we can say that by definition, thinking outside the box cannot be focused thought. It has to be a broadly painted picture. This ability to think broadly is probably an inherited gene or trait that comes from somewhere within one's ancestry and can't be taught or it would be. This type of framework of thought is in the original makeup of a particular type of wiring or mind. Some of us can think outside the box on a consistent basis, in fact, my mind is always thinking outside the box. What we have stumbled onto is probably the most vital key to our very survival and which is missing in our present form of education. We have not realized there are two fundamentally different types of minds; that our educational system is more or less a one size fits all system. It makes no difference if one goes to Harvard or to a state university. We are teaching the same type of mind; it is only the degrees of the same type of mind that allows one to excel in a particular academic field. However, we have to realize that our entire educational system is teaching the same type of mind so we will continue to get the same type of answers no matter what college or university you go to. That is what Einstein must have meant when he said 'we can't fix our problems with the same type of thinking that created them'. Lacy, he must have discovered what we just did. That means our academic idea of intelligence is woefully lacking in depth and is very misleading."

"Jimmy, that means we are going down the wrong road. Man has taken the wrong branch in the road. So the underlying framework, of how we think, is fundamentally different in both types of minds and dictates what we see. Perhaps we can define our type of thinking as a type of fuzzy logic. That means abstract thought is in the association of the pieces of thought but processed differently in the two different frameworks of thinking. Oh Jimmy, I could kiss you. We really are putting the pieces of the human puzzle together. I just have to tell Dad. So what is common sense then?" It must be a close relative of being able to think outside the box."

"Lacy, abstract thought is formulated in the hypothesis and, therefore, different in both types of minds. Let's come back to common sense because we are getting a little ahead of ourselves. I want to continue with our thought about man and his seeming inability to face reality. Will you ask your Mom if she is free to drive over with you at ten o'clock tomorrow?"

"Jimmy, I will in a minute but I just want to continue with our thoughts for just a minute more. This is so exciting. I just love to learn and to solve problems. Alright, so, are you saying the reason we live in or close to a fantasy world goes back to our ancestry of a billion or more years ago?"

"Lacy, let's put the pieces together. We know our cells divide giving each daughter cell the same DNA. Therefore, we can say the original cell or mother cell had the same DNA. That means we can look at the original cell a billion years ago, which a species came from, and conclude that all animals are inheritors of their original DNA. That original single celled organism was a reactive organism living in a world of light diffusion through water. It lived in a world of light and dark. It lived in a shadowy world. It developed cells that were receptive to certain light frequencies found in water. It didn't look for causes it just reacted to symptoms since it was sensual. This single celled organism lived in these surroundings for well over three billion years. We can't begin to comprehend how long a time frame that is. When you realize that man doesn't even show up on the radar screen of life on Earth, that man lives only for the moment and that his mind is very myopic and sees only his own little world around him and that the world around him exists for only a split second in time; something that happened over a period of three billion years or more is way out side his ability to comprehend. Each species is a product of its original cell dating back to the beginning of life. We are just a conglomeration of cells all carrying the same DNA with some cells specializing for certain reactive functions."

"So are you saying the proof of your hypothesis can be seen in an entire species because the whole species reacts in the same way to its biological wiring? That is to say, both its basic instinctive and physical reactive impulses."

"Yes. A species' DNA goes back to the tidal pools in the very beginning. All species and all animals react to their immediate surroundings or dangers. They never were meant to look for the causes but just react to the immediate symptoms or dangers. Mother Nature built onto that original cell. That is why our technology takes us out of our historical heritage. Technology is another dimension that goes beyond our natural abilities that we inherited. The solution to this dichotomy between man, technology and nature is to integrate technology in a way that does not overload the mind of man and even complements it and works within the mind's natural framework and within the framework of Mother Nature. So much of our technology is not integrated with man's abilities or needs that man is getting lost and overwhelmed by it. It is overloading our minds and in doing so forces our mind to limit what we listen to and also limits our mind from the observation and understanding of the world we live in. It is very dangerous because we are getting farther away from our natural world. You can't go outside the world our mind was built to handle."

"Jimmy, we try to reach the United Nations often enough to know how complex this organization is; and how complex it is to find what we are looking for. This is an example of too much information for our minds to handle easily. If I understand you, what needs to be done in this case is have a search window so we can type in the main thoughts of our question allowing us to narrow down the choices available to us. That would get us to another list of choices compiled from the first list. Then there needs to be another search window where we could enter more defined search words to narrow it down even further. Finally, there should be an on- line help button next to our final choice to contact that department in real time for the information we are searching for. It certainly would save a lot of time and keep us from tearing our hair out not to mention the increase in productivity we would see."

"I think that is a good example. If all organizations would just use technology to complement man's abilities it would make it not only easier to communicate with them but we would have a much more connected world. Our communications' systems are breaking down throughout our whole society because we can't get through, we just get automated menus and we are often left without an answer but red in the face and full of hostility. Technology has to complement our senses not work against them."

"Jimmy, I wonder why man doesn't see this dichotomy between the way technology works and the way we work?"

"Scientists call man the irrational animal but we are taking this irrational animal out of his natural surroundings and expecting him to act in a rational manner in a much more complex world. Without a game plan, a vision of where we want to go we are just thrashing around and Lacy, man doesn't even understand himself which should be our first priority. Lacy, we have jumped way ahead of ourselves."

"It's scary Jimmy. We are just starting our lives and yet we can see the problems we will have to face. Man doesn't understand himself and yet he is trying to run before he can even crawl. We were never meant for the type of world we have created."

"Lacy, our generation will be forced to make a complete one hundred and eighty degree turn if we are going to survive."

"The first thing we have to do is update the way we govern ourselves Jimmy. Our system just doesn't work any longer and patches or trying to kick our problems down the road a little further won't help either, even our President called our government dysfunctional."

"Lacy, here is an example of the dichotomy in man. We continue to follow our dysfunctional system instead of updating it for the times. We want to follow someone, something, even if it doesn't make sense. We will follow our dysfunctional government to our grave if we don't change it. We are a total dichotomy in nature. On the one hand we want to act as a pack which is a natural instinct in the animal world but on the other hand we want to do our own thing. Man is apparently a complete split in nature. However, it leaves man in a very vulnerable position of living in two different worlds. We live in a world made from our ability to understand nature enough to manipulate it, giving us technology, but we don't live in a world where we can see the end result, so we are flying blind."

"By saying the end result Jimmy, you don't mean the end result of the actual manufactured product or action, you mean the consequences that the product or action has on everything else. For every action there is an equal and opposite reaction. We don't live in a vacuum, so it follows, therefore, that there is some sort of chain reaction caused by every change we make."

"Very good Lacy."

"And Jimmy, if many people are not wired to see or chose not to see then that is the reason they chose a leader by a popularity contest. Their basic original instinctive senses of strength, size, shape and melody take over."

"Good Lacy. We have a system based on the blind leading the blind. Our leaders do not have a road map or a vision of where we are going and we don't have a universal understanding of the world in which we live so we are flying completely blind. If we want to survive we have to demand our candidates and our president give us a plan and a vision of where we are going for at least the next thirty years accompanied by three, ten year incremental plans on how we are going to reach our thirty year goal. Each administration would then give us their four year plan which would tie into the ten year plan. If we had our visionary thirty year goal backed by ten year plans that would keep us on course to reach our goal, just think of what it would mean to our whole economic system. Spirits would rise, companies could plan and therefore expand, our unemployment problem would evaporate, the stock market would soar and our government would get the needed additional revenue to pay down its debt. It would also mean we would have continuity from one administration to the next. Everyone would be a winner."

"Jimmy, I bet the first candidate to come up with a comprehensive thirty year plan that includes the solutions to our major problems including over population, would win the election hands down. Your idea seems like such an easy solution that solves so many problems. It would also mean we could get rid of our useless congress and two party system which would probably save billions. Why haven't people seen this before?"

"The real question we have to ask ourselves is why any of our candidates or our president want to be president when they don't have any solutions? They don't have a good solution to one major problem in my opinion. I don't understand why they are even running for the presidency other than ego. We have major problems to face and I haven't heard any good solutions mentioned from the candidates. In fact some of the solutions would be like pouring gasoline on a little campfire to put it out. It is beyond me. Mitt Romney went to Harvard Business School and I know he knows what a business plan is. But I haven't heard any mention of a business plan for our country. It would establish his vision and where he wants to take us and how he is going to get us there? I wonder what he is thinking about and I wonder what President Obama is thinking about? He went to Harvard Law School and yet we don't have a business plan from him either. We are flying completely blind. What is wrong with Harvard? Their educational system must be flawed. Our whole educational system must be flawed. Why can't our graduates think, other than how to make a buck? It certainly casts a dim light on our educational system, I think."

"Jimmy, the way we elect our president has to change. This beauty contest of minds, void of solutions, gets us nowhere and our problems are snow balling. Our country and our little planet have critical problems and unless we find solutions it could mean the end of man much faster than we think. It is driving me nuts and all my friends at school are worried sick too. Everyone is worried sick. We are the new generation that no one seems to be thinking about. All these fat heads with all their so called credentials are driving our country and our planet into the ground. It really sucks. I think all these people are blind as a bat. Somehow we must have gotten all these characters out of casting for Alice in Wonderland."

"Lacy, my stomach is in a constant knot. I have already been through so much in my life that I just want to break down and cry but I can't. It seems like everything is a fight now. All I can do is just grit my teeth and cry inside. What has happened to our country? We call ourselves the United States but we seem to be fighting each other tooth and nail, everyone is going in a different direction. No one can agree. How can we all pull together if we don't know where we want to go? How can the president and the candidates be so blind? The very first thing any company has to do is write their business plan. The bankers won't even talk to you without your business plan. A business plan outlines your goals, your vision, and how you are going to get there. We have to demand that the very first thing our candidates do before we vote for any of them is to write a business plan for our country; a plan on where they want to take us. A thirty year plan with ten year incremental plans that every administration can tie into with their four year plan."

"Jimmy, unfortunately, we aren't old enough to vote yet."

"We can tell our parents not to vote until we get a thirty year business plan. Our future is on the line Lacy. Why would anyone hire a captain of a ship unless they knew first where he was going to take them? Our whole political system is on the bridge waving without seeing the rocks dead ahead."

"I agree, Jimmy. It is so sad to think our colleges are graduating people who can't see past the end of their nose. We are printing so called credentials that everyone flashes as fast as we are printing our fiat money. We must have stepped onto the Wizard of Oz movie set. Changing faces in an election is useless if we are just getting a different face with the same type of mind. I think you and I have to start a solution dump or a solution game where everyone can email us their best solutions and we could pass the best ones on to the President and the candidates who are so myopic it gives everyone a headache not to mention the fact that we are on the wrong road."

"That's a good idea Lacy. We need to get everyone involved because we don't know who or where the best solutions will come from. Our solutions aren't the only ones. There may be far better ones out there; we just have to find them."

"We could compile all the solutions for different problems also and see how many of the same solutions we get for a particular problem. I think that would really be interesting too."

"Lacy, what happens if we get so many we can't handle all of them?"

"I think we are getting ahead of ourselves, Jimmy. I think we have gotten a little side tracked. I want to go back to why our system is so blind."

"Don't you think you better ask your Mom if she can pick me up tomorrow?"

"Just this one last question but I'm pretty sure she can. Why doesn't the electorate see our government as being dysfunctional and demand our government change?"

"I think there are probably several reasons. First, most people are just followers. They don't realize that our type of government requires work on everyone's part. They actually have to get up and do something. They have gotten so lazy they would rather stuff themselves with calories sitting in front of the T.V or monitor which is bankrupting our medical system. Second, we live in a highly complex world now and we ask people to vote on issues they don't really understand and haven't researched. Everyone is so overloaded with information already and we only have so much time in every day that we listen to the same old story from our candidates; it builds a dangerous and false foundation of hope."

"We no longer can have a blind electorate Jimmy. If we want to vote then we have to be given both the pros and the cons on the real issues by our academic community easily accessible over the Internet and by TV and easily recorded so we can listen to them over and over."

"And Lacy, once we think we understand the pros and cons to the real issues then we all have to pass a test, in the language of the country we are voting in. We have to show we have enough understanding of the issues to make our own determination of which of the alternatives will get us to where we want to go. After all, you can't get into college, you can't fly a plane, you may not be able to get a job and you can't even get a driver's license for a motor scooter without being able to pass a test. Why do we allow everyone to vote without understanding the issues when our lives depend on knowledge of the issues? It's the same thinking that created golden parachutes. Here take command of my company, ruin it, throw our hard working people out onto the streets and we will still pay you a king's ransom. We are asking people off the street to vote on the future of man and of our planet. Our vote is not only worthless but detrimental if we don't understand the issues. Ask yourself, do I want someone who doesn't understand the issues voting on my life and the lives of my family and the future of planet Earth? To make matters even worse, do you realize one in eight voter registration records have significant errors with many people who are dead still on the rolls according to MSNBC?"

"Jimmy, I think we have forgotten that just because we have technology doesn't mean it works without an up to date infrastructure keeping it updated and that is very expensive. Can you believe, with all the money we spend on technology that some of our systems and information are not current? Think what would happen in a depression when the infrastructure of all our electronic systems couldn't be kept up. It would be curtains because bad information in will give us bad information out. What good is our technology? Everyone knows that garbage in is garbage out."

"Lacy, it is hard to believe man is so near sighted. It follows through to our economy also; man doesn't see around the bend, he has no common sense. The problem, our economic system creates, is the tail starts wagging the dog and it is true for any economy the world over. Economies get to a point where they can't support themselves unless there is continued economic growth. That means either a rising employed population or rising productivity if people have enough money to purchase it, however, with limited resources on a tiny planet we can only grow so much and our growth will decline as our raw resources decline. With a stagnant economy the government reaches a point where it has to continually stimulate the economy to generate enough demand so it can barrow to pay for what it already purchased. There comes a point when we can't grow anymore and the piper still has to be paid unless everyone everywhere defaults on their loan obligations and we start the game over. We live on a very tiny planet. Things never change. A cat is a cat and always will be a cat. A crocodile is a crocodile and always will be a crocodile. Man is man and always will be nearsighted man."

"Jimmy, I think there are going to be a lot of losers that made a bad investment or, I guess, I should say a bad gamble. They bet wrong."

"Lacy, if we are to survive we have to build a system that people can understand and relate to that accounts for man's weaknesses and we don't have any time to waste."

"The question is can man conquer his greed. He is like a monkey with his hand caught in the cookie jar, Jimmy, and he won't let go. Look at our ineffective congress. These are grown people and they still act like childish bullies in a school yard. I've never seen such a blatant display of greed and total blindness even when our national interest is at stake and it's not just politicians here in the U.S., but all over the world. Many politicians are drawn to politics because of their wiring and they seem to be wired to be blind, self-serving, egomaniacs, even Cicero saw it back in 55 BC and that's before Christ. The wiring never changes;

a politician is a politician and always will be a blind politician selling hope to the blind unless we change the system. While there are some outstanding public servants like Mayor Bloomberg, most politicians seem to be in politics for their own career or ego."

"Lacy, the blindness of our system is a huge problem especially as we go forward. Unfortunately, our country's original purpose, over time, degenerated from the good of all, to man's lowest common denominators which are greed and self-interest. Look at what is happening all over the world. The more people we put on our planet and the more we become interconnected the more self-interest takes hold, the more people want what they think someone else has which leads to having more of a say in their government. Eventually survival becomes the focus if we don't solve our problems because of the dwindling supply of cheap raw resources being land, water, food and energy. We all know the instinctive need to survive leads to the disruption of any system and will bypass any laws. Basic survival can lead to chaos and no one wants that. It is not in any ones best interest."

"Nutrition and clean air are or will become harder to find also, Jimmy. So, we need a system that can thoroughly explain the problems and that can also show us the alternative solutions. I think we have to get everyone to agree to a unified planet with a body made up of scientists at the top of the hierarchy, one from each country so everyone feels they are part of the plan. That body has to set the population and environmental goals for the planet, and then the president of each country has to work within that framework, set by the scientific body, to bring about the economic solutions to the problems he was elected to solve. In addition, the scientific body has to come up with a long range thirty to fifty year plan with five, ten and twenty year interim plans. In our country we have to eliminate the congress in its present form which is a waste of time and money anyway. If a country doesn't abide by the laws of this scientific body we have to boycott that country. We have to isolate them by not selling to them or buying from them until they see it is in their own best interest to abide by these laws."

"Lacy, you better check with your Mom to make sure she will be able leave when you want to tomorrow?"

"I am so excited Jimmy. I just love trying to solve the world's problems and I get all wound up. Wait, I will ask her right now. Hold on."

Lacy goes and asks her mother if they can drive over to get Jimmy tomorrow morning at ten o'clock.

"Lacy I have errands to do tomorrow morning so we can do it all in one trip, however, you know that you can't drive when Jimmy is in the car even though I'm in the car too."

"I know, Mom. Jimmy, Mom said she can, so be ready at about quarter to ten just in case it's a faster trip than I planned."

The evening passed quickly with Fred, Susan and Lacy going in and out of the exercise room trying to envision how the equipment should be laid out so the track would make it easy for Jimmy to get to each piece of equipment and to the bathroom.

"Mom, how does the lift work?" asked Tommy.

"Sweetheart, when Lacy makes the harness it will go around Jimmy's back and under his arms and there will be a buckle in the front to hold it on. There will be a loop or ring on the back so the lift can attach to it. Then Jimmy just has to press a button on the control and it will pull him up or let him down. If he wants to move around the track he pushes another button."

"You mean it's like a remote control for the T.V. Can I try it, Mom?" asked Freddy.

"Freddy, it is for Jimmy," replies Lacy.

"I know, but I want to see how it works."

"I want to try it too," chimes Tommy.

"Mom, the more I think about it, what happens when Jimmy is not attached to the lift. I mean if the lift gets in the way when he is doing an exercise he will probably undo it from his harness and move the lift out of the way. His harness will fall down unless there are shoulder straps to hold it up."

"I think that makes sense Lacy, unless Jimmy buckles it tight enough that it doesn't fall down."

"But, if it is too tight it will probably be uncomfortable."

"Lacy, do you have enough material to make straps?"

"I probably don't have enough webbing but since the shoulder straps don't need to be strong enough to lift him I can use some other material. Mom, what do you have that I can make straps from?"

"You can probably use some denim and I have some left over from your skirt."

"Do we have any red denim?" asks Lacy

"No. But the combination of red webbing and blue denim shoulder straps will look O.K.," remarked Susan.

"Mom, can Tommy and me try the lift?"

"Freddy, you and Tommy will drive me crazy unless I let you try it. But it is for Jimmy. Both of you have legs that work and there is no reason for you to use it other than just to try it out. Just think how lucky you are to be able to walk and to be able to run and to play. This lift is not a play toy. It is for a boy who lost the ability to use his lower legs because of a needless car accident. Do you both understand that it is not a toy?"

Both boys nodded.

"Also, you don't have a harness. You will have to see if Lacy has enough material to make one that you can use to try the lift out."

"Lacy, do you have enough material to make us a harness?" asked Freddy.

"Freddy, let me measure your chest and Tommy come over here so I can measure yours too. Tommy, lift your arms up. Mom, can we get some more webbing when we pick Jimmy up because I have enough for Freddy or Tommy but not enough for both of them."

"Can't you make one that will fit both of them?"

"Freddy is a good bit bigger than Tommy but maybe I can put enough holes in the belt part to fit both of them or maybe

I can use a different type of fastener. But both the kids have
to understand the lift is for Jimmy and he needs this lift to get
around and they don't."

"We know," said two little boys with long faces.

Saturday arrived amid much anticipation. The whole house
was up early thinking the installer could arrive at any time. Fred
was busy moving the exercise equipment around after having
thought about the proper arrangement overnight. He placed the
equipment so the treadmill was next to other leg equipment and
all upper body equipment was grouped together. Free weights
were in one end of the room while Fred's pride and joy the PTS-
3 dual action Smith cage universal machine customized for Fred
was in the other. His old rowing machine which was no more
than two cut off oars on arm brackets with a seat on a track in
the middle was next to the highly sophisticated universal machine.
Susan came in and looked at the arrangement. "Fred, you have all
the equipment in groups, wouldn't it be better if you have them
in the order of use? If you have them in two rows so you can start
on either the upper body or lower body and go right through a
complete workout, hitting lower body consisting of legs then the
mid-section of gluteal muscles, abs and oblique muscles followed
by upper body of arms, back, pecs and lats finishing with the
neck, you could have the complete workout in two rows. That way
Jimmy could go down each row."

Fred just looked at Susan. "Susan, if you want a complete
workout you can use my universal machine all in one location. If
you want to work different parts of your body in different ways
you can go to that section and have everything right there."

"Oh! Well, if you think that's the best way."

The phone rang at 8:30 and the dealer called to say the
installer was on his way and should be there in about ten minutes.
You could feel the excitement mount. It wasn't long after the
phone call that there was a knock at the door and the day began
with the whole family including Mussy showing the installer the
exercise room. After a comment by the installer that the room

should be empty so his crew could put the track up, Fred, could see that his day would be moving equipment around. The installer wasn't happy but said he could manage if Fred could move the equipment out of the way.

Lacy and Susan drove over to pick Jimmy up. "Jimmy, I've decided we need to put shoulder straps on your harness."

"O.K., why?"

"Well, I was thinking you may want to unhook yourself from the lift to do some of your exercises and when you unhook your harness it will fall down."

"Or Lacy, I could just take the harness completely off and leave it attached to the lift. That way, instead of having to reach around behind myself to unhook or to re hook, I could just put my harness back on and it would already be attached to the lift."

"We sound like Mom and Dad this morning arguing about the layout of the exercise room."

"Lacy," replied Susan, "we were not arguing we just saw two different ways to arrange the equipment. In life there are usually several ways to accomplish the same thing and it is not worth the time or energy arguing about it as long as both will get you to the same place. But you can also see that decisions that are not made together often lead to different conclusions."

"Jimmy, do you want shoulder straps?" asked Lacy.

"Let's try the harness without shoulder straps. If I find the straps would be better we can always add them."

"That makes sense."

The day passes as Jimmy and Lacy work on their harness, Fred is exhausted from moving the equipment around and the boys watch the installers put the track up in the ceiling. Susan walks over to the exercise room and notices Mussy looks a little anxious.

"Boys, Mussy looks like she wants to go outside. I think she has to piddle; will you please take her out before we have an accident."

"Mom, can you take her out, we want to watch the men put the track up. They are about to make it go into the bathroom."

"Tommy, they will still be here when you get back. Just take Mussy out for five minutes and let her do her thing and get a little exercise. You need some exercise to. I want both of you to go out and run around because you both have been watching the installers all day."

"Come on Mussy we have to go outside," says Tommy. "You have to come to Freddy."

"Take a tennis ball and throw it for her. She loves to chase a tennis ball, just don't throw it anywhere near the water because she will find a reason to go in the water," remarks Susan.

Susan goes into the kitchen to see how Lacy and Jimmy are coming with their harness. "Is the sewing machine able to sew two piece of webbing together, Lacy?"

"Mom, I'm having a hard time. I haven't used this sewing machine before and I don't really know what to do. Will you try and see what you can do?"

"Let me sit in the chair for a minute and I will see what's happening here. The needle seems to be the wrong size. It probably needs a larger needle size which I don't have. I'll run down to the store and get a size 16 which I think will work for you."

"Will you get a stronger thread also? This thread may be a little lightweight."

Chapter Fourteen

Currencies

"Jimmy, let's go back to our study of Europe and trade around I AD."

"Lacy, I want to look at currencies that were used at that time to see what we can learn about the movement of people and goods also. Can I use the kitchen computer?"

"Let me bring it over and I can use my pocket brain. It certainly would be nice if they would build a large monitor into the wall of the kitchen or family room of houses when they build them. If it was a fifty inch monitor you could attach two or more keyboards enabling more than one person to use one screen."

"I wonder why they haven't done that Lacy. The screen could be divided into three or four partitions so three or four people could use them at the same time. It certainly would make it more family friendly. You could have a T.V. show in one partition while someone else could be playing a game in another while someone else was Googling or Binging something."

"Jimmy do you know currency, in some form, dates back about ten thousand years BC. It is so amazing to me, that we think we are so modern today when our financial system has its root in a system that dates back thousands of years before Christ. We have just made it easier to spend more than we have, putting us into debt."

"In fact, Lacy, early currencies were really more of a type of barter. Things that had an intrinsic value like cattle or nails were used. Different countries and different societies or groups used many different types of currency even beads or shells all of which had an intrinsic value to that group of people. However, all of these mediums of exchange decreased over time in their importance because they either were difficult to transport like cattle or were not widely accepted as an equal exchange by everyone."

"Jimmy, it is so interesting to realize that so called ancient man even though he lived thousands of years ago finally chose a medium of exchange or currency that everyone could agree to accept in trade for something else. Gold and silver were viewed as having an intrinsic value because they were scarce and because they could be used in creating beautiful things that people either worshiped or used. Here we are thousands of years later and man has not changed his views on value. We still view gold and silver as precious metals with an intrinsic value and a form of currency."

"Lacy, the more we study man, the more I am beginning to think that we are not the modern geniuses we think we are but just more foolish. People two thousand years ago chose a currency based on its beauty and scarcity which gave it value. Today, we just run the printing presses and create as much worthless paper as we want to pay for our huge debt. Our fiat currency has no intrinsic value other than the value we are willing to place on it for the exchange of goods and services."

"Jimmy, it's scary to see that man has watered down, debased, everything over time."

"That's because of greed and our own misunderstanding of what money or currency was or is today. Man originally established currency as an equal to what it represented. He made gold and silver into coins which could be easily carried around or transported. If we had a ship full of corn, for example, it would have been equal to a set amount of gold and silver or vice versa, therefore, currency represented a store house of value. Every trading partner along the trade route understood that equality. Then man started to debase his gold with lesser metals and the equality was broken. The question then was how much gold was in that coin which lead to different currencies having a different value. Then someone in government thought of keeping all the gold and issuing paper. The paper was supposed to be backed by gold. Then governments didn't want to give up their gold so they started taking on debt. The more debt they took on the less their paper currency was backed by gold. In fact, our own President, Richard Nixon, in 1971 ended the ability for U.S. dollars to be converted into gold. Prior to this the Bretton Woods agreement tied all nations' currencies to the value of gold which kept currencies relatively stable. I think Nixon's move was a horrible mistake. So Lacy, you can see, over longer periods of time, man's perception of a storehouse of value changed."

"Jimmy, you mean man completely lost the concept of a storehouse of value and went wild with the printing press. While man can create something he turns right around and destroys it. What sense does that make? Once you break that equality you ruin or distort its value. The more of anything reduces its value. Eventually, you have more currency chasing fewer products which debases the currency even more. We have gone far beyond Rumpelstiltskin and spinning straw into gold. Jimmy, we all know the more straw spun into gold will only debase the value of gold until finally if you spin enough straw into gold, gold will become worthless and straw will become worth more for its intrinsic value for bedding uses."

"Lacy, unfortunately, the same holds true for humanity. Look at all the unemployed. Look at all the people our system puts into the streets because they can't pay their mortgages. People have become no more than a book keeping entry, a digit, an obituary. Too much of anything ruins its value. It is a very sad tale that we have not learned. Any time you unbalance a system, the system no longer works. Our Wall St. alchemists haven't even learned this. The more money they create in their flawed alchemy, in trying to think up ways to generate more fees, only adds to a huge pool of money that has few places to go and which finds dwindling returns. We are drowning in our own money. There are many people and institutions that have tons of money but nowhere to get the returns they once received. Too much of anything has a declining value and yet we are throwing people out of their homes and ruining lives and weakening our economy because they don't have the money. Where is the balance in our logic? Does this make sense? There are so many critical projects, like the rebuilding of our infrastructure, that need to be done and yet, on one hand, we have a large pool of unemployed workers who can't get a job and, on the other hand, we have so much money in individual and institutional hands that doesn't know where to go and that garners a smaller and smaller return. Our money is becoming worthless and yet we just watch it pile up. Again, I ask, does this make sense?"

"Jimmy, it doesn't make sense, either economically for our country or from any humanitarian point of view but it also shows man's inability to see his problems and to come up with solutions. After our civil war, when the confederate currency became worthless, we had a horrible economic problem where people were wiped out financially so we know that the value of a currency depends on the strength of its economy. I think a solution would be to enact a stiff tax on money that just sits and is not used to employ people."

"Lacy, the tax would have to be greater than the interest earned so it would be pointless to have it sit instead of being invested in the employment of people and the solving of our problems. But if we want businesses and our banks to invest they have to have a reason to invest, we can't expect them to take a wild gamble."

"That means Jimmy, we come right back to the very basics of our problem which is our government. What good is our government if it has no plan, no road map? Everything depends on a business plan, a vision for our economy so businesses could plan ahead and we could feel more secure in our future. It would also mean we would have more faith in our government to solve our problems. Once investors had a better vision of our future they would start to invest."

"It seems so obvious Lacy."

"Jimmy, it all comes down to a structural change in the way we govern ourselves. We have to demand from our President that we have a thirty to fifty year plan so we all know where we are going. We elect a president because we trust what he says, is what he will do. We have elected a president who was the editor of the Harvard Law Review. It would seem to all that he has the intelligence to lead us in the right direction. We needed someone who could unify the whole country so our currency would have the strength and good will of all around the world. And yet, his very first piece of major legislation divided the country. Why didn't he hold town meetings throughout the entire country to see what reaction he would receive from his health care proposal? Why didn't he give a copy for review to our universities and economists for their feedback? The real problem and maybe it was because of his inexperience, was his program was not explained in detail so everyone understood it. For a politician, his first political step was almost political suicide and certainly did not unite us. I wonder if he even read it all and understood it or discussed it with his wife. If he had talked through the whole problem and solution with others he would have seen it was not a workable plan on a national basis. Either he didn't understand it well enough to be able to explain it or he was completely out of touch with what the people wanted. Either way it was political suicide. It will be almost impossible to regain that trust we had in him."

"Lacy, we go back to the same old problem. Man doesn't have any common sense. He thinks he knows what he doesn't know."

"Jimmy, Mom always says to remember the word K.I.S.S., keep it simple stupid. We make our legislation so complex we can't understand what we are even saying. Man has not learned there is only so much time in every day, that we get lost in our own words, that we all see things a little differently and that to communicate to everyone means keeping it short, simple and to the point. We have to learn first, to define the problem, not the symptoms. Then we have to learn to take each problem and give the pros and cons to each solution for that problem and finally sum the problem and the solutions up in a short easy to read concise package so everyone understands it and is on the same page. And Jimmy, it can't take all day."

"Lacy, your Mom's right. But the people we send to Washington don't seem to be able to do the simplest things. We are obviously sending the wrong people."

"Jimmy, it's our political structure that is wrong and has to be addressed and changed. If we realize that all people think and see things a little differently than each other then there is no way our present system can work. Our country and our world have become far too complex making it much too difficult for people to agree on the same thing. I think your idea is the only way we can create a democratic system that will work, which is to elect a president on the problems he outlines in his campaign and his solutions to those problems, nothing else. If we don't like the candidates' game plans we have to be able to ask for more candidates and refuse to vote for the ones we don't want. We need a game plan, a business plan for the next thirty to fifty years with ten year incremental plans that allow us to reach our thirty to fifty year goal. Then each administration could make out its own four year plan that ties into the ten year plan. To paraphrase one of our greatest leaders, Dr. Martin Luther King Jr., 'show us the promised land'. We also have to change our law to enable us to be able to fire the president if he doesn't follow his campaign goals and I mean on the spot. We could complain to a "Board of Review" that would either put the president back on track or fire him. Our congress has to be given back to the states. Since this nation is now fifty states and has grown to be so large, with so many different needs, in so many different types of climates, with so many different nationalities, which are represented in different percentages within each state's population and with a wide divergence in age groups, wouldn't it make more sense to let each state put together its own heath care plan for its people? Why are we making this a Washington issue when, I think, it should be a state's issue? Why aren't we looking at our health care problem from different angles? Why aren't we asking questions? After all, seventy percent of our fifty states now have a population larger than our entire country was when our present political system was devised."

"Lacy, our whole system needs to be revised and updated for a different time and place which is becoming increasingly complex. I think we are leaving a lot of people behind the learning curve; and it is not only our system but our individual beliefs which, in many cases, were established centuries ago which also have to be updated for far different times than existed just fifty years ago."

"Jimmy, we don't seem to realize how fast our world is changing. Everyone should look at Do You Know 2.0 on YouTube to realize that our old way of thinking won't solve our problems today. We have to look at our whole world from different angles. We have to ask ourselves what is intelligence? Do our colleges and universities know what intelligence is? Obviously, what their definition of intelligence is must be incomplete or the world would not be in the mess it is today with all its problems."

"Lacy, our educational system is graduating so many administrators that we are sinking the boat. Where are our leaders, our visionaries? I think it is clear our schools and universities are very myopic in their definition of intelligence and education. Total absolute intelligence, which doesn't exist on Earth, is made up of different types of intelligence, the most important ones being the wrapper of common sense and being able to think outside the box. Both of these abilities are in the basic structure of a mind and can't be taught. The way a mind is structured in the womb dictates how that person processes information. Therefore, we have to be able to test for the type of intelligence we need if we are going to survive. While the human doesn't have total absolute intelligence there is no reason we can't understand the different types of intelligence that different people possess and combine those people with the different types of intelligence to come closer to true intelligence as a unified decision making non-political group."

"Jimmy, when we look at what man is doing to himself; we always come back to common sense as being the problem."

"And don't forget discipline, Lacy. Man lacks the two most important assets he needs to survive."

"Jimmy, if people don't have faith in a country and its future and therefore its currency, the value of that currency goes down."

"Originally, Lacy, as we know, currency represented something else like grain or cotton, something that was needed to survive and, therefore, of intrinsic value and which was stored until it was purchased. Until that time came, something was needed to show ownership and hence the term store house of value."

"And therefore Jimmy, the major areas that used this storehouse of value originally were in agricultural areas."

"I think that's right. The Fertile Crescent around the far eastern edges of the Mediterranean was where currency really became important because it facilitated trade all over the Mediterranean and Black Sea countries. Because the power of countries went up and down and because there was always a threat of invasion by another country's armies, there was an inherent distrust of each other, therefore, a currency was needed that transcended these worries."

"And that is why gold and silver became so important, right Jimmy? They represented value to everyone everywhere no matter who was in power."

"And Lacy, that seems to have held true right up until today."

"Boy, we certainly haven't come very far, have we? Other than much larger populations, fewer resources and polluting our air and our water, it sounds about the same over 2000 years later."

"Remember Lacy, man is man and always will be man. Things don't change because his wiring doesn't change. We may move things around but it really is like a shell game of finding the pea of knowledge under what looks like different shells in a different order. We have to update our political system so that it accounts for man's weaknesses and can guide us in a totally new time period. Probably our biggest change in 2000 years has been the discovery and use of electricity. However, if you take electricity away we are right back two thousand years ago."

"And, of course, electricity uses hydrocarbons, in many cases, to generate and that is killing our atmosphere. That's what makes our problems today so critical, Jimmy. We have to change, we don't have a choice if we want to survive and yet man can't see that adding more people every year is going to put enormous pressures on our whole system. We can barely handle our electrical needs now. Fifty percent or more of our electricity is generated by coal. We know coal is a hydrocarbon which causes greenhouse gas. I really don't know what man is thinking about."

"Lacy, add to that the cost of maintaining and upgrading our electrical grid which is also a huge issue. We talk about it, we have all these grand plans but, as yet, we haven't done anything. We basically still have the same grid we have had for the last one hundred years full of patches and we know populations have spiraled out of control during that time not to mention usage. We want to power our houses with solar and wind and yet our infrastructure, many scientists say, is not technologically ready for a mass migration to alternative sources of energy. We have really boxed ourselves in with a dysfunctional political system, a huge debt burden that is ready to bankrupt us and a population that is exploding out of control. Lacy, I think, we have to conclude that man is a horrible strategist. He is as blind as a bat when it comes to his future and the future of the planet Earth. We really need a moratorium on all births worldwide for ten years to get everything worked out and ready for a bigger population if it is even possible for the planet to handle more. It maybe that in order to survive we will have to wait for someone to die before we can have a child.

In other words, we may have to wait for an open slot in order to bring a new child on to the planet."

"Jimmy, it is so upsetting. I have been brought into a world that is totally alien to me. It takes the whole idea of romance out of life if we are so worried about our populations."

"Lacy, you can still have romance and love. It just means both of you have to take the necessary precautions not to have a child unless it is planned for well ahead of time. Many different organizations have been saying the same thing for a long time. This is nothing new. Many couples have already planned a family well in advance; now we have no choice. We have to listen and we have to act much more like the adults we are supposed to be. If you have only one child, it will take so much pressure off the family and also off society and the Earth. I think everyone is worried sick about how our beautiful little planet can sustain more people. We all have to be much more realistic in our thinking and planning including our government which has totally ducked the whole population problem. Our most critical and serious problem and our government, the government that is supposed to lead us, has completely ducked it like it didn't exist. It is tantamount to letting the planet go right down the drain and not doing anything about it. It is so upsetting to realize that politicians only really care about their own skin. Even our president called our congress dysfunctional. Why would the president continue on with a dysfunctional congress? Why would he continue to have a dysfunctional anything? Why do we even allow it? What good is a government that doesn't watch out for and guide its people? Aren't they elected to watch out for the good of our country, our planet and its people? What is the problem with us for not demanding that our governments take the necessary responsibility to find and tell us about our problems and what we have to do to solve them, whether we like it or not. If we don't solve the population problem, it is the end of man on Earth. What could be more critical and more important to all of us? Instead of fighting wars in far off places that are bankrupting us, why aren't we facing the biggest threat of all which is over population? We are our own worst enemy. What if all of us didn't pay our taxes and we all claimed we just overlooked it just the way you, our governments, have overlooked so many of our problems? What happens if we tell our governments, we will remember to pay our taxes when you, our government, remember to act like a responsible government?"

"What happens if man can't change, Jimmy?"

"Lacy, you better learn to cook and sew and also how to preserve foods because, if man can't change on a dime when he has to, we will turn the clock back 2000 years if we survive."

"It's almost like we took a momentary step ahead before we may be forced to go back."

"Let's just hope that all governments see it is in their own best interest to unite as one when it comes to populations and environment. Anyway, Lacy, currency depends on the willingness of the seller to take something else in exchange for what he is selling. It is similar to barter except instead of a product or service man took currency which he could then barter for something else."

"And Jimmy, because it facilitated trade over a wide area, many different countries developed their own coins based on gold and silver."

"Believe it or not, Lacy, they even developed a copper coin which was of lesser value for smaller purchases. So Lacy, things really don't change. The adage "the more things change the more they stay the same" is still true today."

"And Jimmy, speaking of things always staying the same, the development of currencies led to, guess what, money men; banks and bankers, loan sharks, and credit. Can you believe? If there is a way to make a buck, man will find it or dream it up."

"Not only will he find it but he will start to ruin it by debasing it. He started to use lesser quality metals like bronze. Lacy, doesn't it sound like we have seen this movie before?"

"It is absolutely amazing how things repeat even over thousands of years, Jimmy. What gets me is we pay fortunes to people to develop the same things with a different twist that we had thousands of years ago. We call it progress or technology but we really are just using an electronic machine to do the same things faster. Take away the electricity and we have gone absolutely nowhere."

"In fact, Lacy, if you take away electricity coupled with our creation of a huge complex society based on debt, we really have gone backwards, not forwards. All these so called advanced economies are in debt. Their printing presses can't work fast enough. If we take away electricity, man would be cooked."

"You mean toast, Jimmy and it's not funny. Here we are over a period of 2000 years and we have been going around in circles chasing our tale. We have built a whole complex world around antiquated basic and blind human systems and philosophies. There has been no leadership, just politicians who pander to the electorate so they can keep a job. Talk about depressing. We are adding more people to a broken and blind system that is on the brink of collapse. The answer hinges on uniting the world around controlling populations and reducing our pollution and protecting our environment. It's going to take everyone yelling and screaming and demanding a change or no one will listen. If we can come together as one planet then we can easily spread the wealth. We could put solar collection and distribution centers in those countries that have year round sun and transport that energy where ever we need it. They would get paid just the way oil rich countries are getting paid now. Instead of a country needing a huge military their military could be reduced saving billions. We don't need debt; we need people who are taught the right priorities. The only way we will survive is if we can unite as one world and tackle the problems together. Our standard of living will also have to come down throughout the world until we control our populations. The fewer people we have on our beautiful little planet the higher the standard of living there will be for all."

"It seems so obvious Lacy and yet people are very distrustful of each other. Banks even have a hard time lending to each other because they don't trust each other. Can you believe, here we are more than 2000 years later and even our banks still don't trust one another. It hasn't changed over thousands of years. As you pointed out, that is why gold and silver were used as currency. We have to realize everyone is wired a little differently; everyone wants to make his world in his own light and that is why different countries were formed, why different religions and sects were formed, why they make different car models in different colors, because mankind wants to think independently and think he is different. Man has not changed over thousands of years and that is why our planet is having so many wars and conflicts. The more people we put on our planet the more people want to show their individuality and freedom and equality which leads to more wars and conflicts. Man is very territorial. We want to defend our own territory. You can see it in the animal world also. Male cats, for example, in the Panthera genus, do not get along. In fact they will try and kill each other if put together. They need their own room to roam. People have a very hard time getting along with each other especially males. By adding over population to the problem we are just compounding the problem."

"And, Jimmy, it all goes back to how we see things which goes back to how each of us is wired. But man also innately wants to act as a pack. I think if we can get the ball rolling we can get all countries to join in one united effort. No country wants to be seen as not wanting to help save the planet and mankind; it would not be in their best interest. I think there needs to be the proverbial carrot in front of the horse."

"And that carrot, Lacy, is survival. If we can only get people to see that nature's solution to over population is far worse than what man's common sense and discipline could dictate, then there is a possibility we can unify the planet around a solution. Since we all know, that any animal, which over populates, reaches a point where it outstrips its food supply with the consequence of starvation, the obvious solution is to limit populations. In nature, populations are regulated by nature. Since man has acted as if he was above nature and not regulated by nature the only solution is for man to place a self-imposed limit on himself. Everyone knows that a finite space can support only so many of any living creature and that every space has its limit. So consequentially, we have to ask ourselves how close to extinction do we want to go before we take action. How much pain and suffering do we want to inflict on each other before we see the light?"

"It's so depressing it just makes me sick. How much time do you think we have?"

"Lacy, it really is gut wrenching to think man has pulled the rubber band back as far as it can be. It is very scary to think that we could be the last generation of man on Earth. I get a headache when I think about it. I want you to look at the facts and figure it out with me. The availability of food depends to a large extent on weather and water and to a lesser extent on distribution and storage. The Earth has seen year after year of increasing temperatures over the past ten years. There is a high probability that man is, to some extent, causing the Earth to heat up by dumping so many pollutants into our atmosphere."

"Jimmy, it seems all tied together. If we unbalance our ecosystems there is a direct cause and effect relationship. For every action there is an equal and opposite reaction. The ecosystems will try and re-balance themselves. It may be that an increase in the sun's activity coupled with our dumping so much greenhouse gases into our atmosphere has and is causing a fast and unequaled period here on Earth that heats the Earth to the point it will reduce the yield of our crops or even burn them up."

"Lacy, scientists tell us that the increase in the sun's activity has not increased in the past ten years and yet our pollutants in our atmosphere have. So while we may want to point to the sun's activity as the cause it certainly is debatable since our planet continues to heat up."

"That's a good point Jimmy, but I will give the skeptics the benefit of the doubt. So we don't know how much of the rising temperatures are due to the sun's activity but we do know two things. We know the higher temperatures are creating new heat records almost yearly here on Earth and we know that our atmosphere has more CO2 and other pollutants than ever before. Common sense would tell us there probably is a correlation between the two. Jimmy, do you realize that seventy percent of our fresh water is used for agriculture? That only leaves thirty percent for everything else. The more people on Earth means, more food, which means more water. Where are we going to get more fresh water? Fresh water is a finite resource. That thirty percent has to cover not only human uses but also the water used in the making of many of our metals and in the production of oil and gas we use for energy. If we run low on water it will shut down our energy producing capability."

"So your conclusion is Lacy?"

"My conclusion Jimmy is, we can't base our present thinking on the past because we don't know if we have altered our climate and if we have to what extent. What is obvious is we live in a universe of constant change so the past may not be indicative of the future and we certainly can't plan on it."

"So Lacy; if I understand you correctly, we can't base our populations on the Earth's past ability to produce food and energy. We are in a new period, manmade or not, where the whole ball game could change on us."

"Yes, that is what I think. The only course of action that makes sense to me is, to plan everything for the worst possible outcome short of a total collapse, of course."

"Lacy, our next problem is our basic energy source. There are alternatives to oil like sun, wind, geothermal and natural gas even from such sources as methane hydrates. However, we are mostly talk right now. We are starting to convert to sun, wind and geothermal in some places but it is scattered and represents only a small part of our whole energy needs. We think natural gas can help out in the shorter run but again we are mostly talk. I don't see our energy companies rushing to install natural gas tanks at their gas stations. Electric cars are a possibility but again we have not overcome the storage problem yet. Perhaps the biggest breakthrough of our generation will be the ability to store electrical energy over long periods of time in small batteries. However, batteries are dangerous to our environment which means we will have to have very tight control on them and they will have to be recycled. So, while we are a lot of talk and wishful thinking, we don't see a huge mass migration away from oil."

"And Jimmy, while oil shale offers potential with some analysts thinking the U.S. will be able to export more and more oil, there is only so much oil on Earth and much of the world like India and China and the many developing countries are all using more and more oil every year. Our oil shale is just part of the whole pot of oil which we are using at an ever increasing rate with the end result being higher energy prices. But the big problem the Earth faces is we are still using oil which is a hydrocarbon which is saturating our atmosphere and, therefore, our oceans. Our oceans are more acidic than they have been in three hundred million years according to scientists. Also, much of the world is in debt and trying to cut back or reduce spending which means less capital to convert to alternative fuels. And, Jimmy, we are also adding approximately another 70,000,000 people to this planet every year. If we say, only eight percent drive, that is 5,600,000 new drivers every year."

"Lacy, if each of those 5,600,000 new drivers drives an average of ten miles per day and gets an average of twenty-five miles per gallon, the world is using an additional three quarters of a billion gallons of gasoline every year. On top of that, the sixty four million that don't drive still require gasoline for the transportation of food, clothing and many other services that each requires."

"Jimmy, no matter how much oil is in the world, we are going to run low enough on oil that the price will go out of sight bankrupting economies around the world. So while we would like to dream of a world that is not polluting its atmosphere and oceans and is not dependent on oil, that is not what is happening at least not at a fast enough pace. So, here again, we can't plan our populations on wishful thinking."

"It is so scary, right Lacy? Why bring a new helpless life into a world that is so uncertain and one that we may not be able to feed. With oil gyrating in price and the outlook from our top energy analysts for much higher oil prices down the road, there is no way to know if our economies will crash and whether we will be able to just feed ourselves."

"Jimmy my stomach is in a great big knot; but this is the hand our generation has been dealt. I just want to yell a lot of four letter words at all those stupid politicians. The next problem is our infrastructure which we all depend on. We know our roads and bridges need to be updated and, in some cases, completely rebuilt. Our electrical grid is the same grid we have been using for the past one hundred years just with a lot of patches in it to manage our bigger populations and economies. We have big ideas on what a new grid would look like but we see very little action and limited funds to make it happen. Jimmy, I read an article, not long ago, written by energy analysts that cast doubt on our present grid system to be able to accept all the energy from conversions to solar and wind. So, we are putting the cart before the horse. If we don't have the electrical grid system to take all the energy from a switch to solar and wind then what are we thinking about?"

"Lacy, talk about a bunch of wishful dreamers. That means each of us is going to have to convert our own house over to solar because the infrastructure may not be able to connect everyone to the grid. But, here to, our future is so un-certain, we can't plan a future on it. Let's look at our oceans next. Here is certainly one of our most important if not the most important ecosystem on our planet. It produces almost half of the protein the world needs. We know the atmosphere and our oceans are tied together. CO_2

is absorbed by the cool waters of our oceans. If the oceans warm they give off some of the CO2 that they had been storing."

"So, they are a warehouse for excess CO2, Jimmy. If the warehouse gets to hot it can't hold as much CO2 and it is given off back into our atmosphere which already is holding so many pollutants it is having a hard time holding any more. The question is if the oceans can't hold any more and our atmosphere can't hold any more, what happens next?

"Lacy, plants absorb and use carbon dioxide, CO2, so maybe plants can take up some of the excess."

"The problem is, Jimmy, we are cutting down our forests, especially our rain forests at an alarming rate. So instead of our forests being able to store some of our CO2, we are tearing that warehouse down. With all the development going on around the world we are destroying the plants that help control the CO2 by using and storing it. With too much CO2 in the oceans they become acidic which has a bad effect on living organisms. We are not only over fishing our oceans and polluting them, putting a huge strain on that whole ecosystem but we are changing the make-up of our oceans by making them more acidic. The question is how much more acidic can our oceans and seas become without ruining the whole ecosystem? Look at what acid rain has done to our lakes and ponds. Those lakes and ponds were once full of many different types of fish and now many are close to being dead. The end result is we are doing our best to kill our most important ecosystem. Even the phytoplankton which absorbs so much CO2 and gives off oxygen is being destroyed. Phytoplankton is also at the base of the whole food chain which all the other fish depend on and ultimately man. Since 1950 we have lost forty percent of our phytoplankton scientists tell us. Without phytoplankton man cannot survive. So, here again, we are living on a razors edge with just our present populations. On top of this the oceans are becoming so full of trash especially plastics that we find our wildlife wrapped in it or dead because they ate it."

"Lacy, it makes me so mad I'd just like to wring the necks of everyone making a buck from producing plastics especially when you realize they are as blind as a bat. They could easily make plastics out of polymers that are bio degradable."

"Jimmy, I didn't know that. What can they use to make plastics that are eco- friendly?"

"First, we are tearing down our rain forests so we don't know all the sources that could be used but we do know that tapioca root produces a polymer resin that can be used to make plastic bags and which bio-degrades in under a year. Compare that to other types of plastic that take thousands of years to bio-degrade. Plastic bags are a huge problem for our oceans as well as on land. Why aren't we making plastics out of bio-degradable plastic alternatives? We have a huge problem with drugs coming across our Mexican border because Mexicans need to make a living. Why can't they grow tapioca plants that we could buy to make plastics from instead of using oil in the production of plastics?

"What are people thinking about, Jimmy? You mean we are killing ourselves because we are too lazy or to set in our ways to find alternatives?"

"Lacy, it's enough to make you sick. What has man been thinking about? Doesn't anyone listen to the scientists? Are we totally deaf, dumb and blind? Where have our politicians been? Everyone must be living in a different world somewhere. There is so much money that doesn't know where to go and yet there are more things that need to be done than ever before. The whole world has to transition to a completely new time frame and outlook. I can think of hundreds of new projects that have to be done that would get high returns for their investors without hurting the environment. I don't know what is wrong with our companies. Who are they hiring? Obviously the management they are hiring is the wrong management. Where are our leaders our visionaries? We don't need more baby sitter administrators. No wonder our past leaders like Lee Iacocca are having nightmares."

"Jimmy, it is hard to hold the tears back when we see what man is doing. Clearly, our whole system including our political system, our academic system and our financial system is totally working against itself and mankind. We have taken our eye off the ball. We are so worried and focused on making a living that we have forgotten the most important thing, our environment. How can we call man an intelligent animal? He is, in fact, a suicidal animal like lemmings."

"I hate to say this Lacy, but in the next ten years we are going to put close to another one billion people on this planet if we continue to grow at a rate of 1.2 % per year. That equates to a new country every year for the next ten years. Even if some people want to argue that we can bring our growth rate down to 1% or .9% it won't change the equation much."

"How can we handle more people Jimmy, when we can't even handle the population we have now?"

"We can't Lacy. In the next eighteen years, at a growth rate of 1.2% per year, we will add another 23% to our populations. If we can't control our populations they will just continue to spiral out of control exponentially until the end comes which wouldn't be long. Our country is one of the richest countries and yet MSNBC reports that about half of our population is classified as being in poverty or in the low income group already. Here, in one of the richest countries, we have had a dramatic rise in the need for food stamps. Scientists tell us there is no way our systems can adapt to such a huge change in such a short time span if at all and that the price of food will have to spiral higher. There is no way we can create 23 percent more fresh water; there is no way we can increase the harvest from our oceans by 23 percent, in fact, our oceans have to be shut down and allowed to rejuvenate just to be able to feed Earths present populations; there is no way we can add 23 percent more pollutants to our atmosphere and there is no way we can create 23 percent more food from the land, that is already losing its nutritional value from over production. The most arable land left for agriculture is only approximately

ten percent and that land is not as productive as the land now in agricultural production. We use fertilizers but they do not replace the micro-nutrients that are essential to life. In fact, fertilizers are a two edged sword. Too much fertilizer and it runs off into our streams and rivers and finally into our oceans creating dead zones where nothing lives or grows. In Africa they are finding that agro-ecological farming can increase food output substantially but that type of farming is not conducive to large industrial type farms. If we over tax the planet's ecosystems they will collapse and life on Earth will be over."

"Jimmy I think I'm going to be sick" said a scared young girl. But can't we bring our ecosystems back by having a moratorium on eating sea food for eight or ten years, can't we somehow put the micro nutrients back into our soils and can't we purify and take out the pollutants in our atmosphere? The U.S., is only four percent of the total world population, why should we be worried about the rest of the planet when we are the bread basket to the world?"

"Lacy, it is up to man everywhere on this planet. Nothing will help us if we can't control our populations. We may comprise only four percent of the world's population but the oceans and seas are an interconnected ecosystem. What happens in one area can affect the whole system. Not to mention the connection between our oceans and our atmosphere. Our atmosphere is interconnected with our oceans as we can see by El Nino weather patterns that can affect everyone by creating very severe storms and droughts. Our whole Earth is interconnected in some way. Don't forget, Earth is a huge mixing pot. The United States has some of the most productive farmland in the world and we export a great deal of it to feed the world. If our agricultural breadbasket is hurt by drought or floods, the world will suffer and people will die by the millions. We have to understand our Earth is one big mixing bowl and even the amount of dust that is blown across the oceans from Africa affects the weather in many different places. So you can't say it's another country's problem. We are so inextricably intertwined with our Mother Earth that our lives depend on our understanding nature and our ability to live within the confines of nature. All countries are also closely tied economically, so if they have a problem we feel it here. Man has created his own economic ecosystem that ties all of us together. It does no country, anywhere, on Mother Earth, any good to overpopulate. By adding another billion or more new mouths to feed will create enormous pressures everywhere causing catastrophic conditions. The Chesapeake Bay, here in the United States, is a good example. It is the largest estuary in the United States and a breeding and spawning ground for many of our most valuable fish, not to mention our famous blue crabs. A few years ago the striped bass populations were being over fished and declined to a critical point. There was a moratorium on fishing for striped bass established by the Maryland and Virginia fisheries under the Department of Natural Resources. It took seven years for the striped bass to re-establish their populations in the Chesapeake. Ecosystems are resilient, if they are given a chance, and the time to come back. But even in the Chesapeake, which is closely watched, it is an ongoing fight every year just to try to keep the ecosystem stable."

"Jimmy, I was reading about The Chesapeake Bay Foundation and its fight to save the Bay. They say they are fighting a constant war. The pesticides and herbicides as well as the fertilizers put on by farmers within Maryland and in the surrounding states run off into the Chesapeake. Nitrogen from the fertilizers causes algae blooms. The algae blooms suck up the oxygen in the water creating dead spots where nothing lives or grows. The marsh grasses which are vital to the ecosystem and to fighting erosion have largely disappeared causing a big problem in the whole ecosystem. The farmers haven't been able to control their run off going into the Bay and the fishing pressures are an ongoing problem, whether it's crabbing or fishing or the oysters. An unhealthy Bay weakens the whole ecosystem allowing diseases to take hold and decimate the food stocks we depend on for our own survival. When you realize the Chesapeake Bay is a small piece, of the whole ecological pie worldwide, and is closely monitored and yet every year it is touch and go as to the health of that ecosystem and that is just with our present population."

"Lacy, an ecosystem is intricately interlaced and delicately balanced. Ecosystems are resilient and can come back given the needed time if they are not continually over taxed to the brink of extinction. Once they collapse it is all over. By adding so many more people, when our ecosystems are already taxed to the nth degree, will just over tax them causing them to collapse and stop functioning and once they go we are sure to follow. I don't understand why farmers aren't required to circle all their fields with a cost effective porous pipe buried under ground that would catch the runoff and cycle it back to underground tanks that the farmers could again use. It would save them a fortune in fertilizer cost and help save our ecosystems."

"Why don't we have environmental laws that mandate that farmers make this investment Jimmy? If their cost goes up they will just have to pass it along to us. Aren't our lives worth any added cost?"

"Good question Lacy. People are just so myopic they can't seem to see the forest for the trees."

"What about our soil, Jimmy?

"Our soil is a different problem but one that maybe the easiest to fix. Farmer can rotate their crops with clover and alfalfa which are rich in micronutrients. Micro-nutrients are found in abundance in our lawn clippings also. We have to start collecting these clippings and start putting them on our fields to increase their micro-nutrients. But how and when we do this is the tricky part. Our grass grows in the summer but that is when the crops grow. Maybe we can pelletize grass clippings so we can put them on when we need them or we can put them on when fields are in rotation. It really is a logistics problem that our colleges and universities should be able to solve. If we can pelletize our grass clippings we could sell them and home owners could make a little extra money. Don't forget, Mother Nature spent hundreds of millions of years building our soil; like everything else in nature, the problems man causes are not easy to fix."

"And Jimmy, if we can put the micro-nutrients back into our soils we can live from the cereal grains, fruits and vegetables while the seas rejuvenate if we will only give them the time."

"Lacy, it can be done. Our next problem is the pollutants in our atmosphere and it's a huge problem. We first have to collect them, which is no easy trick, then we have to be able to warehouse them somewhere they can't escape from or they would go right back into our atmosphere. On top of this, we have to eliminate them from going into our atmosphere in the first place. It is a complex problem and one not easily solved. However, if we can turn to alternative energy fast enough and eliminate the vast majority if not all of our carbon fired power plants world-wide including China and India, it would be a step in the right direction. Don't forget Earth is a giant mixing bowl and what China and India do effects everyone everywhere."

"And that means these developing economies have to convert to alternative energy sources also. So if we can control our populations we have a chance?

"Lacy, if man acts now and acts together, as one unified planet and faces reality head on, like it or not we have a chance. Don't forget, U Thant, Secretary General, of the United Nations said back in 1965, if we don't control our populations within the next five years it will be too late". That year, 1965, in which U Thant spoke, was 47 years ago. We have to act now; we don't have any more time to talk about it. To bring our populations down we really need a moratorium on all births for eight or ten years and then only one child per family. When women go to the hospital to deliver their child, they automatically get their tubes tied and fathers get a vasectomy."

"Jimmy, that's not something that anyone wants, we don't want it, but what choice do we have?"

"Lacy, I know it sucks, however, the survival of everyone, the world over, depends on it. Everyone has to ask themselves, do we, do I want to survive? Do I want to see my children starve to death?"

"Jimmy, even here in the U.S., one in every two people is in poverty or in the low income group already. That tiny little helpless bundle of joy depends on us for the right answer. Our governments are bankrupt so we can't count on them for help. If our answer is the wrong answer nature will unleash a punishment so cruel that no human wants to be part of it or to see it happen."

"Lacy, it is gut wrenching and the more I realize how critical our problems are and I look at our solutions to them the more my stomach becomes a bigger knot but we didn't face this problem years ago. Man won't face reality. There is no perfect solution and no one is going to like the solutions. But they are not going to like dying either; they are not going to like starving to death either, they are not going to like to see children in rags in the street emaciated from starvation either. We have no choice now but to take the least devastating solution which is limiting every family to one child."

Tears formed in Lacy's eyes until she could hold them back no longer and she started to cry. Jimmy's emotions also formed in pools of tears and he reached out to Lacy and pulled her to him. She collapsed in Jimmy's lap and buried her head on his shoulder. "This isn't the world I dreamed it would be or the world I wanted, Jimmy," she sobbed. "Jimmy, I'm scared."

"Man has horribly mismanaged himself and our beautiful little planet," replied Jimmy softly with tears starting to roll down his face; putting his arms around her.

An eternity seemed to pass as the tears ran down their faces. Their tears told their agony.

Susan drove up the driveway. When she opened the door to the kitchen, she was shocked.

"Lacy, is everything alright?"

Lacy looked up and nodded with tears falling to the floor.

"What happened?" asked a mother who obviously could see that things were not alright."

"Susan" said Jimmy in a choked and muffled tone, "it's my fault. We were taking a look at our future and it doesn't look very bright."

"Why not?"

"Because man has placed his own greed and self-interest above our planet's life."

"He has always done that, Jimmy. Man lives for the moment, but somehow we are still here. What got you both in tears?"

"Mom, man has pulled the rubber band back as far as it can go. It can't go any farther. If we don't change, life is over."

"Lacy, you can't let it get you down."

"What do you mean, Mom? Everyone has dumped all their lack of common sense and discipline on my generation and you say I can't let it get me down."

Susan was silent while her mind grasped what her daughter was seeing. Her worst nightmares that she always forced out of her mind were coming home to roost. All of man's fantasies; his inability to see his problems, his inability to face his problems, kidding himself and pointing the finger at someone else, caressing each-others egos, his blind greed and self- interest and constant denial, all of it was being dumped on her daughter's generation and our planet. She could only think of "oh what a tangled web we weave when first we practice to deceive". Man has been kidding himself; He has been deceiving himself and now all his poop is about to destroy him.

"Lacy, I'm sorry, I said that. We all want to dream, we want life to be perfect, we want to be able to spoil our children and get them to believe in the same fantasy world. I think you are right, the time has come, we are at the brink and our only hope is that all women see the horrible mess we are in and come together to protect our little planet. There is no force like a female protecting her cub or cubs. It is up to us said a deeply angered and hurt mother with determination, we have to have the discipline it will take."

"That is a huge burden to place on women, Mom."

"Lacy, the human female is the most dangerous and the most powerful force on Earth. Only she has the power to overpopulate the planet or to save it and that is just a fact. That power only we have and we are as dangerous as a loaded gun. I agree, it is a shared responsibility and the male has to get a vasectomy but until she gets her tubes tied she is extremely dangerous. As long as she is driven to reproduce there will always be an army of willing males ready to accommodate her. This is not something I ever wanted to say. But you and Jimmy have discovered the horrible truth that man has been living in a dream world of deception. He has deceived himself. He can't see; he has no idea what he is doing. He is and has been completely blinded by his greed and ego. He has no long term plan, no road map, no five, ten and twenty year interim plans, he doesn't have an understanding of how everything is interrelated, he is flying completely blind and that is true for both our planet and our nation. There has to be severe penalties imposed by society if a couple has more than one child whether we like it or not. The consequences of continued overpopulation are so devastating to man that what other choice do we have?"

"Susan," said a choked Jimmy with tears in his eyes. We have to cut the birthrate to the point it equals the death rate just to stabilize populations. But our planet can't even sustain our present populations over time. We are like a plane full of passengers with no destination, no directional instruments and limited fuel. Our time is very limited. Just take a look at www.worldometers.info, a population clock in real time. Man's problem is, he thinks he knows what he doesn't know and what he does know, he doesn't want to face. What we do know is that we can't go another eighteen years, especially with an increasing population since our ecosystems can hardly sustain our present population and that is only on a short term basis. We know that if we continue to over tax our ecosystems they will collapse. We know that ecosystems are interconnected so if one goes it triggers a chain reaction through many other ecosystems. We can look at phytoplankton in our oceans. If we kill our phytoplankton due to the warming of our oceans caused by greenhouse gases or a combination of greenhouse gases and higher sun activity there would be a whole chain reaction throughout the entire ocean complex, killing it. Phytoplankton has decreased by forty percent, reported by scientists that study phytoplankton, since 1950 and it may be due not only to the warming of the oceans but to over fishing. Because phytoplankton is at the bottom of the food chain our whole ecosystem depends on them. We are living on a knife's edge. Look at our own financial ecosystem. It is crumbling right before our eyes. If we take away the middle class the whole system collapses and that is exactly what our system is doing."

"And Jimmy," replied a teary Lacy, "once we lose faith in our governments and our economies both here and abroad our currencies will lose their value. With the value of our currencies decreasing fewer people will be able to make purchases and pay their bills. There is a whole chain reaction that could crumble our economies overnight. We don't realize how interconnected everything is. It is the same old story. Man can create something but then he turns right around and kills it or debases it. Man is his own worst enemy."

"Lacy, if we don't or are unable to keep up our data infrastructure our computers will give us garbage out crumbling the whole electronic age of computers."

"Jimmy, the whole world is sitting on a huge mine field since we rely on computers to do so many functions for us. For some reason man overlooked the fact that computers can't think or produce their own energy or fix themselves. They rely on man and an economic and financial system that can afford them."

"Lacy, once we started to accept currencies without any intrinsic value backing them, we lost the meaning of a storehouse of value. Man can't eat paper and it won't protect him from the elements. Paper is truly worthless and yet we have built a whole complex civilization on something worthless. Our system makes Bernie Madoff look like a childish prankster."

"Talk about blind, Jimmy. But we are doing the same thing as Bernie Madoff. Once money became hard for him to raise, he did whatever it took to continue to survive. We are doing the same thing. In order for us to continue on we are raping whatever can be raped instead of analyzing our problems, finding the solutions and changing; no matter the hurdles, no matter the difficulty and no matter the emotional pain. Look at our debt here in the U.S; it is greater than our GNP, that's our gross national product, the value of all our goods and services produced. That can't continue and still have a currency that other nations want to hold."

"Do you still want to continue with our research and the unraveling of the human world, Lacy; asked Jimmy?"

"Yes, it is so interesting and yet so depressing. If we close our minds to learning more, then we are sticking our heads in the sand and pretending our problems don't exist. If we do that, life is over. Crying won't do any good. What is done is done, but now we have to face reality and change as hard as it maybe. All of us are going to have to make the hard decisions. These are tough emotional problems that demand a cool head, a warm heart and an open mind. It will take discipline and we aren't going to like the steps that have to be taken to survive."

"Lacy, it is going to be tough and sacrifices will have to be made by everyone."

"Jimmy, we are going to have to look at the world and ourselves in a whole new way. All our systems and views will have to be updated. We have to be able to set limits on our populations whether we like it or not and all people have to be taught from the youngest of ages that Mother Nature rules and we can only partake in her beauty and plenty if we play by her rules. We know we can't continue using the same old thinking. There are so many questions that have to be answered. If we don't continue to unravel the way man thinks, we would be doing the same thing blind man has always done and we would be hypocrites. Jimmy, we are looking at a repeat of the sub-prime mess just in another area except this time our lives are on the line. No one wanted to see the housing collapse until it was too late. Man does the same thing over and over and over and he never learns. Mom, I'm alright, don't worry. I'll pick myself up but we have to get everyone to see that our populations can't continue growing without killing all life on our beautiful little planet and scientists have been telling us that but no one seems to listen. We have to act; we can no longer just talk and spew hot air around and dream. Our scientists are the environmental Greenspan of the coming environmental collapse if we don't listen this time and act now globally."

"Lacy, the United Nations needs to host a joint meeting with the heads of all the religious groups and our leading environmental scientists and hash out how many people Mother Earth can support on a sustainable basis for the good of all. It also means our social Internet sites have to pull everyone around the world together so we all realize that our planet is tiny and finite and that our ability to live within the confines of Mother Nature will dictate whether we survive. China has a one child policy. Why can't all nations? Isn't that the least painful solution?"

"Can we do it Jimmy?"

"Lacy, man can do anything if he puts his mind to it. The question is will he do it? There is a solution to every problem. We just have to find the solution and be willing to take the medicine."

Author Biography

*T*he author graduated in business and economics from college and went to work for a management consulting firm specializing in Fortune 500 companies. His travels took him all over North America including Canada. It was a rigorous schedule of meeting deadlines and traveling five days a week, sometimes from coast to coast. His schedule prompted the author to switch gears and jump from being a staff consultant to working for one of the largest Wall St. brokerage firms as a broker.

The author has always had a very keen sense of and about nature. He also questions whether a direct lineage to Benjamin Franklin on his mother's side gives him a slightly different perspective in the way he sees things. As a young child growing up, the world made little sense to him causing a difficult adjustment in his views. He saw the human world out of touch with the natural world around him; there was a dichotomy when there should have been a union; man was part of life and therefore part of the Earth's ecosystems and yet man was polluting and destroying his own environment.

Growing up, the author was a top junior sailor and tennis player which gave him an awareness of how important physical fitness is to both mind and body.

Index

Form for submitting your solutions.

On page number _____ the following problem is: _____

_____
_____
_____
_____

My solution is _____

_____
_____
_____
_____
_____
_____
_____

Circle one of the following: I want to remain anonymous, I want my name published.

If you agree with the characters solution you can put "I agree" in the solution box above.